Praise for

WHAT TO KEEP

"Striking . . . sparkling . . . chick lit for smarties . . . One of the chief delights of Rachel Cline's lovely, understated debut is her smart, self-respecting heroine Denny Roman, who never clamors for attention. And thereby earns it."

—*Entertainment Weekly*

"Delves into familial and romantic minefields with compassion and humor." —*People*

"Zings along with cinematic flair . . . probing . . . exquisite . . . a mad tangle of personal histories, full of characters who are as tangibly real as they are completely AWOL."

—*Los Angeles Times*

"Sharply observed and paradoxically tender . . . smart, witty . . . Held aloft by astute psychological insights and deadpan humor, [*What to Keep*] moves to a satisfying denoument."

—*Publishers Weekly*

"[An] insightful and briskly narrated mother-daughter drama . . . [with] plucky characters and neat plot turns."

—*New York*

"A smart, ruefully funny debut . . . perfectly observed details of ordinary life that coalesce to offer a realistically hopeful and genuinely touching finale."

—*Kirkus Reviews* (starred review)

"Wry, well observed . . . harbors much wit and insight, as well as numerous passages of handsomely phrased prose . . . droll and perceptive." —*Newsday*

"Smart and witty . . . a wryly funny novel that feels completely fresh . . . depicts offbeat, memorable characters; and offers a perceptive, nuanced take on familial relationships."

—*Booklist*

"A poignant character study and a moving meditation on the changing definitions of family . . . Denny is an appealing and compelling character. . . . Readers should consider themselves fortunate to be able to take this journey along with her." —Bookreporter.com

"A charming look at the different combinations of people who can make up a family . . . Cline draws readers into caring about her flawed but likable characters while passing on some worthwhile life lessons." —*Library Journal*

"Eden 'Denny' Roman of Columbus, Ohio, is the creative, intuitive, somewhat directionless and emotionally unmoored daughter of two neurologists who are hopelessly brilliant and accomplished. . . . I'm rooting for her; you will too."

—*Elle*

"This one-of-a-kind novel will keep you fascinated."

—*Lifetime*

"A sweet melody played with hipness and humor, *What to Keep* shows how life shoves us forward whether we're ready to go or not. The silent, courageous, and reasoned decisions made by the women in this book prove, once again, who the real heroes of ordinarily life are."

—JAMES MCBRIDE, author of *The Color of Water*

"This witty and affecting novel tells its story glancingly, its progress only gradually revealing the truth at its center: that accidents, half-choices, and patched-together solutions can lead us, as surely as their opposites, exactly where we need to go." —ANN PACKER, author of *The Dive from Clausen's Pier*

"Intelligent and entirely original, this story dramatizes and makes plain sense of the complex formations of what we call family, rendering the nuances of each character with an honesty that reaches straight to the reader's heart."

—ELIZABETH STROUT, author of *Amy and Isabelle*

WHAT
TO
KEEP

A NOVEL

Rachel Cline

BALLANTINE BOOKS / NEW YORK

2005 Ballantine Books Trade Paperback Edition

Published in the United States by Ballantine Books, an imprint
of The Random House Publishing Group, a division of
Random House, Inc., New York.

BALLANTINE and colophon are registered trademarks
of Random House, Inc.

Originally published in hardcover in slightly different form
in the United States by Random House, an imprint of The Random House
Publishing Group, a division of Random House, Inc., in 2004.

Grateful acknowledgment is made to the following
for permission to reprint previously published materials:

Hal Leonard Corporation: excerpt from "You Belong to Me," words
and music by Pee Wee King, Redd Stewart, and Chilton Price,
copyright © 1952 (renewed) by Ridgeway Music Company, Inc.
All rights reserved. Reprinted by permission of Hal Leonard Corporation.

Interview with Rachel Cline (appeared on cable television show
Books & Authors, 2004) copyright © 2004 *Books & Authors.*
Reprinted by permission of *Books & Authors.*

LIBRARY OF CONGRESS CATALOGING-IN-PUBLICATION DATA
Cline, Rachel.
What to keep : a novel / Rachel Cline.
p. cm.
ISBN 0-8129-7179-5
1. Women dramatists—Fiction. 2. Mothers and daughters—Fiction.
3. Children of divorced parents—Fiction. 4. Columbus (Ohio)—Fiction.
5. New York (N.Y.)—Fiction. 6. Stepfathers—Fiction. I. Title.
PS3603.L555W47   2004
813'.6—dc21   2003054810

Printed in the United States of America

Ballantine Books website address: www.ballantinebooks.com

24689753

Book design by Casey Hampton

FOR MY MOTHER

the reader, writer, and student of life

BOOK ONE

NEUROGENESIS
1976

1

Lily wakes up with a cupcake hovering before her eyes. Denny holds it there, has held it there for a while in fact, waiting for her mother to (1) wake up, (2) make a wish, and (3) blow out the candle. Not so hard, you would think, but it is for Lily. She stares blankly at the tiny flame, and Denny, who at twelve and a half is nearly too old for this sort of thing, is forced to intervene. "Mom," she says, dropping the word into a second, disappointed syllable as Lily's eyes blink, again. "Mom, make a wish. Happy birthday."

Ordinarily, Lily would be the one waking Denny up, so Denny is surprised to find her mother as hard to retrieve from sleep as she is. But that's just how it is. Since her parents' split two years ago, Denny has been in charge of their domestic reality—the here and now of social perception: what other kids' parents are worrying about, what's worth watching on TV (*Little House*), whether or not there is lip-stick on Lily's teeth, and when it's safe to turn left on Broad Street. In return, Lily makes money, buys groceries (by proxy, but more on that later), drives the car, and tells Denny when to turn off the TV.

Lily and Denny Roman live in Bexley, an amiable suburb of Columbus. Unlike the way most suburbs relate to their cities, Columbus has grown *around* Bexley in concentric rings of shopping centers, parks, hospitals, universities, insti-tutes, and bedroom communities. Every ten years or so, the latest ring seems to degrade into slum. Bexley itself is only a mile or so from the old, original downtown (and state capi-tol), but it somehow retains its beauty and its property values. Its houses are large, its schools are excellent, and its trees are immense, forming a canopy over the broad streets. Some of the streets are so wide they have their own grassy median. It's a very old suburb but it has a faint theme: the street names have a Brittanic sound, and many of the houses are distinctly manorial. The Romans' house at 2424 Sherwood Road—just two blocks from Main Street—lacks cupolas and sleeping porches and isn't as large as many in the neighborhood, but it isn't small, either. It is built of gray clapboard with white trim, black shutters, and one little dormer window, on the third floor, looking out at the vast Ohio buckeye tree in the front yard. It is a fine house, built in 1907, and has never needed major repairs.

As Lily rubs her eyes and fumbles for her glasses, Denny nibbles at the pink-frosted cupcake. It's a Hostess Sno Ball, a coconut-flecked demi-globe of pink marshmallow that sur-rounds a wad of chocolate cake. Inside the cake is a tiny inner bolus of something called "creme." In short, it's a food that would give pause to almost anyone over the age of sixteen.

"Perhaps a Sno Ball is not the perfect breakfast food?" asks Lily.

Denny shrugs but halts her attempt to tear off a flag of marshmallow flesh. She stares at the cupcake, replacing it on the plate with its twin as Lily blunders into the bathroom, now awake to the day.

"They're like tits," says Denny, though Lily can't hear her with the shower running. It's not a remark likely to reach Lily's sense of humor, anyway. Denny picks up the two cupcakes and holds them, breastwise, up to her own largely featureless chest. She steps to the mirror as Lily sticks her head out of the bathroom to ask something that she instantly forgets at the sight of Denny's pantomime.

"Look, I developed!" says her daughter, slyly.

"I see that," Lily replies with a nod. The doorbell rings.

Denny raises her eyebrows.

"I have no idea," says Lily.

Denny goes to the bedroom window and looks down. "It's Dad." She's still holding her cupcakes at the ready.

"Go offer him a Sno Ball," says Lily. "And, for God's sake, don't tell him where it's been." This cracks Denny up. Lily returns to the bathroom, not sure she was making a joke. She looks at herself in the steaming mirror and remembers that she has a nine A.M. haircut appointment at Lazarus, downtown. For most of her life, Lily has studiously ignored her appearance—she was pretty enough in her teenage years to take it for granted that she didn't have to fuss. However, since turning forty she finds herself taking a more careful look: She is far too pale, and verging on bony; her wispy blond hair is neither long nor short, and the layered cut that—if properly blown dry—was supposed to look like a less trashy version of Farrah Fawcett's has never been, and will never be, properly blown dry. Moreover, her eyeglasses have worn a pair of purple indentations into the sides of her nose and a formerly inoffensive beauty mark on her cheek has become, decisively and seemingly overnight, a mole.

Denny opens the front door for her father, who looms in the doorway. Charles is tall and slender and mostly bald, prematurely so. His eyes are light brown and crinkly but so far above Denny most of the time that she feels like she never sees them. He wears wire-rimmed glasses but not the John Lennon kind. His are rectangular. Usually he wears turtlenecks under his tweeds, but today he is wearing a shirt and tie. Denny knows he was once physically close to her, she even vaguely remembers it. Now he looks down at her and forgets to smile.

"Mom's in the shower," says Denny. "Want a Sno Ball?"

"Isn't she going to Chicago today?" asks her father.

What Denny doesn't know, and Lily doesn't remember, is that Lily *is* supposed to go to Chicago today, on her birthday, because it's also the annual meeting of the AAN (American Academy of Neurology) and Maureen paid Lily's $500 deposit long ago. The whole point of having someone else manage this type of thing for you is so that you don't forget, even if it *is* your forty-first birthday and you *are* feeling strangely petulant and vulnerable. Unfortunately, sometimes even Maureen's systems break down.

Maureen is Lily's gateway to the world. In some respects,

Maureen is Denny's make-do Dad—the second opinion that makes being a single mother bearable for Lily. Maureen is also a small business that began four years ago as an answering service and grew with the times. Mostly, she works for doctors (her father was an endocrinologist). Now she not only fields calls but acts as a travel agent, bookkeeper, personal shopper, UPS drop and pickup site, contract post office, appointment secretary, and dispatcher of taxis, ambulances, and messengers. Maureen does not do pet care. Maureen and Lily sometimes speak several times a day, as do Maureen and Denny, as do Maureen and Charles (another client). No one really grasps the full extent of Maureen's involvement in this stubby little former family, except Maureen and, maybe, Denny.

"No one else in my class has a Maureen. Why not?" Denny asked, when she was eight.

"Well, there is no one else like Maureen, Denny. Just like there's no one else like you. Put your shoes on."

"You're not answering my question. Does it have something to do with religion?"

"No. What do you mean?"

"I don't know. Sometimes that's why people's families are different."

"Well, we're not that different. Come on, let me tie that. Lots of the other people in the neighborhood use Maureen."

Denny retrieved her sneakered foot from her mother's busy hands, wanting to tie her own damn shoe, though that is not what she said. She simply performed the task, somewhat laboriously, while formulating her response to her mother's statement, which was:

"We don't 'use' Maureen. We 'have' Maureen. That's what you always say. I think it's different."

Lily didn't know what to say to that observation, and anyway, it was time for school.

And it is time for school, again.

Charles stands awkwardly in the kitchen that used to be his, waiting for Lily to finish her shower and for his suddenly alarmingly chic-looking daughter to go upstairs and get dressed. Denny is a little bit short for her age and has enormous black-brown eyes. When she flips her long blondish hair back from a fully bent-over position, it transforms her into a sex goddess for about forty seconds. Then the hair flattens back down and she is a small girl with big eyes, weird coloring, and a defensive stance. The sight of her in her nightgown (a worn black J. Geils Band T-shirt that clearly never belonged to either of her parents) reminds him that Dolores Haze—a.k.a. Lolita—was also about twelve. Coincidentally, on the way over, he had just been thinking with relief that his daughter was finally old enough to be left alone in the house for one night, adequately provisioned with foodstuffs and phone numbers. Now he is thinking she might also be *too* old for any such thing.

"How's work?" asks Denny, swirling her orange juice.

"Fine," says Charles. "How's school?"

"Fine, too. We're doing dissection this year in biology."

"What are you dissecting?"

"Well, first we did a clam. I think next we get an earthworm."

"Not much to see in a clam."

"No kidding."

"Do they give you a cat eventually?"

"Dad!"

"Some kind of mammal?"

"Is a pig a mammal?"

"Of course. You know that."

"At the end of the year we get a fetal pig."

"That's good. Pigs are much closer to humans than you might think."

Denny's not sure that closer to human is good, in her book, but that's how things are talking to Charles. "Yeah, I guess so." She washes her orange juice glass and puts it in the drainer. "I better get ready for school."

Denny's room still harbors most of the toys, games, and books of her early childhood, a condition that she is on the verge of doing something about. Returning to this domain after that typically unsatisfying exchange with her father, she sees it anew as the room of a child. Even the collection of clippings from the *Dispatch* that are taped to the wall over her desk, which only recently seemed to her to lend that corner a serious, newsroom quality, now seem to broadcast the childishness of their subject matter: the fate of the Columbus Zoo's orphan polar bear, Otto. Today, the headline CAN OTTO SURVIVE ADOLESCENCE ALONE? sounds as dopey to her as before it had sounded antic and clever. Denny can't yet deep-six Otto, but, possessed of a ruthless new attitude toward childish things, she instead collects the row of trolls that are lined up on her windowsill and drops them individually into the bottom drawer of her desk ("Good-bye, Lolly; sorry, Skeezix; see you later, Lance"). She scans the room for more victims, but can't figure out what to do with all those picture books about talking animals beside her bed. Among those books, however, is the white leatherette diary that Maureen gave Denny on her last birthday. Denny takes the diary from the shelf and opens it, using the little brass key that is tied to the lock with a matching white grosgrain ribbon. The pages are blank. When Denny received this gift, she had more or less ignored it, but suddenly it has appeal. The idea of the lock is particularly compelling, although she doesn't know from whose eyes she'd be locking it, really. She selects a purple Flair pen from the collection of markers in a mug on her desk and sits down on her bed to write.

She rejects the convention of beginning "Dear Diary"; *diary* sounds too much like *diaper.* Her book will be more like an official record, like the Captain's Log on *Star Trek.* She writes the date at the top of the page, then:

Today is Mom's birthday but I'm not sure she cares. I care, though. I got cupcakes but she didn't eat them. Then Dad came over. He was dressed up for something. We talked about dissecting mammals. Yuck.

Lily comes downstairs and finds Charles standing in the middle of the kitchen doing absolutely nothing.

"Do you want some tea? We have Earl Grey."

"Oh—"

"Oh?"

She measures two spoonfuls of loose tea into the pot without waiting for his answer. Charles doesn't usually stop by at this hour, but when he does stop by it is always without prior warning—there are still some joint investments that need her signature or a book that's his but still on her, formerly their, shelves.

"I thought I could read your paper on the way to Chicago."

Lily's brain swims to the surface: paper, airport, Chicago! She feels as though she's been kicked—and, in a way, Charles looks like he has kicked her.

"It's at the lab."

"Aren't you coming on the same plane?"

"No."

"Isn't your talk at three?"

She turns off the soon-to-scream kettle and empties it into the teapot. She thinks, He has no idea it's my birthday and that I've suddenly gotten old—he can't know how humiliated I feel to have forgotten this conference. As though she believes that "forget" is what she did.

Charles *does* know it's Lily's birthday, but that's not what's on his mind. Someone he knows reviewed Lily's paper and told someone else he knows that she was on to something interesting, possibly even big. Her research is about the events that finally differentiate brain cells from other cells as they develop in the embryo; it's long been established that neurons are the only cells the body never makes more of and Charles assumes Lily's analysis will help explain why.

Lily did not completely forget the conference or the paper, she just ignored them so furiously that it had almost the same effect. She doesn't want to stand in front of all those smug, bespectacled men and feel her face turning red with the effort of not weeping. Though she has spent the past two years

fantasizing about how one day she would triumphantly present this research, her calm certainty has now deserted her.
Lily suspects this is because she's pregnant. She didn't expect
to be, she's not sure she wants to be, but she is.

Charles has been watching her think, an old habit.

"So?" he now asks.

"Excuse me?"

"So what's in your paper?"

"It moves," she says.

The fetus is not old enough to move. This is a reference to
Galileo's supposed last words about the earth relative to the
sun. Back then, the idea that the earth could move was
heresy. Charles resists the reference because he, himself, is
too mired in the current orthodoxy of no new brain cells,
ever.

"What moves?"

"Nothing."

"I hope you're not talking about neuronal reproduction."

"Don't you have a plane to catch?"

"Because that would be career suicide, Lily."

If Charles wasn't so substantial visually (he's not just tall,
he's dark and handsome), you might have to call him an
enigma. Lily, of course, knows Charles intimately, but she's
not convinced that that ever did her any good. Most of the
time, the part of her brain that deals with Charles supplies
the message *Oh, that's just Charles* to any and all behavior the
man enacts and that's the end of it.

"No, trying to be a neurosurgeon and a mother at the
same time—that was suicide. This is just research."

Lily had gotten angry with him once. Denny was four.
Lily was trying to prepare for a procedure, Denny was trying

to finger paint, and Charles was listening to Schubert lieder. About every five minutes, Denny would finish a painting and need a new piece of paper made ready. She visited Lily for this service. Around about page five, Lily asked Denny to ask her Daddy for his help, which Denny did. Charles did help, and in fact wound up finger painting, too. Denny's squeals of delight at their collaborative efforts soon became impossibly distracting to Lily. She closed her door, which didn't help much, and she was even more distracted when the giggling and jabbering stopped. Ultimately, it was the silence that drew her out of her room to find the remains of what had once been a small girl's well-contained project grown to six-foot-man size. Wet paper, newspaper, drying paint, miscellaneous finished and unfinished works littered the kitchen, and Charles had apparently taken Denny out for a walk. By the time they returned, Lily had cleaned up the mess and, in her frustration, thrown away the newspaper drop cloth, which—as it turned out—was Charles and Denny's collaborative magnum opus. Denny burst into tears. Charles promised her they'd make another one right away (i.e., Get out those paints again, Lily). Lily tried to go back to studying. It was hopeless.

Denny doesn't remember any of this, except, dully, the sound of her mother shrieking through the bedroom wall much, much later that night. It's true that Lily had gotten mad, but though she was furious inside, what she did was, mostly, sob. It didn't sound good to Denny and it didn't sound good to Charles, who could barely comprehend his role in the tragedy except to understand that what had seemed that morning like an episode of domestic bliss was also, at least in Lily's eyes, a deep and vicious betrayal.

Charles, an independent sentient being, obviously had the

power to offer alternative interpretations, but he did not, perhaps could not, realize that power. Things might have turned out differently for Charles and Lily if he was a guy who ventured interpretations; but he is a guy who observes until the data is overwhelming and only then acts. At that point in their relationship—that night after the finger-painting catastrophe—Charles's one remark cast a shadow on Lily that instantly recalled every withering comment she'd ever ignored from a colleague, professor, resident, or man in the street. "Stop making a mountain out of a molehill" was what he said. There's a limit to the amount of passive tolerating a pale yet intelligent woman can do. Lily had done it and she was done and she wept inconsolably. She withdrew from her surgical residency later that summer, but it took her another five years to withdraw from Charles.

Lily raps impatiently on Denny's door. "Are you almost ready? It's time to go!" Denny is still on her bed, wearing her J. Geils Band T-shirt and writing in her diary. She is seriously behind schedule and getting dressed now seems like an impossible task. Not that she has a lot of choices—with a mother who hates to shop and no real income of her own, she's pretty much stuck with whatever Sears is minting this year. What she'd *like* are some platform shoes and big curly hair, like the kids she sees on *Welcome Back, Kotter,* when she finishes her homework in time to watch it. What she's got are corduroys and turtlenecks and—at best—a yellow crocheted vest that's supposed to tie cutely between her breasts but succeeds only in hanging like a deflated canary cage. Does the fact that her father forgot to look her in the eye or smile properly upon greeting her exacerbate Denny's what-to-wear crisis? No and yes. Her mother's confounded reaction to the cupcake didn't help, either. Not that Denny's young ego is that fragile or that either parent has been actively remiss, she's just at that very particular point in life where one is at odds with just about everything.

When Charles, Lily, and Denny were all living together in the house on Sherwood Road, they acted as one another's very specific checks and balances. Lily used to err on the side of looking forward, Charles on the side of self-absorption, and Denny on the side of passion. (Of course, no one identifies their six-year-old girl's willfulness as "passion," but Charles and Lily did recognize in Denny an emotional immediacy that was genuine, relentless, and entirely new to both of them.) After her parents' separation, Denny found that the only adult to whom she was neither confounding nor overwhelming was Maureen.

Maureen never minded playing the monster or the policeman and even had some imaginary characters of her own—memorably, a wise old caramel lollipop named Ish Kabibble. (When Denny was seven and had big new front teeth, Maureen had commandeered her partially consumed Sugar Daddy. Because the thing was pocked with bite marks and Denny had pulled the top to a tapering end with her incisors, Maureen pretended it was a silly man with a Brylcreemed forelock. She had it say things like "Buy low, sell high" and "There's no such thing as a bad watermelon." Maureen didn't remember the real Ish Kabibble, the nonsense poet–trumpet player, though she'd seen him once on television at her uncle's apartment when *she* was seven or eight.) Lily and Charles, both brain surgeons by training and ambition, were lousy playmates. They were goal-oriented. They wanted a procedure to follow. They wanted to get it right, whatever it was.

Denny once tried to introduce Ish Kabibble to her mother. It was after dinner, when the consumption of a lollipop was certainly allowed. Lily just scowled at the sticky brown ingot as eight-year-old Denny waved it around, trying to give voice to the wise old Borscht Belt comedian whose cadences she could hear in her head perfectly but could not adequately convey to her mom.

"I don't understand," said Lily. "The lollipop is an old man?"

"No, Mom, he's a lollipop-man. But he's caramel, so he's more like . . . he's not from the normal world."

"He's a Martian or some kind of spaceman?"

"No, more like, I don't know, the circus. See, he has sayings, like he says, 'I resemble that remark.' "

"Oh, he's Groucho Marx."

"Mom! He's not a person."

It was frustrating having someone so literal-minded running the show. Later that year, remembering the talking lollipop debacle, Lily took Denny to the circus, but Denny hated it. The three-ring aspect drove her crazy. Was she supposed be watching the clowns or the lions? Anyway, the clowns weren't funny—all they did was bonk one another on the head. There was no one in the whole Ringling Bros. family even remotely like Ish.

Finally, Denny recollects that there is, in the giveaway

box, an angora sweater of her mother's that shrunk when Lily somehow managed to throw it in with the sheets and towels. This sweater will look neither boring nor childish; there's an outside chance it could even look sexy. Denny's a good way off from having breasts, but there is something newly swollen around her nipples—the flesh around the nipple, which is called the areola. Denny learned this word just last week while speed searching for information on puberty in one of Lily's old textbooks.

Lily hasn't consulted anyone about her pregnancy, not even Maureen, who knows everything. Last week, however, during a five-minute "quick check-in" about the following week's laundry, groceries, postal requirements, etc., Lily told Maureen she'd begun to think that buying both whole and skim milk was unnecessarily extravagant for a household that numbered exactly two. The only wrinkle being that Denny sniffed suspiciously at skim, and Lily, after her own mother had survived a minor heart attack, had decided that maybe she was not immune to cholesterol, after all. At which point Maureen couldn't help laughing (the rhyme) and Lily—having unburdened herself of the substitute fear that she might be depriving Denny her due as a child if she forced her to give up milk fat—was simultaneously unburdened of other, deeper fears: that she is too old to mother another "real" child, an infant; not to mention the fear that something is seriously wrong with her if she truly desires such a thing. She wasn't such a wizard at it the first time. And what about the fear that Denny is old enough now to participate in the rearing of her unborn sibling and might just be better at it—more passionate—than Lily?

Denny would viciously resent the intrusion of this or any other infant. She is nowhere near prepared to be a surrogate mother. Denny is, after all, only twelve and a half. She may talk like a canny sophisticate, but she is a kid, a child, still learning how things work in the world of adults.

Lily is shifting allegiance internally. As her womb prepares to nourish a new symbiote, her years of intermittent but intense emotional symbiosis with her first and only child are slowly being reabsorbed. It's true. Even medically trained Lily won't bring herself to look at her own circumstance this clinically, but there it is: Denny is no longer her baby, whether or not the fetus survives.

2

So, how *did* Lily get pregnant? It's not like she's got a lover. There's no special light in her eyes or bounce in her step. In fact, knowing Lily and discovering the fact of her pregnancy, you'd have to wonder if she didn't slip up in the lab and get some profoundly potent test-tube-reared spermatozoa on her hand shortly before a trip down the hall.

The truth of the matter is that, not quite three months ago, Lily had sex with a guy on a plane—a guy she hadn't seen in five years. His name is Phil. She first met Phil when he was a graduate student. He was really a kid (twelve years younger than she); a sweet kid who clearly admired her and with whom she was relaxed and comfortable but that was it. She had even recommended him to Charles as a smart, competent researcher. Then, at a conference, they had wound up together in a hotel elevator one morning, and then they sat together at the talk, and then, as they left the hall, Phil had quite unconsciously put his hand at her elbow as if to steer. She found herself leaning against him ever so slightly. When she woke up the next morning—with Charles—she had felt as though she was madly in love. It was a total surprise to wake up with her heart full of Phil. He was all of twenty-four and she was thirty-six and theoretically happily married.

Nothing else happened. Phil had taken a post-doc somewhere else. Dallas? But in the months immediately following her breakup with Charles, Phil started appearing in Lily's dreams. First, she dreamt that she was leaning against him in a sailboat. Then there was the one where he took off his shirt and had skin made of velvet. That morning, awake, she remembered the time she had asked him to retrieve a notebook she had left at home. She was writing a grant application that had to go out that night, and he stuck his head into her lab to say hello to one of his classmates, and she begged him to do her this favor. She wrote her address down for him but forgot to tell him, at first, that he could find the house key under the bust of Zeus by the front door. She went to the window to catch him on the way to his car, and saw him from the back, doing a kind of Fred Astaire sliding lunge, alone in the parking lot. It slayed her.

And then, a few months before her forty-first birthday, she was flying home to Columbus from Houston and saw Phil—six feet two in the exit row—staring at her like he'd seen her coming from a long way off.

She'd been to her cousin's wedding. At the last minute, Denny had decided to stay home and spend the weekend with her father, so Lily was alone. The wedding had been her first real confrontation with the family since the divorce and she was exhausted from pretending everything was fine. They were not the sort of people to pry, far from it, but in some ways that made it even harder to be among them. Two-thirds of her uncles and cousins were wildly successful physicians and the rest were utter wrecks, so the middle ground was dangerous. Fifteen years ago, when she got the neurosurgery residency, it had elevated her above suspicion. Before that, her life had been all upward trajectory. But she knew, even if her relatives didn't, that recently she had been falling. She loved her research, but they probably would consider it crackpot. To the women, she was a failure for not having a second child and for separating from Charles. At least her father was dead—she didn't have to face him.

Lily's mother, Anne-Marie, was and always had been a bit mystified by her daughter's prodigious intellectual abilities and drive. Anne-Marie had a fixed idea of Lily that was unshakable but not exactly supportive or warm. And, since she'd recently been ill, she stayed home from the wedding. So it was really just Lily's aunts, uncles, and cousins. Lily had smiled and chatted heroically with them, she thought, and had drunk only two glasses of champagne. Looking at the third glass, she decided to fly home that night instead of staying over, using Denny as her excuse.

Lily and Phil ran out of things to say to each other after about ten minutes, but they still kept grinning and blushing, and when the captain turned the cabin lights down for the movie, they started to neck. Can neurobiologists neck? Phil was not twenty-four anymore, either. Despite the lingering

Howdy Doody quality to his wide eyes and freckled face, he looked like a real person now and, in fact, he was: had his own grant, was on his way to having his own lab and his own post-docs, and no wife. This made it possible for Lily to let herself follow him down the airplane aisle and into the impossibly tiny lav. Airborne sex was an idea that had never in the least appealed to her and it didn't appeal to her then, either, but Phil did; and it appealed to Phil. There was one good thing about the tininess of the room, she thought, which was that it made looking at each other's bodies more gymnastic than it was worth. Given the fish-tank quality of the light, Lily was grateful for that. Phil was grateful for Lily, who, despite her usual slightly cockeyed and unkempt appearance, was oddly self-possessed when it came to sex. She was a little like that fantasy librarian who, behind the Coke-bottle lenses and the tight chignon, is a frisky sex kitten. Phil giggled when she pulled apart the cheeks of his ass as she ground herself into him. Lily!

Getting disentangled and reasonably presentable was another matter. They did it in shifts. Lily half turned her back and sat on the toilet seat as Phil washed himself in the sink. He handed her a crunchy paper towel and she gently dried him from where she sat, glancing up once to see how he was reacting. He was watching her with a childlike look of wonder on his face. Flustered, he scruffled her hair like a Little League coach. Then he zipped up, said "Bye," and left her alone. Lily sat, dazed, in the now large-seeming cubicle. Her panty hose were on the floor and she nudged them gingerly into the trash receptacle. Her skirt was around her neck like one of those collars they put on dogs after surgery. She looked completely ridiculous, but she refused to become ashamed. When she finally got herself reassembled—without benefit of comb, brush, or makeup—she slid out of the bathroom and into an empty seat in a dark row at the rear of the cabin, where she promptly fell asleep.

Phil, back in the bulkhead, eventually came looking for her but, seeing her bobbling head, he let her be. She woke up with a jolt as the plane touched down. She would have been the last one off, but Phil waited for her up front and walked with her down the jetway, his hand once again gently resting on her elbow. He stopped, spooked, just before the end, and asked her, "Is Charles . . . ?" but she shook her head.

They parted at the curb; neither had much luggage. Phil was picking up a rental car and driving on to a family reunion near Marysville. She did not offer her phone number, because it was the same one as always, and it was in the phone book. She did not tell him she was single, because she couldn't think of any way to do so that made sense. And they didn't kiss at the curbside, because they were in Lily's hometown more or less. So Lily went to long-term parking and Phil went to Hertz and that was that.

Until about a month later, when Lily missed her period. She knew she was pregnant. She'd had premonitions of it several times since seeing Phil, some of which were more physical than mental. But she couldn't find a way to consider what this might mean to her, let alone to Phil, or Charles, or Denny. It was so disconnected from anything real in her life: her patients, her research, her daughter, her house. . . . "Baby" didn't fit in anywhere, except where she was loneliest and least verbal.

At four in the morning, lying in bed, she pictures nursing again. Driving home from work, she smells the inimitable smell of baby scalp and almost swoons. But she does not speak of it, or plan for it, or ask herself how or why she could fit it into her life. She assumes it will go away by itself, not meant for her, really; just briefly on loan from the library of souls. In the daylight, Lily adamantly disbelieves the superstitious things that others say about why sometimes the sperm hit home. She knows better than to suspect herself of unconsciously flexing her fallopia, beckoning some iota of Phillip Coughlin's green-flecked-iris gene toward her ripest ovum. The idea that her fortieth birthday might have sent some panic afoot in her reproductive anatomy is ludicrous to her: She has a child, and one is plenty for a single working woman. The species cannot expect her to do any more of its work than she has already done. At least not with her loins.

She doesn't call Phil or even try to. She has a vivid, fond memory of their encounter and holds on to it fiercely, fearing it might easily be her last of the type (passionate encounter, not sex-in-the-sky). Her life is too full for a boyfriend. She does, once, picture running into Phil again, years ahead, with her beautiful grown-up daughter and her tall, freckled geek of a son. And if she is still single then and so is he, maybe she'll marry him. She'll be past fifty. What difference would any of this make then?

In a perfect world, Denny would be spared any impact from Lily's condition or the rash act that precipitated it. But the fact that Lily has been keeping this secret from her, perhaps the first real secret, is the ultimate legacy of Lily's poorly anticipated forty-first birthday.

On the morning of that birthday, Lily drives Denny to school in their pale blue VW squareback. It's close enough to walk, but lately they're always running late at the getting-dressed point and particularly today, because of Charles's visit and Denny's foray into the giveaway box. Lily didn't really get a good look at the sweater until just now, when she reached across Denny's chest to pull the passenger seat belt outward (a motherly reminder). In so doing, her forearm glanced Denny's fuzzy chest and this sensation struck her as quite familiar in an unfamiliar way. It also reminded her of a story she'd heard the day before at the clinic—about a man who, inconsolable over the death of his wife, had shaved his own legs in order to be reminded of her as he lay alone in bed. The story had made her cry, though she didn't look up from the data she was supposedly transcribing at the time. But the sweater provokes a different response.

If she could tell the truth, even to herself, the sensation is sexual; but of course she can't tell that truth. Instead, she turns to Denny a little too abruptly and takes a careful look at her daughter's prepubescent front, straining in angora. Before Denny even thinks any words to herself, she sees the judgment in her mother's eyes and her little chest begins to cave in response. The question Lily ultimately coughs up— "Are you really comfortable in that thing?"—is not, as Denny can clearly see, what Lily is thinking. That's something more like, "How dare you dress yourself as a woman?"

Denny says, "You put it in the giveaway box. You said I could have it."

Lily can't backpedal fast enough to catch up with her own

thoughts, let alone soothe Denny. She's trying too hard to cover up too much. "Better go, you'll be late," she says.

So Denny goes to school self-conscious and angry, and Lily, after taking a moment to watch her daughter safely into the building, fails to see the oncoming station wagon that buries its right front fender in the driver door of her VW with a thunderous crunch. The noise, a cross between a thump and a clang, certainly sounds like death, but Lily is only knocked unconscious for a few seconds—a minute at most. She revives enough to exchange paperwork and reassurances with the other driver, an old Italian man who is nearly weeping with anxiety and regret. Talking to him through the driver window while he stoops to look into her eyes, Lily is unaware of the damage to her car and oblivious of almost everything but the man's alarmed face. She goes into doctor mode instantaneously. Her voice is soothing, her manner serene.

Although her cheek is bleeding, her door won't open, and she knows better than to drive with a head injury, Lily proceeds downtown to her hair appointment in a kind of trance. She parks on High Street, right in front of Shaw's Jewelers.

Maureen has made an appointment for Lily at Richard's salon inside the venerable F. R. Lazarus department store. There is a well-meaning urban-renewal campaign in progress downtown (with the slightly apologetic slogan "Columbus— We're Making It Great"), and most of the central shopping district, with the exception of the flagship Lazarus store, is slated for demolition. No ground has yet been broken, but just in the past year or so, the formerly busy neighborhood has begun to feel desperate. Bexley people have largely stopped shopping there, although no one openly admits this. They are not racist, after all, and that would be the implication. In fact, Columbus's inner-city dwellers would prefer to shop in the newer malls, too, but they'd have to take two buses to get to any of them. Lily is unaware of all this and Maureen knows only what she reads in the daily *Dispatch,* which tells a brightly optimistic story of the changes downtown. It's not as if by sending Lily to Richard's salon Maureen has put her in harm's way—it's just that, even six months ago, Lily would certainly have run into people she knew there, and one of them would have realized she was dazed, or even seen the accident and asked about it, and Lily might have gotten to the E.R. a lot sooner.

First period, Denny has homeroom with half of the kids in her grade. For the most part, she hates them. If they were in the grade above her or even the grade below she probably wouldn't feel that way but they are not. She has been being misunderstood by these very specific youngsters for seven years now and, at this late date, she cannot be bothered to imagine that they contain any hidden aspects that might interest her, now or ever. Her best friend, Julie Moyer, moved to Boston over a year ago, leaving Denny with a macramé bracelet to remember her by. Now Denny really says hello to only three people: Beatrice, a fifth-grader who believes Denny to be a goddess (literally—even Denny doesn't quite get it); Juanita, a Harley-riding lunch lady with a gimlet eye; and Henry Goldblum, a profoundly introspective geek who, posing as a standard-issue math-and-science nerd, passes undetected in the social maelstrom of the Bexley Middle School. (He and Denny once built a very successful fort together when they were about six, and this bond persists as "Hi" and "How ya doing?") She also checks in with Maureen two or three times a day, not for emotional support or anything—just as a matter of coordinating her ride home, her dinner time, whether there is anything to pick up at Maureen's, that kind of thing.

Denny sits in homeroom wondering if everyone else will find her sweater as horrifying as her mother seemed to— next period is usually English, but that has been superseded by play rehearsal because the premiere is tonight. (There is a final dress rehearsal this afternoon, as well.) After that, she has biology lab and then lunch. Because of the tight-fitting sweater, Denny considers whether she can avoid confronting any of the truly mean girls in her grade before lunch, and whether hiding in the bathroom would be any safer. Unable to resolve this question, she begins a letter to Julie in Boston. The letter is all about Lily, but it's not a complaint about Lily and the sweater, or even about Lily and Charles. It gains momentum with a phony-sounding squall of concern for her mother.

The poor thing barely even noticed the cupcakes I brought her, and I could tell she was way too tense (pair of tepees) to appreciate the song I was going to do. Then, she left the house with her shirt buttoned wrong and had the nerve to make a comment about my sweater. I don't know what I'm supposed to do when she's like that. It's very sad, don't you think?

There was *supposed* to have been a song, but the Sno Balls by themselves had failed so miserably that Denny bailed on the impression of Marilyn Monroe serenading JFK that she had worked up last week after school, with considerable help from Maureen.

"Why Marilyn Monroe?" Maureen asked her.

"Because she was the sexiest woman on earth?"

"Uh-huh. And that has what to do with your mother, exactly?"

"Well, nothing. It's just a show. Mr. Wood says dramatic characters should be the 'est' of whatever they are—biggest, smartest, most."

"Uh-huh."

"And Mom always says she'd rather have a present that I made than one I bought."

Fair enough, decided Maureen.

"Well, to sound like Marilyn, you have to sing in like a whisper: 'I wanna be loved by you, by you and nobody else but you.' "

Denny listened skeptically to this demonstration. "Do you think Mom will get it?"

"Why not?" she asked. Then she told the story of how Marilyn had to be sewn into the jeweled gown she wore for the president's birthday because it was too tight for a zipper.

As homeroom wears on, Denny recalls an earlier plan for Lily's birthday: she was going to cut out during lunch and obtain a puppy from the pound. Possibly in one of Maureen's taxis. Maybe that would have been a better idea, after all. Lily

grew up with a collie named Bert, about whom she remi-
nisced from time to time with Denny. Among other things,
Bert was purported to eat peppermints. Since her mother's
lack of free time had always been the reason that Bert had no
successor, and since Denny herself is now old enough to walk
and feed a dog, Bert II at first seemed the perfect present for
Lily. Furthermore, in Denny's fantasy, Bert II would have
been trained to snarl ferociously at the appearance of Faith
Jackson, who Denny hates more than anyone in the entire
seventh grade, maybe the world.

Faith is not one of the mean girls. She's on the quiet side
and will probably grow up to do something genuinely good
for humanity—like teach school in Appalachia or run a rural
health cooperative in Zaire. But she's not a saccharine goody-
goody, either. What she is is someone who seems to intu-
itively finesse every circumstance that Denny finds
insurmountable. The "My Summer Vacation" essay, for example: Denny tries to make hers funny and clever and succeeds only in being cryptic and suspiciously negative:

The Lake at my grandmother's house is really just a
pond but everyone there calls it "the Lake," anyway. I
guess "pond" just sounds too hick for them. In my opinion, for something to really be a lake it has to have fish,
or at least frogs or minnows. The pond just has water-
striders and blue-bottles, and other giant, weird bugs.

Faith writes a fairly straight-ahead report of a day at the
state fair and comes across as placid, optimistic, and good
with facts:

If you have never seen all the things that can be made from cattle besides meat, you are really missing something. Even the film for your camera is made from gelatin and there's a pudding called "Junket" that has a cow enzyme in it. Cattle products are everywhere!

Denny could puke. Another example is *"Repetirle"* in Spanish class. Faith, whose accent is hopeless, responds with total commitment and simple accuracy, which earns her immediate praise. Denny grinds her gears in an attempt to "sound" Spanish in form and content and therefore, of course, hardly says anything at all. Faith's bag lunch always contains a bag of chips, a piece of fruit, and a treat of some kind, in addition to the sandwich. Denny's rarely has more than one element and that element is usually a sandwich of either peanut butter or bologna. Once, Lily had run out of the above and sent an actual can of tuna fish and a stack of saltines wrapped in tin foil (but no can opener). Faith happened to observe this particular lunchroom faux pas. She was not derisive, just amazed.

"Wow," she said, "do your parents own a grocery or something?"

"My parents are brain surgeons. They don't have time to cut up carrot sticks. Want to make something of it?"

Denny likes to tell people her mother is a brain surgeon, even though it's no longer true. Lily *was* trained as a pediatric brain surgeon and she *did* practice when Denny was younger, but now she spends two days seeing patients at the clinic and the rest of the week at the lab, doing research.

When Denny was three or four, she used to play with blocks on the floor of the living room while Lily studied her next surgical patient's films. Lily laid out the slides, X-rays, and micrographs side by side on the floor. Of course, Denny was not allowed to touch them—that's what the blocks were for. Working from flat images, Lily would memorize the shapes and spaces between the microscopic vessels clustered around tomorrow's tumor, aneurism, or plaque. (An ability to visualize the surgical field in three dimensions is the defining skill of the brain surgeon.) "This little boy has a tumor on his trigeminal nerve, which will be very hard to get to," she would tell Denny, starting out as though her daughter might actually follow along. Lily continued to describe the problems she saw in increasingly technical terms. She might tell her daughter what job a particular structure performed, but she never named the consequences of a possible error—there was no talk of rendering her patients comatose or blind, in spite of Denny's very frequent question, "Why?"

In her own mind's eye, Denny turned the landscapes her mother described into a kind of gray-matter theater, where characters like Spinal Process, Plaque, and Dendrite played hide-and-seek and sang songs about memory, sight, taste, smell, speech, and hearing. She could tell that much was left unsaid, but this just added to the sense of drama.

Why does Denny, at twelve, still cling to the old version of her mother's job? Because it cost her so much. Denny trained herself to accept Lily's frequent long absences by cultivating a fairly gruesome vision of Lily at work, sawing through the scalps of all the *other* children, who thrashed and bled copiously. The god of neurosurgery was a vengeful god, in Denny's mind, and the sin of needing Lily was apparently high on his list—you could pay in flesh or in a feeling of abandonment that stole over you unexpectedly. Though Lily ultimately reorganized her career and her life for Denny's sake, her daughter's early adaptations were as vigorous and enthusiastic as Denny herself.

Lily's hair is now neatly chin-length and close to dry. It is light blond (naturally, give or take a streak) and unusual in its contrast to her olive skin and green-gold eyes—the product of a Polish mother and a father whose family started out in Sardinia. At the moment, in spite of her near-perfect hair, Lily is not looking her best. The adrenaline that kicked in to get her out of the accident and over to the salon has worn off and she is feeling shaky. Richard, her stylist, seems oblivious—grooving along to Morris Albert's "Feelings" as he blows her hair dry. She thinks she heard him sing along using the words "feel me," but ignores it because he is clearly gay and she knows herself to be in an odd mental state. Richard really is concerned about Lily—and he did sing "feel me," but only because he thinks those are the real words. He knows today's her birthday because Maureen told him so when she made the appointment, and—romantic that he is—he thinks Lily's present bruised appearance is the result of the particular flavors of loneliness and loss shared by middle-aged divorced moms and queeny men in their thirties as they face the insults of age. Flicking off the dryer with a flourish, he puts a hand on Lily's shoulder and looks into her eyes in the mirror.

"You look gorgeous, don't you?"

Lily smiles a crinkly, Charlie Brown smile that is not too convincing.

"Can we give you a little birthday present? A facial, maybe? Or a pedicure?" Lily doesn't much like the idea of someone paring away at her feet. She has no idea that a facial involves equally invasive levels of scrutiny.

"Maybe a facial is a good idea. I'd like to lie down for a while. But won't it ruin my hair?"

"You couldn't find a better place to ruin your hair, honey. It's like breaking your leg at the hospital."

Lily has not exactly forgotten about the plane she's supposed to be on, or the paper she's supposed to present, but the last thing she needs today is a roomful of neuroscientists and she is stalling. What her research has uncovered is something no one wants to hear: her mockingbirds don't just learn new tunes, they grow new brain cells within which to store them. It's not bad news from the point of view of being a neuron owner, but Lily's colleagues don't think like neuron owners. This is probably why she has never really gotten along with very many of them, besides Charles.

The neuroscientists don't want the fundamental assumptions on which they've built their own research being picked apart, especially not by some thin blond woman who never laughs at their jokes. This is why a facial sounds like a good idea.

CHAPTER

4

Denny's drama teacher is a hip young man with a big laugh and a reddish goatee. Rufus Wood is profoundly, utterly charming and the immediate ally of every child who enters his classroom. He never condescends, and he is a wellspring of the type of wisdom, knowledge, and perspective that galvanizes most children's respect. He knows how to balance a salt shaker on its edge in a pinch of salt, for example, and has also shown the class how to give breasts to the Land O'Lakes squaw by tearing and folding the cardboard box in a certain way.

Many of the girls have painful crushes on Rufus, and his idiotic influence will shadow their early decisions and impulses about sex for years to come. Denny is still largely immune to the demands of her own sexual desires. (She does have them, they just haven't yet cracked the surface. There's nothing that distracts her from her homework or, for that matter, from her idealization of her mother. She doesn't even like horses.) But unlike most of her peers, Denny was suspicious of Mr. Wood before entering his class. His cultlike following of seventh-graders past alerted her "otherness" sensors.

Wood's students were always in high spirits when she passed them tearing down the hall or the stairs. They became infected with Wood's particular form of slang and accompanying worldview before Thanksgiving, without fail. They spoke of the kids outside their coterie as the "Idonwanna-knows," an imaginary tribe of Native Americans (no offense) with a mysterious set of rituals and beliefs. Rufus Wood is so charming and charismatic that even his colleagues tend to fall in line with him, though they sometimes recognize the source of his insights in, say, late Laing or early Zappa. Rufus is so delighted with his own tiny tribe of followers, so whole-heartedly amused by the antics of the PTA and of his friends and enemies on the teaching staff, that no one can really think ill of him for long. Even Denny.

Especially since the day they started making "guerrilla theater" out of *Damn Yankees* and Denny became both one of the chorus of ballplayers and (not that she *cares*) the understudy for the role of Lola. Since then, Denny has been giving Rufus a tentative chance. The fact that the part of Lola went to Virginia Cecci, the only girl in the grade with actual breasts, has somehow escaped the class's radical analyses. Feminism is not part of the lesson plan. It's true, Virginia can also carry a tune. But still . . . she's a long way from compelling when seen from across the school auditorium.

Rufus Wood has noticed how, when sitting at a desk, Denny twists her hair, chews her pencil, and rolls her eyes. He was a nail-biter, himself. But Denny backstage is another matter—she is placid, almost catlike, sitting on the floor with her shoes off. When the lights go down, she drops further into this meditative state: her limbs are slack, but her eyes focus like those of a night predator. She loves the sense of being "inside" the world of the play—not just the drama but the whole backstage environment. It's like a secret club, or a very large family with lots of rituals and traditions. Since her own family is tiny and has no rituals or traditions that she can identify, she longs for this.

This morning, Rufus sits beside Denny in the wings—she with her legs folded, he with heels planted and forearms on knees. At one point, he drops his arm slightly, just enough to glance her thigh. Probably, this excites him a tiny bit. Denny, too, though for other reasons in the long run. Or are they?

"Did you see that?" he whispers.

"What?" asks Denny.

"Virginia's double take. Paul took her arm; he's never done that before. See, she's still wincing."

Of course she had seen it all, but she hadn't interpreted it, and now she feels as though she's been let in on a secret. There is nothing in adult life like the swelling of self that's provoked by this kind of inclusion in the adult male world when the hemisphere you otherwise occupy is solely child-female. If Denny were a lab rat, this is a lever she would press again and again. So, there is more than a little collusion from her in Rufus's game of physical-intimacy-that-supposedly-bespeaks-intellectual-parity. It's just that his end is so much simpler, really. The delighted gaze of a twelve-year-old girl, whether on you or near you, has the power of gravity itself.

There is nothing "wrong" going on here, be certain of that. On the contrary, this is education at its purest: student and teacher intent on the same enterprise, relying on each other's unique comprehension of the task at hand. But it's darn close to being wrong. Does anyone really know exactly where that boundary is unless they cross it?

Onstage, Paul Rappaport, a small, blue-eyed kid with a nice tenor voice, is rehearsing the role of Joe, a middle-aged man who has accepted an offer from the devil to be made young again in order to play baseball. Paul sings "Good-bye, Old Girl," Joe's poignant farewell to his loyal, old wife. The house is dark, the wife is asleep, the cab is waiting, and Joe's combination of denial and tenderness is such that, were he not singing, the adult women in the audience would have to groan and howl in disgusted recognition, "You 'have to go'? To be a baseball star at fifty? Give me a break! And quit calling me 'old'!"

Denny finds the song excruciatingly sad. It so neatly encapsulates her fantasy of how difficult it must have been for her own hero-dad to leave when he and Lily decided to separate. She's gotten pretty good at not really listening to Paul Rappaport sing this song.

Now Rufus turns to her and whispers, "Do you think Paul understands what he's singing about?" This inquiry is uncomfortably close to the mark of Denny's private train of thought—she feels exposed. In keeping with their "approach" to the play, the class has discussed this scene at some length and is fully aware of the irony imparted by having the over-the-hill-and-magically-made-young Joe played by a twelve-year-old boy not yet at his physical peak in any respect. Rufus isn't asking if Paul gets the irony—he's attempting to probe the extent of Denny's identification of Joe with her own absent father because, like any connoisseur of local gossip, Rufus knows the whole story of the neurosurgeons who couldn't quite separate but nevertheless divorced. He is prying. And he is also trying to help. In short, Rufus is acting almost like a real adult.

Denny desperately, and secretly, wants to have a big part in this play. Denny, therefore, wants to believe that what Rufus really meant was, "No one understands this story better than *you*," despite the fact that the story, as a whole, resonates for her only faintly. She understands this scene because she has so often imagined, on her father's behalf, the agony of leaving your own home because of more pressing, or at any rate less negotiable, obligations.

Charles left because Lily told him they could no longer live together in silence in front of their daughter. It didn't occur to him to reframe their problem as something a little less absolute. "Let's play Monopoly after dinner" might have been one solution. But framing the problem was Lily's role in their marriage. Anywhere else, Charles was so certain of his superior intellect, he rarely even formed his sentences as questions. He was a statement guy. The question he might have asked Lily, "Why can't we try to talk to each other?," would have admitted ignorance, or possibly even anger. Instead, he chose to view the end of his marriage as some heroic duty that should not be mentioned, some subparagraph of the Hippocratic oath known only to those who are bound by it: Do no harm, but also show no weakness. Therefore, what Denny saw on the day he left was a six-foot-four-inch man stifling tears as he rolled up seven pairs of socks to carry away to an undisclosed location later revealed to be the Y. Denny sat on the floor and watched her dad at his dresser, and begged for a fuller explanation. She got none, but that isn't something she remembers with any rancor, yet. She just remembers how stuck he looked and how—what is the word?—how noble.

CHAPTER

5

Maureen doesn't remember when she realized that her life, as the word is commonly understood, had ended. She is not dead, she has simply stopped living. The transition was extraordinarily subtle. Maureen is a shut-in at age thirty-five, but she stills applies eye makeup every day.

Last winter, weeks and weeks went by during which she had every intention of, for example, walking to the mailbox on the corner instead of leaving her outgoing mail clothes-pinned to the boxes inside the door to the two-story brick building on Bexley's Main Street where she lives and works. (Its ground floor houses the barbershop, the florist, and a ladies' clothing store called Fashion Bug.) She certainly never made a conscious decision to stop going to the grocery store. She didn't even like the delivery kid—and that was five or six delivery kids ago. Some had been obnoxious, one had been outright menacing, claiming to have a score to settle with her about a scratch on his car—he mistook her for someone he had sideswiped in a parking lot recently. But by then groceries-by-phone had become so habitual that she never bothered to consider the surly, purple-lipped adolescent who might appear when, list complete, she said, "thanks" and "good-bye." She never considered who would be sent to her along with her careful enumeration of citrus fruits and cans of soup. She is not afraid—she has the cabbies on her side. All she has to do is pick up the radio handset and speak.

A sideline of Maureen's business is dispatching and managing a rogue threesome of independent taxicab drivers who recently defected from another dispatcher's frequency. With the business generated by Maureen's doctors, their spouses and children, along with the occasional package to the airport and, not to be forgotten, actual fares that hail from the street, the hacks do just fine and are no trouble at all. In some ways, the cabbies are Maureen's best friends. They demand nothing. There is Rhonda, a chain-smoking grandmother of sixty-five with a dyed red bouffant hairdo. Rhonda specializes in long hauls to West Virginia and Cincinnati—she's got grandchildren in both places. Rhonda brought along Dude, a former rodeo rider from Jackson, Mississippi, who is a recovering alcoholic. Dude is quiet and careful—he was a mean drunk and has five grown children who don't speak to him. He's also dying of liver cancer, but he doesn't know it because he hasn't been to a doctor since he got out of the service in '68. Finally, there is Oumar, a Mauritanian refugee. He is so dark-skinned he practically absorbs light. Oumar's family is still in Africa. He came to Columbus because a Peace Corps kid he met ten years earlier invited him. When he got to town, the kid was long gone but his parents let Oumar sleep in their son's then-empty bedroom for two weeks, and so Columbus is where he lives. Maureen and the drivers have potluck supper together, at Maureen's place, once every month or so. They eat, they play gin rummy, and they watch the late movie.

One night not too long ago, they watched the John Ford picture *The Searchers*. Each of them understood, and misunderstood, different things in the film. Oumar was mystified by the concept of the Texas Rangers—in essence a self-ordained private police force. "In this country, Texas, you do not have the rule of law?" he asked his companions.

"Texas only became part of the U.S. in 1845," Maureen answered, proud to remember the date, "right before this movie is set. It's not like that anymore," she added hopefully. She knows that Oumar believes everything she says. She has cousins in Houston. They vote Democratic.

Oumar accepted Maureen's answer but was still uncomfortable with the ethical landscape of the movie. There were so many different types of clan membership in it (family, tribe, Confederate states, Union Army, Texas Rangers), but none of them conformed very closely to what he had known in either Mauritania or in Columbus, Ohio.

Dude had an encyclopedic understanding of the origins and customs of the Texas Rangers but was disgusted by the film's sloppy geography. It seemed to him that scenes were set where they were set only "for looks," with no regard to the actual lay of the land.

Rhonda was fine with the Rangers, the geography, and

believed John Wayne—"the Duke"—to be a godlike figure, but she had no patience for the love story between a blond schoolteacher type and a handsome "half-breed" young man. For Rhonda, the idealized interracial love affair undercut the "real" point of the movie: the Duke's quest to rescue his niece (the young Natalie Wood) from Scar (the evil Commanche war chief) and his subsequent determination to murder the girl after he learns that she has become Scar's squaw. This storyline, to Rhonda, was the essence of American grit. "A man's gotta do what a man's gotta do," she echoed dreamily.

Maureen watched anxiously as her weekly family gathering threatened to devolve into an idiotic race war. The racial aspects of the story flew right by Oumar, however. (To his eyes none of the purported ethnics in the movie were other than Caucasian, and he never listens to Rhonda, anyway.)

Maureen has other friends she speaks to once a week or so who have not seen her in person in over a year. Lunch dates are made and broken, prospective men are lined up and set adrift by scheduling demons, and somehow—quite unconsciously—Maureen maintains the illusion of participation in the world around her. No one thinks of her as a cat lady or a lost cause. No one offers to come by and take her "out of that place," because no one realizes she hasn't been. To them, "that place" is just a charming little strip of stores on Bexley's Main Street. Because Maureen subscribes to *Rolling Stone,* because she mentions meaning to check out the new Lazarus at the mall, because she works out on the stationary bike and listens to the news on the radio, her speech never quite acquires that underwater quality one expects from a shut-in. So she passes. It helps that the phone has always been her instrument.

Her telephone manner, even with friends, is preternaturally alert and mercurial, like her face. She looks like the Irish colleen she is named for, in spite of having been raised by a Protestant woman with absolute contempt for the Irish and their religion. Maureen's phone manner is uniquely suited to Maureen's unique form of work: Maureen, Inc. She got the idea from the busy allergist whose office she used to run. He was always threatening, affectionately, to clone her. Then, one afternoon as she was eyeballing an incredibly expensive photocopier in the office supply catalog, she saw how the better idea was to clone him. And so she did.

Although Maureen thinks that her clients have, in many ways, been the root cause of her retreat, she doesn't blame them. That their demands are relentless is only what she has offered to tolerate for steady pay and no visible boss. Her ability to interpret, negotiate, and address those demands is a point of professional pride as well as a sucking sound around her soul. This is her rationale, even if it is a pack of lies. The unfathomable side effect of always "being there" for her clients is that she must sustain occasional blasts of almost unbearable intimacy—moments when she not only knows "too much" about her people and their loved ones (for example that Dr. Allen's wife, Amy, tried to hold her breath for the duration of any trip to the bathroom that involved a bowel movement), but when she also can't help but surmise how they deeply, secretly feel and what they want most fervently from life. These incursions are what's killing her, at an imperceptible rate.

Revelations come to her without warning from the accumulation of tiny details that should, by common sense, divulge nothing. Just by accretion, the time of the weekly tennis game, the amount of the donation to the Juvenile Diabetes Foundation, and the sudden need for four new tires would collide in Maureen's brain and result in the wrenching conviction that Arthur Keves's father had been tortured by Nazis and left his son with an overwhelming fear of the dark. And then she would know the truth of her discovery as well as she knew her watch was five minutes slow. She also knew with equal certainty that this was something she could never address, let alone fix. Sometimes she thinks it's genetic, that her emotional antennae came along with her exceedingly thin, freckled skin (and her curly brown hair and green eyes) from those Druids or Celts about whom her father was such a sap.

So Maureen stays away from encounters, confidences, and any kind of witnessing that takes place in person with clients. Obviously, she cannot avoid a certain amount of information gleaned over the phone, but without visual substantiation she is largely able to forget, or at least ignore, those clusters of detail. Lily's pregnancy, nevertheless, is something that she has not only intuited but that haunts her. For all Maureen knows, Lily and Charles have still been occasional lovers. She knows enough about both their schedules to doubt the presence of any other contenders for either of their attentions. Except Denny, of course.

Maureen's only rule is that she doesn't do pets. This began as an entirely reasonable boundary—she doesn't baby-sit, either. At some point, however, the no-pets rule became a litmus test of her unacknowledged depression. Maureen has to ask herself, in less vigilant moments, if the real reason she doesn't do pets is because pets go outside and she doesn't. When this question leads, quite logically, to counterarguments about hamsters and turtles, Maureen has to suspect herself, at least momentarily, of being insane.

Denny and her lab partner, Josh Walker, are dissecting an earthworm. Denny has very little stomach for slime, but, as the daughter of physicians, she pretends well. Inside the earthworm, believe it or not, are eggs. For some reason, Denny finds these tiny pearlescent globes even more nauseating than the earthworm's feces, which are also readily apparent along the featureless, all-purpose earthworm canal.

Josh catches a glob of the egg-goo on his dissecting tool and flings it at Denny. He has been mightily distracted by Denny's tight-fitting sweater since she sat down opposite him, and this is his inarticulate response to its stimulating fuzz. Denny shrieks, as who wouldn't? What's worse, she flinches, and therefore has no idea where the unborn earthworms may have lodged. In her hair? In her eye? In her mother's sweater? She would very sincerely like to claw out Josh's eyes, but she starts to raise her hand, instead. Josh stops this immediately, grabbing her arm.

"Oh, come on, you're not going to tell on me!"

"Why not?"

"I was just goofing around. Come on, Denny. It probably didn't even land on you!"

This piece of highly comforting information inspires a compromise.

"So, then, let me do the dissection and you take the notes."

Josh complies but now feels he's probably been swindled, and when Denny gets far enough ahead of him in the lab instructions that he's in danger of not catching up, he returns to the offensive.

"Since when are you so interested in earthworms, all of a sudden?" he asks.

No response from Denny as she tweezes the entire digestive-reproductive tract out of the earthworm.

Josh continues: "Why are you making me take the notes? You don't even like science."

"Maybe," says Denny, pausing for emphasis, "it's because I've got half a brain."

She doesn't even look up from the process of teasing the worm's own tiny neural node from its slimy home. Josh is now not only incensed, but Denny has left him so far behind that he has nothing left to do but stare directly, relentlessly, at her chest, which, much too late for it to be recognized as an actual rejoinder, gives him the following idea.

"Maybe so. You've sure got only half-tits!" This, of course, succeeds in getting Denny's attention.

"Shut up!" she yells, loud enough to be heard across the room.

Josh, encouraged, begins a whispered incantation: "Half-tit, half-tit . . ."

Denny, still under the uncomfortable impression that there's earthworm spawn on her somewhere, and now increasingly enraged with her mother, the sweater, the earthworm, and Josh Walker, yells, "More like an eighth, you idiot!" and pulls the sweater up over her head, exposing her essentially flat chest to Josh for at least a count of three.

More or less the whole class witnesses some portion of this display, and after a prolonged moment of shocked silence, the boys begin to hoot and holler. Denny turns to the jeering idiots. "I'm twelve years old. I've got mosquito bites—what's the big freaking deal?"

Miss Boles, their severe African American science teacher, strides up to Denny and Josh's lab station, blocking the view that lingers so substantially in the minds of the seventh-graders.

"Eden?"

"Yes, Miss Boles?"

"Are you quite finished?"

"He was making fun of my . . . chest."

Even now, there are remnants of a hormonal gleam in Josh's eyes.

"I don't doubt that," says Miss Boles, "and I'm sending you both to Mrs. Rainey—but you, Eden, are going first. Right now."

After listening skeptically to Denny's story, Mrs. Rainey issues a detention. Since Denny can't stay after school tonight or tomorrow because of the play, Mrs. Rainey also asks her for a written explanation—an apology—due tomorrow morning.

The only good news is that the tale of Denny's outburst will not reach Mr. Wood until tomorrow. Otherwise, Denny would soon be chafing under some nickname like "Hot Stuff" or possibly even "Skeeters." Rufus believes the hours between final dress and opening night to be sacrosanct and will not stray from the stage area into the faculty lounge between now and then. This guarantees, however, that what he will hear about the incident tomorrow will be even worse for Denny, having been elaborated and embroidered that much more. And her defense, or apology, or whatever it's supposed to be, will be useless, revisionist history.

Everything will be different tomorrow, anyway, she tries to cheer herself: She will have made up with her mother; she will have lived through watching everyone else's curtain calls from the wings tonight; and she will have finally changed out of the sweater with its itchy neckline, sweaty armpits, and invisible veil of earthworm spume. But wait, she can run over to Maureen's right now and solve that last problem first.

Denny's real name *is* Eden. Maureen knows this because she gets the mail from Denny's school before Lily does. Still, she finds it out of character: whether its origins are biblical, Hollywood, or idyllic Old South, it makes no sense for Denny or her parents. Maureen even entertained a passing fantasy of Lily and Charles as former members of the Woodstock nation, wishing their way "back to the Garden," but Denny was born before anybody'd ever heard of Yasgur's Farm. Luckily, Denny suits Eden just fine, and as there are no romantics, no Baptists, no hippies, no southerners, and no starlets in the family, the name carries no obligations.

Though she dials Lily, Denny's principal reaches Maureen. (In Mrs. Rainey's official version, the epithet "half-tit" is omitted, as is the earthworm, and Denny's transgression becomes the uncomfortably clinical "exposed herself in science class.") Maureen knows Kristina Rainey, though the principal herself is not a client, and Mrs. Rainey knows Maureen. Maureen is at the other end of quite a few phone calls in Mrs. Rainey's life, and not just the disciplinary ones. Mrs. Rainey may not drive—she left the scene of a fatal collision two years ago, coming home from Christmas shopping on a snowy night. She gets her rides from Maureen's taxi drivers. Mrs. Rainey wants to make sure that Maureen tells Lily about the written explanation she has asked Denny to provide—it's a tough assignment and Denny will need adult help, suspects Mrs. Rainey, especially because she will be getting home late, after the play.

Maureen listens. She knows Lily is about to get on a plane and she knows Denny is a kid she knows how to talk to and can probably even "reach" if it comes to that. She therefore excuses herself briefly, then calls back to report that she has spoken to Lily when of course she has not. Her only uneasiness derives from her certain knowledge that Lily has no idea that Denny's play is tonight—and that she ought to be back in time for it. The play was not really on Maureen's radar until now and, hence, not on Lily's. Of course, the flyer has been stuck to Lily's fridge for several weeks, but no one reads the flyers on their fridge, do they? Anyway, Denny has been downplaying its importance. But now, it's as if Maureen is the mother of Denny, and Lily, and Mrs. Rainey all at the same time. She feels that responsible for the lapse in communication. Before she can sink too far into this thought, the phone rings again and it's Charles, at the airport. The plane's boarding and Lily isn't there. Ordinarily, she's at the gate early.

"I'm sure she'll get there," Maureen assures him. "Do you want me to page—"

"I already have. She didn't respond."

"Why did you do that?"

"Why shouldn't I?"

"No reason. Just—you never do. Do you?"

"Does she leave her pager with you?"

"I'm sorry?"

"How would you know whether or not I page her?"

"I wouldn't. I'm sorry. I'm trying to do two things at once here and—anyway, I don't know what to tell you."

"They're saying the flight is ready to board," says Charles, "I'll try you again when I get there."

"I'll get her on the next flight," she tells him, quickly retrieving her current copy of the *Official Airline Guide* to determine exactly when that flight might depart.

In the back of Maureen's mind, a memory is now emerging: a transmission from the police operator that came through earlier. The operator's staticky description of a light blue VW station wagon athwart traffic on Cassingham Road comes into Maureen's mental focus. The morning's welter of grocery lists, quarterly tax returns, pedicures, and passport renewals recede to the background. Lily, with her circumspect manner and her tidy putt-putt of a car, is the world's safest driver; but then again, now she is driving for two.

Maureen believes that she understands Lily in a way that no one else can. It's true that having access to the factual and temporal ephemera of Lily's life—her appointment calendar, business correspondence, grocery lists, etc.—is the kind of thing that literary biographers build great stories from. But Maureen's belief is a bit more fervent than that, and supersedes her degree of involvement with the others in her clerical care. It would be easy enough to call it envy, or some adult version of the adolescent girl's crush on the history teacher with the great way of crossing her legs. But Maureen looks at Lily and sees neither a heroine nor a role model, and certainly not a version of herself. (Maureen, at five-foot-seven and 140 pounds, could more or less contain two of Lily.) What Maureen sees in Lily is an unfinished story.

Her father told her once that everyone is an unfinished story, until the day they die. Maureen knows she herself could leave her apartment, someday, or kiss the delivery boy, or write a book. But Lily has an aura of incompletion that gnaws at Maureen's desire for closure—despite her forty-one years, she's almost infantile in her abstraction and her pallor. Partly for Denny's sake, but even more in the hope of someday resurrecting her own life, Maureen believes there is an unexpressed trait in Lily, some late-onset strength that has been masked by the noise in her life so far—patients, insurance, teaching, conferences, even child-rearing. (All the things that Maureen herself takes the brunt of.) Maureen has been waiting for Lily's big left turn, but she never expected it to be an actual crash.

Sometimes Denny comes over to Maureen's after school, ostensibly to do her homework. Denny has quietly diagnosed Maureen's problem by observing the number of ordinary things for which Maureen employs agents. They are things that would be infinitely easier to do oneself, like choosing fruit or having keys made. Denny has also realized that this observation isn't something Maureen would want to discuss. Maureen's half of the tacit bargain is that she feels responsible for Denny far above and beyond the children of other clients.

It's easy for Maureen to canvass the emergency rooms and ambulance drivers, but she doesn't learn much. Yes, there seems to have been an accident involving Lily's car, but Lily herself has not turned up. Not knowing Lily's actual whereabouts is starting to cloud Maureen's sense of the orderly process of the day. It's a little like that feeling of having misplaced your keys.

At which point, her downstairs buzzer rings.

"It's Denny."

Maureen buzzes her in while surveying the work area for any telltale jottings from her recent survey of hospitals and ambulance drivers. She wouldn't want Denny to conclude that her mother is unconscious or worse.

Denny knocks impatiently at the door and Maureen opens it to see a whole different kid than the one she saw last time Denny came by. It must have been several months ago. Denny seems four inches taller, with bone structure emerging from her child's face and long messy hair that falls almost sexily in her near-black eyes, now red-rimmed. She stands with her arms crossed defensively across her chest and looks imploringly at Maureen.

"I need to borrow a shirt," she says.

"Mrs. Rainey just called."

"Yeah, I figured she would."

Maureen leads Denny into her bedroom and pulls open a dresser drawer full of shirts. This was the very source of the J. Geils Band T-shirt that Denny was wearing earlier this morning. Denny has secretly been waiting for an opportunity to return to this treasure trove of things far cooler than anything in her mother's giveaway box. She digs in avidly, retrieving first a sweater dress that—on Denny—becomes a midi-length cardigan.

"I should get rid of that," says Maureen. "It's hideous and always was."

Denny nods, accepting Maureen's opinion as a ready replacement for her own. She really just wants to cover her shameful upper body with as much fabric as possible. Maureen pulls out a red cloth shirt with cowboy snaps and stitching.

"This would look pretty cute on you, don't you think?"

"But it has darts," says Denny, showing Maureen the seams sewn into the shirt to allow for the breasts Denny doesn't yet have.

Maureen scowls at the offending seams.

"Try it on," she says. "Screw the darts."

Denny giggles, removing her mother's sweater in one quick motion and leaving it behind her on the floor. She takes and puts on Maureen's red shirt, snapping the snaps as she sidles over to the mirror on the back of Maureen's bedroom door.

"Wow, it does look cool." She turns to Maureen. "Can I have it? Really?"

"Sure. I haven't worn it in ages."

Of course Maureen hasn't worn anything but sweatpants and a T-shirt in ages, but Denny is not supposed to know that.

"Thanks." Denny flops down onto the bed and sighs.

"Hey, don't you have to go back to school now?"

"Not *right* now."

Maureen's phone rings. Maureen starts to worry that the call will be a report about Lily's whereabouts and not a good one. Should she pick up? It would be worse if they heard it come in on the answering machine, or over the emergency radio frequency. She looks at Denny, who looks back with an expression that clearly says, "Why don't you pick up the phone?"

Maureen jogs into the other room and does just that. It's Lily.

"Where are you? Are you okay?"

"I'm still at Richard's. They gave me a facial as a birthday present. I've never had one before."

A facial? Lily has the skin of an infant.

"But didn't you just have a car accident?" Maureen lowers her voice to ask.

"It was minor. I'm fine."

"Really? You sound a little . . . odd. Low affect."

"Since when are you a neurologist? I'm fine. Listen, that's not why I called. I called because . . ." Lily has forgotten why she called.

"Charles called."

"That's it. I wanted to let you know I'm not going to Chicago."

"What?" Maureen peeks down the hall to check on Denny—she's in the bathroom running water, out of earshot. "Lily? Why not?"

"I need to do more research."

"Well, sure. I mean, it's work-in-progress, right?"

"I think— There are still things I know how to fix."

"Is that what you want me to tell Charles?"

"Why do you have to tell Charles anything?"

"He noticed you weren't on the plane, Lil. I'm sure he's going to call again when he gets to the Drake."

"It's none of his business."

"Okay." Maureen is unconvinced.

"Okay—okay, good-bye."

Maureen hangs up the phone and realizes she forgot to say "Happy birthday." She's off her game. Returning to the bedroom she finds Denny lying curled up on the bed—at first Maureen thinks Denny's sleeping because of the way her torso rises and falls. Then she walks around to the other side of the bed and sees that Denny is weeping silently, with her knuckles in her mouth.

Maureen sits down on the bed and puts her hand on Denny's shoulder. She's afraid to ask what the matter is. She's used to a tough Denny who doesn't do things like suddenly start to cry.

"How am I supposed to explain what happened?"

"You mean, the thing for Mrs. Rainey?"

"I don't know why I did it! I don't know what I was trying to prove!"

"Well, you could just say that, couldn't you?"

Shame wells up in Denny because not knowing, irrationality, is really the cardinal sin. She can't tell her mother a story like that!

"My parents aren't coming to the play tonight, are they?"

"What?"

"They're at that conference. They don't even know it's tonight." Denny isn't blaming Maureen, and it's not even really about the play.

"Well." Maureen also forgot to mention the play to Lily. Again. "Chicago's only an hour away."

"Yeah, but they're going to have to have dinner with their colleagues and everything."

"Maybe."

"The kids all hate me now, because of what I did in science. They're going to make fun of me. It's going to be horrible."

"You know, there are two ways of looking at something like this . . ."

"Yeah, the cup's half full? Really?"

"Don't be a wiseass."

Denny wipes her eyes.

"Rainey gave me only the five-second version of what happened. Why don't you fill me in?"

Denny sits up. She looks at Maureen and fights back a momentary smile. "It was pretty unbelievable."

Ten minutes later, Denny is on her way back to school in Maureen's red cowboy shirt. Maureen has not exactly promised to deliver both Charles and Lily at the school play, but she is determined to make sure that at least Lily gets there before the curtain falls.

The story that Denny told Maureen was pretty close to what really happened, but she still has an odd, tight feeling in her belly as she walks back toward school. The trip to the principal's office was not her first. She could pick Mrs. Rainey's perfume out in a crowd, at this point. She intensely dislikes Mrs. Rainey, but she isn't sure why. Something about her imposing front—literally, she has breasts that jut out of her like machine-gun turrets. And sometimes she hugs. Not Denny, at least not lately, but Denny sees her walking through the halls and stopping to chat with the littler kids, and when she stoops down to hug one, Denny feels a little bit sick. Mrs. Rainey is not someone you are allowed not to like—she was an orphan in Poland or something. When Denny was sent to her office this morning, Mrs. Rainey looked meaningfully into her eyes and asked, "Well, Eden, what have you done?" And Denny told her a version of the truth, but not the same version she told Maureen. Maureen got all the good details, like getting the earthworm egg in her eye, and why—though it was nearly instinct at the time—flashing Josh Walker was the perfect revenge.

"It showed him exactly how wrong he was to think of me that way," Denny said with conviction, "and it showed him that I am fearless."

"Fearless?" asked Maureen.

"Impossible to intimidate?"

Now, walking up Cassingham Road, Denny recalls that exchange and feels uncomfortable. She is utterly possible to intimidate—it's just that when she's intimidated she acts out instead of retreating. No one seems to understand that when she is making up dances during recess or splashing the other kids in the pond near her grandmother's, her goal is really not to attract attention, it's to fill her brain with something besides fear and anxiety. Well, perhaps some of her teachers and Mrs. Rainey have started to catch on by now, but her mother never witnesses this aspect of Denny's "real life," which only happens in school or elsewhere outside the house.

Now Denny regrets that she didn't let Maureen tell her the possible second way to look at this situation. She tries to think of how she can explain it to her mother. It's neither the funny version she told Maureen nor the terse version she gave to Mrs. Rainey. What is the right version? What would hold Lily's interest? Instinctively, Denny knows that her mother is interested in men—despite the fact that no man is particularly "around," except her father. But she also senses that playing up the idea that Josh Walker was flirting with her (in that retarded way that boys do) is not the right tack. For Lily, she needs to exhibit control and balance. How can she retell the science class story as an illustration of her tremendous self-possession? Could she somehow say that she had planned the whole thing? Could she portray it as a matter of principle? She writes the scene in her head:

"Mom, you're going to get a call from Mrs. Rainey—you probably already have. I don't know why they thought I was misbehaving, because I wasn't; I was *protesting* the inappropriate behavior of my lab partner."

"Protesting" is good. Actually, this version is sort of true. But Denny doesn't think she could really get it past her mother.

Certain things always trip Lily's radar, and one of them is anything that sounds like someone behaving sexually toward Denny. Lily is determined to protect her daughter from the incidental harassments and impositions she experienced as a child. She has taught Denny to listen to her instincts and that if something seems or feels "wrong" to her, it probably is. Of course that statement's a hall of mirrors when you're eight, which was Denny's age the first time Lily introduced the idea. By twelve, Denny had determined that whatever sense it made it was not worth trying to think about. Sometimes, everything feels wrong.

Of course, no one at Denny's school thought to call Charles. Yes, he's out of town, but this is not always the case, but it *is* always the case that no one calls Charles. Not when Denny is bad, not when Denny is good, not when Denny is sick, not when Denny is well. Denny herself doesn't call her father very often, though she might like to see him more than she does. He's not the kind of guy you can just yak on the phone with; his silences are voluminous. But that's no excuse for Mrs. Rainey and that's no excuse for Maureen—they have a much better excuse: Lily is Denny's mother and when it comes to school, health, food, and clothing, they know as well as you do that mother takes all.

After the breakup with Lily, Charles sought professional help. This is something not even Maureen knows about, because Charles drove all the way to Cincinnati to see a man whose research had interested him. The man had referred Charles to a female colleague, also near Cincinnati, and in Dr. Mink, Charles met his match. Not that he is anywhere near changing his behavior, but he's begun at least to notice it. Sometimes he even sees how it has an impact on those around him that was different from what he intended. For example, this morning as he drove to the airport he realized he had forgotten to wish Lily a happy birthday—not even forgotten, simply not bothered. And he also realized that not bothering was cold and, in effect, unkind. He would never not bother to wish Denny a happy birthday—especially since Maureen could be relied upon to remind him when it came around. All those thoughts were conscious. Eddying beneath them were sad and conflicted feelings about Denny's headlong rush toward teenagerdom.

"Do you have any sexual feelings for Denny?" Dr. Mink had asked him, not long ago.

"I don't think so. Not really."

"Tell me about the last time you saw her."

"She came over for dinner—we were making spaghetti, and listening to *Traviata,* and Denny was jumping around and pretending to be Violetta, and we were having a great time."

"Go on."

"Well, I corrected the way she was cutting the onions—she was sawing at them and I knew the juice was going to get in her eyes. But what I said was 'No, not like that,' and suddenly it wasn't fun anymore."

"Why not?"

"I guess because I turned into the authority figure."

"Is that an unfamiliar role?"

"Of course not, I'm her father." Dr. Mink nodded and there was a silence until Charles added "Yes, completely. Lily always handled discipline, even when we were married."

"Did Denny say anything about how it sounded to her?"

"She said I sounded like Mr. Spock on *Star Trek.*"

"Did you laugh?"

"No. Was that funny?"

Charles loves Denny more than he has ever loved anyone or anything, ever. But he's a long way from knowing what to do about that.

Maureen doesn't believe in psychological trauma. Nevertheless, it is a fact that five weeks before she stopped going outside she was raped. She herself would never use that word, but it is the best way to convey the experience she had with Jamie, a kid of about twenty who works at Magnolia Thunderpussy, the record store where she used to address her weird (for Columbus) tastes in music. Jamie is a wiseass, a type for which Maureen has always had a weakness, and she had certainly flirted with him (and he with her) on various occasions. But Jamie is also fifteen years younger than she is, and in such a distinctly different chapter of his life that she never considered the possibility that anything would come of their flirting. His youthfulness was evident in everything, from the way he dressed (yesterday's T-shirt was also today's, and then reappeared, inside-out, later in the week) to his profound intolerance of anything bourgeois—a category that for him included items as pedestrian as Dannon yogurt and novels in hardcover. He had lambasted Maureen for her embrace of both these things, on separate occasions.

Still, Maureen liked Jamie, and something about his intolerance in particular appealed to her. Possibly that thing was anger. But he was just a suburban college kid with an ironic flair, hardly anyone to watch out for. She suspected she was more like his mother—in affect and milieu—than like Jamie, despite her enthusiasm for bands like T.Rex and Free. After all, at heart she's a Beatles fan. So, when Jamie suggested they go see a revival of the "swinging London" movie *Darling* at the OSU film society, it only seemed appropriate, in a way. She would represent the mysterious past of parents who had lived through the early '60s as adults—even though she herself had been going to secretarial school while Julie Christie was swanning around in gowns by Oleg Cassini. Oddly, she never asked herself what Jamie represented to her, or why going to the movies with him in the grip of a fantasy that she somehow represented an incarnation of his mother was appealing to her. She just went.

Going to the movie hadn't even really been a mistake. And the first round of tequila shots was also probably not fatal. Leaving her car on campus, however, and traveling to a bar with Jamie in his car, which she did before drinking anything at all—that was her real slip. At least, that was how it always came out when she revisited the problem in her head. And she could never quite understand how she could have known better, at that point in the evening. Was it really that—the single point of failure that fell outside the circle of predictable outcomes—which had stolen her sense of comfort from her? How could she have known?

At the bar, Jamie drank three tequila shots to Maureen's two, and then had a few beers. The type of subtle indication that Maureen was used to supplying when things appeared to be going awry was absolutely imperceptible to Jamie, in his condition. And especially in the midst of a conversation that was otherwise pretty lively. They were telling each other childhood horror stories. And these stories were seeming terribly funny to them both—Jamie had been through two sets of stepparents for each original parent, and each of these had come with his or her own children, pets, and living quarters. He had lived in a bohemian walk-up in Chicago with his dad and the student he left Jamie's mother for; and in a quasi-commune in Hawaii with his mom—once she left their original apartment in Hyde Park; and even in what he described as a "shack" in Galveston one summer with his father and wife number three.

Maureen's parents had divorced when she was nine and her father had died two years later. Just prior to the divorce he had become an ardent Buddhist, which had caused her mother to try to have him declared insane. He said he was going to give all his money to a monastery in Burma. At his deathbed, Maureen's mother, Alice, sat close, expecting him to finally call "olly, olly, oxen free" and drop the beatific mask. Ironically, he hadn't gotten around to changing his will, but the one in force still represented an earlier bout of money-loathing, and his estate went to the Maryknoll sisters—not Buddhists, but not Alice and Maureen, either. Her father had the last laugh, in his way. When Maureen finished her story, Jamie was wiping his eyes—he'd laughed so hard and inappropriately that he was weeping. He also couldn't really stand up. Fortunately, or, as it turned out, unfortunately, the bar was walking distance from Jamie's apartment, and so he asked Maureen to walk him home, where he would call her a cab.

He did not attack her, or threaten her with physical harm. In fact, at first, all he did was smoke a joint with her and then give her a kiss. Maureen, who hadn't been kissed in a long time, knew it wasn't a kiss she was particularly enjoying but thought it would probably be over soon, and was worth experiencing almost as a curiosity. She wanted to remember what it felt like to be kissed and held, and Jamie seemed too far gone to last for long at it—especially if she did nothing to encourage him. And she, too, was drunk. When he stopped kissing her she said she had to go.

He said, "Wait a minute—I want to play something for you."

The something was his latest discovery, *Horses,* by Patti Smith. "Jesus died for somebody's sins, but not mine," sang Patti, and Jamie nodded happily at Maureen as if to say, "She's a genius, right?" Maureen was stopped cold by Patti's nasal Jersey voice and five-star attitude—she wanted to see who could possibly sound like that. When Jamie handed her the record cover she gazed hungrily at the coolest woman she had ever, and would ever, lay eyes on. She wanted to be sneering, skinny, brilliant Patti but she was just large, soft, drunk Maureen.

When the song was over, she again stood to go but Jamie took her by the arm and pulled her into his bedroom. She didn't exactly go willingly, but she didn't know how to resist in a way that wouldn't seem as though she was accusing him of just exactly what she should have been accusing him of. He pulled her down onto his bed and began kissing her again. She considered her options and decided perhaps it would be over soon, and then he'd fall asleep, and then it would be much easier for her to call a cab and go home. But it was not over soon, because Jamie, as previously mentioned, was extremely drunk. Eventually, even passive Maureen began to resist and object, but by then Jamie was determined, somehow, to ejaculate in—or, if necessary, on—her and to compel her to help him to do so, if that was what it took.

Maureen tried curling up in a fetal position and she tried saying "Stop!" and "No!" but none of this was any more effective than Jamie's relentless rubbing, grabbing, pushing, and pulling. Even drunk, he was quite strong. After an hour or so, he did eventually fall asleep. Then Maureen dressed herself, finally released Patti Smith from eternal repeat-play, and sat on Jamie's couch until daylight. At dawn, she walked out to the nearest phone booth and called a cab back to the quiet street where she'd parked her car what seemed like a hundred years before. She didn't tell anyone what had happened—she was ashamed of herself for not stopping it before it started. She was ashamed of herself for parking her car. She was ashamed of herself for sitting up all night on his couch.

Denny calls Maureen from school at around two. She has a lot to say. Due to certain bizarre events, Denny has ascended from understudy to star. Tonight she will play Lola. She knows the script inside out, of course, but is uncertain whether she will still know it at seven that evening, or will even still have the part, then. (She fears that as soon as Mrs. Rainey gets wind of her luck there will be countermanding orders.) So it's really no big deal, but maybe Maureen should tell her parents anyway, if she happens to speak to them.

"So, how did this happen? I thought you were in so much trouble."

"It's kind of crazy. Virginia, the girl who was playing Lola originally, totally broke down crying in rehearsal—it turns out her parents forbid her to be in the play."

"On the night of the show?"

"Well, that's the crazy part. They're these seriously weird, old religious people—some people say they're really her grandparents because of the clothes she wears and especially her underwear. She wears like half-long underwear even when it's hot out. And a slip."

"So they're from the old country. What are they, Greek? Swabian?"

"I'm not sure. She celebrates Christmas like a week later than everybody else."

"So why'd they wait till today to put their foot down?"

"Apparently, she never told them exactly what the play was. She just told them it was about salvation and redemption and stuff. Then, this morning there was an accident in front of school and they had to drive around the other way, where the posters are. And they saw that the show is called *Damn Yankees,* and the drawing of Lola in fishnets, and all that, and they flipped."

"Wow. Poor Virginia."

"Yeah, she was crying and everything."

"But good for you, though."

"It's definitely an improvement over the earthworm catastrophe."

Then there is the part Denny can't tell Maureen: the part where time stops and she permits herself to imagine singing and dancing, in a lace-trimmed leotard, in front of the whole school. Singing and dancing are not part of Denny's everyday round. Wearing a leotard in public, never. In her imagination, she is good at it—well, good the way people are on TV—which is like, sexy, or larger than life? Denny isn't sure. The words all sound off, hence her reluctance to explain to Maureen. Later, she will realize that this is simply the first time in her life that she has visualized herself as an adult and not just pictured her mother but shorter and with brown eyes.

As soon as Maureen hangs up, she pages Lily again, then calls the salon to see if Richard knows where Lily was headed next. What she learns is that, after her facial, Lily just kept adding more services . . . waxing, pedicure, she's been there for hours. Maureen gives Brandi, the receptionist, strict instructions to keep Lily at bay until Maureen can get one of the cabbies to swing by and pick her up—she's not sure what she's going to tell Lily about why she's being taken hostage, but the anxiety of having her just ranging around without a known agenda is more than Maureen can bear.

Oumar takes the radio call. Maureen gets Brandi to describe what Lily is wearing so that she can relay to Oumar the basics of who he's after. Brandi's description goes like this:

"A greenish shirt—I guess it was silk. The kind that goes in at the waist? Only it didn't really hit her right. Anyway, it was green. And then she had some nice-ish gray pleated pants. And those shoes that are supposed to look okay even though they're comfortable and don't. You know, Naturalizer?"

The pants, the only item that failed to offend, were chosen by Denny. All Maureen tells Oumar is "Green shirt, blond hair, glasses, answers to Lily."

Oumar, who is not a native speaker of English, doesn't understand the "answers to" reference, but he's used to it by now. Maureen says it every time she sends him on a pickup. He's under the impression that this is a common locution for quick introductions. He will eventually come to grief on this point, but that's not exactly Maureen's fault.

Brandi's description is no help to Oumar, anyway—he fails to identify and bag the wandering Lily at the salon because when she walks by him, she has forgotten her eyeglasses and is wearing someone else's black jersey dress. The dress was hanging in the little changing room where she went to remove her robe, and so she put it on—to her recently concussed brain, it seemed not worth questioning. She didn't think about what would happen to the dress's true owner—if she had, she probably wouldn't have been able to go through with the theft. Instead, she saw a new version of herself in a tight black dress, and she headed off into the world to see what next might happen to this person.

When the owner of the black dress emerges from her hair-frosting marathon sometime later, she is outraged and has Brandi call Maureen back. Maureen is stumped, Oumar is stumped, too. The cosmetologist, who Lily left tipless, is also a trifle miffed. Now Maureen has Brandi on one line and Oumar on another without realizing that they are both together in one room on the other end. Oumar's the one who puts everything together when he hears Brandi reading back the same American Express card number he wrote on his palm when Maureen dispatched him. He hangs up his line, walks over to Brandi's hutch, and stands with his palm extended upward on her counter, indicating his desire to interrupt. When you're six-foot-two and have nearly purple skin, this action has the desired effect.

It takes Maureen a while to absorb the story about the wardrobe switch. When she does get it, she immediately stops believing that Lily is on the verge of coming back. This is no longer Lily as she knows her. This Lily will require a whole new set of assumptions. Maureen makes a list of things that could have happened:

1. Lily met someone she knows at the salon.
   (Plausible, but not much of an explanation. Why would they swap clothes? Anyway, it didn't sound like the switchee was a willing participant.)
2. Lily met someone she doesn't know.
   (Someone very persuasive who happened to need a quick change of identity. Okay, next.)
3. Lily's accident has had some profound and transformative effect on her personality.

Maureen has heard of something like that, but what does it mean? She tries to imagine how the dark or repressed side of Lily is most likely to manifest. Though simple reversals seem like a good place to start, Maureen soon has to wonder: a basically sincere and moderate person who is not entirely without cunning—what's the opposite of that? Does "kind of self-effacing" become "somewhat forward" or is it "next stop, raving exhibitionist"? She thinks about herself. A rare moment. What would Maureen do? What would she do, if she were Lily? She would leave this town so fast there'd be skid marks. But Lily never even made it to the airport. She'd have an affair. But probably not if she was already pregnant with the child of her ex-husband. She would look for her daughter to make sure that she was okay, especially if she knew that she herself was not.

In fact, Lily is submitting to a free makeover at the Union, across the street from Lazarus.

"You have perfect brow bones," the makeup artist tells her. Lily is ravenous for beauty right now. Not beauty in the conventional sense but some larger-than-life version of beauty that is redemptive and magical. The saleswoman performs well, guided perhaps by Lily's inner appetite. She, too, is a receptive soul whose life has not gone as planned. She chooses to ignore the quite substantial bruise blooming on Lily's forehead.

Lily wants to feel that God, whoever he is, is on her side. She used to get that sense from her work. A child's brain truly is a thing of beauty—not just because it looks so perfect but because it's only half full. A child's brain, even when diseased, injured, or incorrectly wired, resembles pink velvet grown according to an elaborate, unseen plan—an organic Oriental rug whose design will only translate into action in the course of a long and confusing life.

"You look beautiful," says the saleswoman, and Lily replies, "I do."

She gives this consent to the face in the mirror as much as to the saleswoman. She agrees to marry herself to that new face and, more important, to the life that looms before the face. Lily focuses on the mirror with all her might.

The thing that Lily has never been able to see around the sides of is being a mother. Even while working sixty hours a week, even when Denny was asleep, even when she and Denny were always together and their relationship made perfect sense to her, the role of mother did not. Even more than a doctor, even more than a wife, a mother is an "other," whose existence always seems incomplete—and maybe that's why, in Lily's state of burgeoning concussion, it is the first thing she lets go.

To be fair, Lily's old self-image—an accretion of science nerd, doctor's daughter, abstract thinker, eyeglass wearer, left-hand user, and pediatric neurosurgeon—never felt quite seamless, either. In fact, there were whole episodes in her life that had had to be filed separately because they refused to fit (her summer at ballet camp, for one; the college boyfriend who manufactured an early version of what was later known as LSD, for another). But still, Lily's young adult sense of herself had been flexible enough to encompass it all without fissure. It was only when Denny was born that things inside her started to become brittle. During Denny's infancy, she lost control of a lot of minor details, and she's never really had the sense of being in control since. This undercurrent of chaos makes her feel unattractive and helpless in a way she has recently been unable to shake.

After her separation from Charles, Lily made a paltry attempt at meeting other men. It wasn't paltry in her own eyes, of course. It took tremendous effort and focus to ask people for setups, to dress for dates with strangers, to listen to their small talk—she couldn't bring herself to care who they really were. Nor could she stop acting as if they had met by coincidence. In her heart of hearts, she wasn't interested in any of them. And yet she was lonely, extremely. For a month or so, she'd even had a boyfriend—a man named Robert, who was appropriate in all respects: financially stable, well-educated, nice-looking, not egregiously fat or loud or Republican. After they had sex, she would lie there wondering if she was just too old to fall in love with him, or if she would have fallen in love with him if she'd met him instead of Charles, when she was twenty-two. That was a thought that kept her awake—she feared that she would have, and feared further that her relationship with Denny's father may never have been more substantial than the best she could imagine with Robert: polite conversation about the newspaper, perfunctory sex, lackluster hand-holding—how did these things happen?

She and Charles had once been passionate, more than once. In medical school, she would sometimes just stand near him and feel herself become aroused. Reproductive necessity? But it did seem like more than that. They used to stay up late talking about their colleagues, their patients, new surgical techniques, even their own bodies. She couldn't bring back the warm feeling, but she knew she had felt it. Robert just made her anxious, and though she always came when they had sex, it was more like sneezing than merging souls. Was the latter feeling a delusion only possible for people who had never lived through a marriage? She might have felt it in the airplane with Phil, but she has never allowed herself to think about that—not even to recall it, or describe it to a friend.

Maureen checks the list of her duties for the afternoon. It is five items long:

- Siegel parking violation
- Driver totals at shift change
- Cranford billing
- Stationery order
- Find dog-sitter for Harper

Only one of these things really has to be done today, and that's closing out the taxi drivers' shift at three P.M., which is in less than fifteen minutes. And even that could be left till later, if it came to it. But Maureen can't stop reviewing the list, because not reading it will force her to register what she knows was true before she picked up her pencil: she can, and must, go find Lily. On foot? No, that would take forever. She must drive. She has no car. She must borrow a car and drive. She reviews her list again. She calls Oumar.

He picks up the radio handset. "Yes, hello. This is Oumar . . ."

"It's me," says Maureen. "I need a pickup."

"I will get a pencil, Maureen. Hold on, please—"

"No, me. I need a pickup. Here."

"Where's it going?" he asks, assuming he is making a messenger run, as he often does.

"It's me," says Maureen. "I'll tell you when you get here. I've got to get dressed."

"I'll be there in ten minutes. Good?"

"See you then."

Although Dude, Rhonda, and Oumar have all witnessed the same types of evidence of Maureen's shut-in life that Denny has, none of these adults has drawn the same conclusion. Dude has not drawn any conclusions, because he has not noticed anything odd. Rhonda has decided that Maureen is just more evolved than she is, in terms of exploiting the conveniences that modern life has to offer. In Rhonda's worldview, anyone who can afford a dishwasher, or even a microwave oven (a very new-fangled appliance of which she has never seen an example), is a moron if they don't have one. Maureen's reel-to-reel PhoneMate answering machine is the single most impressive thing Rhonda's ever laid eyes on. Oumar assumes that whatever Maureen does is more or less normal American behavior. His sample of normal Americans is small.

Maureen has not gotten properly dressed in a long time. In fact, if any one thing other than her night with Jamie can be said to have precipitated her homebound existence, it is the problem of clothing. She works every day in a pair of gray sweatpants and a million-year-old T-shirt. She sleeps in this outfit, too, except she takes off the sweatpants. She has three pairs of the pants and a large number of T-shirts, most of which are drug advertisements given to her by the sales-people who come to her door expecting to find the doctors who use hers as their mailing address. In her closet, unworn, and mostly in plastic dry-cleaning bags, is the wardrobe of her former life. Suits. Blouses. Shoes with heels. Impossibly wrong—she cannot wear them. In a trunk are her college clothes: preppy Villager blouses and vaguely bohemian smocklike things. She was pretty in college. Gingerly, she extracts a black sprigged-print dress that once was her favorite. Her first boyfriend had once told her that in it she reminded him of Anna Magnani as a Resistance fighter in *Rome, Open City*. She has never seen the movie, but she has always kept a mental picture: a Soviet-realist style image, very contrasty, her head at three-quarters profile with the wind in her hastily pinned-up hair, behind her lots of sky and some filmy palimpsest of Rome. If she is going outside, she needs to feel that bravery.

Oumar pulls up outside Maureen's apartment building and picks up his handset. "Car one ready at pickup."

Maureen, sitting frozen on her bed, hears the radio in the other room but doesn't move. She is wearing the dress, and sneakers, and a heavy pullover sweater, which looks only a little bit eccentric. In her right hand is a composition book. A pen is clipped into the neck of the sweater. Maureen stares blankly into the distance.

"Maureen? I am in front of your building."

Maureen just about sleepwalks over to the radio and picks up the handset. "I'm having some trouble," she says.

"Should I come up?"

Maureen thinks. And thinks.

"I will come up."

"No," says Maureen. "Stay there."

"You're the boss."

"I guess so."

"Good, standing by, then."

Charles sits in the empty conference room where Lily's talk would have been. He looks at his watch. Around him are empty folding chairs; behind him, a withering lunch buffet. The fluorescent lights are turned off. He pats himself down for his address book and pages through it as though it might dispense some information about his ex-wife's whereabouts. It's not as if he doesn't know all her numbers by heart. He realizes he is looking for an idea about who could be with her. Which heartbroken nurse or secretary started crying on her shoulder and made her miss her plane? But that's not like Lily. Who among his colleagues at the hospital could have seduced his ex-wife? But he thinks this without conviction. Something is wrong. There is a bank of pay phones just across the hall, but it seems very far away.

A colleague sticks his head into the room and looks around. Charles looks up helplessly—she's not his wife anymore, he has no explanation. The man pretends not to see Charles and withdraws. Charles makes his way to the pay phones and dials Maureen. Her phone rings once, twice, three times, and then something unprecedented happens. He hears Maureen's voice on tape saying, "Doctors' Exchange is busy. Please slowly say your phone number and the time of your call after the click and this machine will make a recording." Charles doesn't know that Maureen hasn't left her house in the past year and a half but he does know that she is always, always, there when he calls. Even if she immediately puts him on hold afterward, she answers the phone. And he has called at all hours and on all days of the week. This is merely a Thursday at three-thirty in the afternoon.

Maureen is slowly descending the inner stairway of her building, gripping the handrail as she goes. She's heading for that brightness beyond the glass door. She squints as she descends into the glare. As her eyes adjust, she sees the yellow cab first and then, standing right outside the door and peering into her building, Oumar. Maureen keeps going, past the mailboxes, all the way out the door—right past Oumar—and down to the curb. Oumar falls in behind her, intending to open the front passenger door for her, but Maureen has already let herself into the back. She is hyperventilating as she shuts the door.

Oumar gets into the driver's seat. Before latching his seat belt, he half turns to regard the stricken Maureen. Maureen holds her hand out in the gesture that customarily means "wait," and continues breathing rapidly.

"I'm a safe driver. Never any accidents. Where do you want to go?"

Maureen has no idea.

Oumar turns on the ignition. "This is an emergency?" Understandably, he is uncertain.

"I'm sorry, Oumar. I just—I don't usually go outside."

This is not a remark that Oumar can in any way understand. He now turns his whole body to face Maureen fully. Maureen looks away, ashamed of herself.

"I am uncertain what you mean."

Maureen starts to sob. This is very bad news for Oumar. All kinds of conflicts arise. He may neither comfort her like a child, nor tell her to be quiet, like a wife. He is aware that people who see them may believe him to be the cause of her tears, but then concludes that, since she has chosen to sit like a passenger, in the backseat, confusion is less likely. And, of course, she is white. To Oumar, no matter where she sits, Maureen is not a passenger. What, exactly, she is to him is something he cannot fathom. He does not speak of her in his letters home.

"Maureen?" he says. "You must give me your instructions."

Denny is backstage helping Faith Jackson prepare the night's costumes—they are checking for downed hems and torn armpits, ironing out rehearsal wrinkles, pinning shirts to jackets—things like that. Faith is also in Denny's science class and as of this morning she is utterly and completely awed by Denny Roman, a person she had previously barely noticed. It's not admiration, exactly, because she was appalled by and embarrassed for Denny at the time, but she recognizes that there was something incredibly brave—and extremely funny—about Denny's act of rebellion.

Denny has barely spoken to Faith since first grade, when the social winnowing in their class first started to occur. She knows Faith is in her science class, though, and she so badly wants to be forgiven, or absolved, or maybe just yelled at, that she looks up to see what the most popular girl in the seventh grade might be thinking now. Faith is staring unabashedly at Denny. Mortified, both girls look back down at the clothes. Faith sews like a fairy; her stitches are tiny.

"Go ahead, say it."

"Say what?"

"What a joke you think it is that I'm going to play Lola."

"I wasn't thinking that."

"Uh-huh. And chicken have teeth."

"What?"

"Nothing."

Faith forms a mental image of a smiling, toothy chicken and cracks up. "You are really weird," she says.

"What—you've never heard that expression before?"

"No."

Denny got this expression from Maureen, who got it from her mother, who got it from her uncle Henry, who was a bricklayer in Chicago and had nothing to do with poultry.

Behind them, the wardrobe rack starts to move as if possessed. The costumes ripple and jiggle until—"Eden Roman!"—Rufus sticks his head through to look at Denny and Faith, who look at him with a combination of fear and anticipation. Faith has taken this backstage role in order to stay as far as possible from the disturbingly sexual energy that, as far as she's concerned, pretty much oozes from their teacher's every pore.

"You weren't going to start the run-through till four-thirty," Denny objects.

"Yeah, well, when you're the star of the show, you're supposed to be onstage and ready, not ironing. I was just about to start looking around for another Lola!"

Denny looks at him with horror.

"Man, you're gullible."

"Very funny."

"How's the costume?" asks Rufus, eyeballing the red tulle number beside him on the rolling rack.

"I haven't tried it."

"Don't you think you better?"

Denny thinks that, in light of this morning's earthworm episode, she's going to get hooted right off the stage if she tries to play Lola the way Virginia did, as sort of an homage to Natasha Fatale (of *Rocky and Bullwinkle* fame). Virginia's version of "Whatever Lola Wants" lacked style, in Denny's opinion, but that was Virginia. However, once she's got the dress on, Denny suddenly sees how wrong she herself is for the part.

"I look like a kid playing dress-up," says Denny.

"I can fix that," Faith offers. "Look"—she pinches the bodice to show Denny where she can take it in. Denny still looks defeated. "Or—here, you can wear the red bolero over the black dress in Act One and then take it off for Act Two."

"Bolero?"

"This little jacket thingy—Virginia never wore it, but it goes with the red one."

Denny looks at the bolero. Could work.

"Really?"

Lily is sitting at a bus stop, crossing and uncrossing her bare legs. She looks down at them and thinks, "Those are normal. I recognize them," but they don't feel normal in the least. They feel soft and silky and strangely alert—she's been waxed. She's nauseated, has a splitting headache, and she doesn't know why she's sitting there. Every few minutes she vividly recalls that she has an obligation but is unable to place what that obligation is. As she tries to remember, her thoughts wander down various blind alleys, but she is always brought up short by this incomplete sense of duty. Sometimes she even says out loud, "I have to be somewhere," and begins to stand up; but as she stands, she realizes, yet again, that she can't remember where she's supposed to go or why she's supposed to go there. After a while, the cycle of remembering but not remembering has itself started to be memorable, and Lily begins to sense that something is very wrong. Her hands go to where her pager should be—but it's not there. She looks around for her bag, her date book, some way of retrieving the lost fact, but these, too, are missing. She tries to retrace her steps in her head, to track down these missing items, but can only remember seeing her face in the cosmetician's mirror, and how much it surprised her. She will go back to the makeup department at the Union—the store's right across the street from the bus stop. But why? She never buys makeup.

And this is how it is, in Lily's head. Eventually, she begins to weep with frustration. She has no tissues, so the clear mucus that drips from her nose is soon pooling on the bus-stop bench, along with her tears. It's humiliating—so infantile, it reminds her of when Denny was three or four—and a stab of recognition follows. She can see the three-year-old girl on the wood floor, her face red and shiny with tears; she can feel the conflict in her heart over whether or not to comfort her—if that would invalidate the punishment. "I am a bad mother," she thinks.

She looks up at the scene around her. In the distance are a few pedestrians, a woman with a fur coat, an old man with a slow, fat white dog. All she knows are two things: "I have to be somewhere" and "I am a bad mother." She smiles at herself, ruefully. When it comes right down to it, even the best brains are storing some pretty bad fortune cookies. Her years of learning and practice, of reading and judging information—all those X rays, titrations, micrographs, stains—have not made her clever enough to understand what to do next. Using the skills she has learned to visualize the diseased brains of her patients, she can see the nature of her problem but not solve it. Words float over the images—but the words won't come into focus. Lily begins to remember the protocol for evaluating an insult to the brain: The Glasgow Coma Scale. She remembers children answering her questions, struggling to keep their eyes open, and to retrieve their street numbers and mommies' and daddies' names. She is not *comatose,* her eyes are open and she can converse coherently. The word is *amnestic.* She has am—nesty? She has a concussion; concussive amnesty. She can tell that isn't right. Her tears begin to fall again. She stops herself, fighting the regression, wiping her face on the now truly unfamiliar sleeve of the unfamiliar dress.

She knows she is supposed to be somewhere, and she looks at her watch; but as soon as she sees the time, she forgets why she is checking it. Then, a few minutes later, she checks it again. To anyone observing her, she looks like a woman being stood up for an afternoon date, perhaps an illicit one. And someone *is* observing her, a twenty-eight-year-old shoe salesman named Dan.

"You're very beautiful," says Dan to Lily, as he approaches her. He stops at a safe distance, but Lily never saw him coming and she nearly jumps out of her skin. He can't help but laugh at the extent to which this hoary old line has unsettled her. She blinks at him, as though clearing a speck from her eyes. Then she frowns.

"I was just over there"—he indicates Baker's shoe store across the street—"and I couldn't help noticing you. Are you okay?"

Lily is by nature scrupulously honest, not to mention literal, about questions of this sort. Still, she doesn't anticipate the words that slip out of her mouth: "I'm pregnant," she says.

Dan sits down on the other end of the bench, upset by this news. Suddenly, she's not some sexy suburban mom on the loose; she's a lost child.

"I don't know why I said that," says Lily, all business, now that Dan is sitting with her. And then, "Who are you?"

Dan's a nice-looking guy, a member of one of the last professions in America that require a suit and tie. His suit— tweed, almost academic-looking, and nearly out of season for April—once belonged to his father.

"Daniel Willard," says Dan. He cocks his head at her. "Do you— Can I— Are you waiting for someone?"

"I'm divorced," Lily says.

Dan nods, as though this were the answer to his question.

"I'm on my fifteen-minute break," he tells her. "Usually, I just read." He pats his jacket pocket where a paperback is crammed. "Sometimes I smoke; would you like a cigarette?" Lily nods. Dan lights. They smoke. Lily is not a smoker, but never mind.

"Have we met before?" she asks.

"You and me?"

"Ever?"

"I don't think so. I've only been back in town since February."

"Where did you move from?" Lily asks.

"New York City."

Lily nods.

"Have you been there?"

She has to think. She thinks for a long time. Clearly she has forgotten the question. Dan is fascinated.

"Do you want to talk about—the other thing?"

"What other thing?"

"The, uh, baby."

Lily doesn't really remember telling him about the baby. And she's more than a little ashamed of herself for apparently having done so.

"Oh, I'm much too old to have a baby," she says.

"You don't look too old."

"Well, too busy."

"Really?"

Lily looks away, her eyes momentarily fill with tears, which she successfully blinks back.

"Look," he says, "I have to go back to the store in a minute; and I'm sure you have things to do, but . . . I'd like to see you again. Can I call you?"

"When do you finish? With work?"

"Around five-thirty."

"I'll be here."

"Are you sure?"

She nods.

"Can I borrow your cigarettes? And your book?"

"You're just going to sit here?"

She looks around. The day is bright but overcast, there aren't many people around. She looks at her hands.

Dan puts the book and the pack of cigarettes down on the bench beside her. "See you later?"

Lily nods, smiles, but doesn't look up.

Charles has been pacing in the tiny hotel telephone alcove and is now listening again to Maureen's answering machine. He didn't even know Maureen owned one. Ed Pulaski (chief of surgery and must-own-every-new-gadget hotshot) must have given her his when he moved to Denver. Charles was sure Maureen would answer if he called again. He hangs up the phone without satisfaction and, with nothing left to do but pick up his briefcase and go, heads back into the swarm of doctors in the hall. It's a big conference.

In the backseat of Oumar's taxi, Maureen is now breathing almost normally but her body is still covered with clammy sweat. Not knowing what else to do after hearing that Maureen was still pursuing this "answers to Lily" person, Oumar began to cruise the neighborhood. All Maureen has to do is sit there and scan the streets, which are empty. No one walks in the suburbs. It's so stupid of her to have forgotten this. Does this mean she really could have gone outside? If only there were something to be afraid of—instead of all this solitude.

"Is it always so quiet at this time of day?"

But to Oumar, it's not quiet; he is fighting the queue of moms in station wagons forming ahead of them to pick up their kids at the elementary school.

"It's always like this," he says to Maureen. "Now can you tell me where we will go?"

"To the police station. Downtown. Maybe they have her car."

Sure enough, when they pull into the lot, they are immediately confronted with the wreck of Lily's car—towed from its inauspicious parking spot across from Lazarus. The damage to the VW doesn't look to Maureen like something the driver could have survived. The windshield is fractured—cracks radiate from an impact point not far from the steering wheel. The driver door is bent inward—halfway into the driver's seat, it seems. Oumar slows to a stop as they get close.

"Is that the car?"

Maureen nods, transfixed.

"Perhaps it is not as bad as it looks," he says, thinking he has heard these very words come out of Maureen's mouth, more than once.

"I feel sick," says Maureen.

"I will go inside and ask about this car," offers Oumar. "What shall I ask?"

"Ask when and where they found it."

"Yes."

"And if the driver, if Lily, was with it at the time."

Oumar goes into the police station, determined to do what he can for Maureen, who is really the closest thing he has to a boss.

Maureen turns away from the wreck of Lily's car and stares at the flag as it twists in the wind. Charles once prescribed her some pills he said would alleviate her occasional moments of extreme panic—back before she stopped going outside. She had even filled the prescription—in fact, she probably has one in her purse. She roots around till she finds her little tin of aspirin and there it is, yellow and small and over a year old. She swallows it dry.

The day has gotten cloudy and cool. Lily is cold in her thin dress and uneasy in her high heels. Her makeup is streaked and dissolving. She sees other people returning to their cars after shopping, women who look so normal sorting through their keys, scanning for the vehicle they know is nearby, lost in reverie over how they will wear or use their recent purchases. She thinks that's how she's supposed to look, instead of this bare-legged wreck with no bag, no keys, no daughter, no car.

She leaves the bus stop, walking faster and faster until eventually she is half running down State Street, away from the stores and toward home, even though home is three miles off. She doesn't notice the police cruiser following her at pace. At the corner of Third Street she waits for the light, but with the State House behind her and no landmarks ahead, she realizes again that she has no plausible destination. When the light turns green Lily just stands there. Cars behind the police car start to honk. Lily turns to face them— she is weeping again and looks wretched.

The officer driving the patrol car rolls down his window and addresses Lily: "Anything I can do to help, ma'am?"

Lily shakes her head no, but as the car horns continue to honk, her knees start to give way. The cop pulls over to the curb, allowing the cars behind him to continue on. People stare at Lily as they pass, trying to discern the cause of the delay. All she knows is they're all staring at her. She sits down on the pavement and covers her head. The police officer jogs around his car and crouches beside her to help her up.

Dan returns to the bus stop where he met Lily. His book and most of his cigarettes are still there. He looks around but sees no other sign of her. Then he sits down on the bench and half-heartedly recovers his place in *Even Cowgirls Get the Blues*.

Denny is staring out at the empty auditorium, halfway through the final run-through. Everyone has been nice to her so far. Much nicer than she is used to. She really does know all the lines, and the other kids are impressed. The dress she is wearing, the red one for Act One, is dumpy on her, even with Faith's artful alterations. The black one, which is basically a leotard, fits her well, and even on her undeveloped body was distinctly sexy. As she walks through "Whatever Lola Wants" with the blocking, she tries to picture her parents watching her frolic in that vampish black costume. She remembers the critical look in her mother's eyes this morning when she noticed the tight, fuzzy sweater. She remembers her father's obliviousness. Then she remembers baring her chest in the science lab and how strong she felt at that moment. The moment just before she started to feel humiliated.

Paul Rappaport is staring into her eyes as she sings to him—it's so strange to be seen this way. He's even cute. She puts her foot up on the chair next to him and the red dress falls aside to reveal her leg in its high-heeled dance shoe. Paul starts to giggle, but she keeps singing.

" 'I'm irresistible, you fool, give in!' " She throws her head back, an added flourish.

Offstage, Faith laughs. She's a character, this Denny.

Charles, flying first-class, is preoccupied. He reviews the proceedings of the conference—trying to ascertain what he will have missed by taking the early flight home instead of staying for the last session. The woman beside him is looking for a conversational opening with her peripheral vision, but it's unlikely that Charles will grant her one. He can't remember the last time he felt this uncertain. Even the divorce was manageable, in its way. The steps were clear, the momentum ineluctable.

No real ties had been severed—well, except for the sexual one. That was difficult, but he assumed a change would come along eventually. In the meantime, he wouldn't starve. But this—Lily's disappearance, Maureen's disappearance— these tiny fissures were making him unaccountably anxious. At bottom, the agitation was about Denny. He had not kissed her this morning. He had barely looked at her. If Lily and Maureen have both disappeared, where is Denny? What if she is gone? It's an unthinkable thought, but he thinks it. There are reasons that he's a scientist, and this is one: He'd rather know than not. The women who've loved him, including his own mother, want to attribute that thirst for knowledge to some childhood scar, to a time when Charles had experienced not knowing at its worst. And in fact he had not known, until the age of twelve, that he had once had an older brother. Alan, at six, had died of complications from pneumonia. When Charles learned this, he at last understood why so many of his clothes and toys from childhood seemed strangely worn yet also preserved. And he also understood, or so his mother assumed, why she had often become lost in grief or confusion when young Charles crossed various childhood frontiers such as shoe tying, bike riding, and writing in script.

Although learning about Alan had upset him, and he had often wondered about and wished for his lost older brother, Charles's inquiring nature is not a result of that early loss. It is as deeply ingrained as his habit of standing with one foot resting on the wall behind him. It is his opacity that is the learned behavior. By the age of two Charles had found that if he didn't focus his eyes too closely on his mother when she held him, she was much less likely to weep. It worked, and he never unlearned it. Women seemed drawn to this quality of his, and it had worked to his advantage on many occasions with men as well. No one ever perceived him as competing or threatening, despite his looming height and his towering intellect. There were only two people in Charles's life that had not responded well to his abstractedness. His father was one of them, and the other one was Denny. He knew he could lose his daughter by failing to look her in the eye. But he had never quite wrestled this thought into consciousness. He sits on the airplane and closes his eyes. The thought is there with him now, and it is staying put.

All that Oumar learns from the police is that Lily's car was towed in driverless—information Maureen had presumed anyway. What she now has to determine, on Denny's behalf, is whether Lily has come to harm or simply run away. Circumstances have begun to point to the latter and this chills her as viscerally as the prospect of entering the shrill interior of Richard's salon. Her next step should be to retrieve Lily's clothes and bag—discovered by the client in whose black dress Lily wandered off. She only hopes that Lily's things may provide some clue as to where she may have gone, but Maureen is afraid that the trail is already cold, that in her anxiety she waited too long to act. As they drive along the quiet streets, Maureen sings the (wrong) lyrics of "Eleanor Rigby" to herself, "Howww to get over lonely people." When the song first came out, this was how she thought the refrain went—now she sticks with her version, because she does not want to look at all the lonely people, she is one of them.

When they get to Lazarus, Maureen finds herself on the escalator before she realizes her pill has kicked in. Outside, Oumar waits in the car, trying to understand what is going on. As Maureen opens the door into the busy, hairspray-smelling salon, she feels her stomach unknotting, her corset of fear beginning to unlace. Stepping up to the receptionist's podium, she has a sudden and terrible pang of loss: She's left behind fourteen months of her life. Could she really have been freed by one stupid little pill?

Lily's bag reveals no answers, and neither does the woman at the front desk. She wasn't there this morning, and Angela, the girl who gave Lily her treatments, left an hour ago. Maureen watches the frostily lipsticked mouth moving and remembers, briefly, what it would feel like to slip into panic. Instead, she interrupts—

"Will you call Angela for me?"

"I told you, I can't give out employees' numbers."

"I don't want her number—I want you to call her up for me."

"Uh." The girl's mouth goes slack as she thinks.

"Right now," says Maureen.

Richard listens from the other side of the partition, where he is creating the day's fifth Farrah. He whistles under his breath. Enter the dragon.

The receptionist dials. No answer.

"Does she call in for messages?"

The receptionist just keeps chewing her Trident. Apparently not.

In the back of the squad car, Lily is curled up on the seat, experiencing brutal, excoriating cramps. As the car bumps up over a curb and comes to a halt, the officer speaks to her. "Come on into the station; we'll get you straightened out." Lily picks up her head and looks around, dazed by pain. The officer walks around and opens the door for her, but she stays in the car. "Come on, it's warm inside; we'll get you a cup of coffee." He holds out his hand.

"That's mine," says Lily, seeing her wrecked car behind him. The officer turns to follow her glance. "And I've just had a miscarriage in your squad car."

He turns around to face her again, frowning.

"Do you think I could clean up a little before I go inside with you?"

"I'll get you a towel," he says, walking away without shutting the car door. He has no intention of returning. He will send Linda. And he will find out the name of this person the broken VW is registered to, and he will call the hospital and ask them to send an ambulance. A number of unpleasant things have happened in his squad car, but this is one he never anticipated, and that makes it the worst.

When she arrives at the Grant Hospital Emergency Room, several members of the staff recognize Lily but, without her glasses and with her fluffy blond hair and in her tight black dress, she looks different. One of the nurses asks an intern if Dr. Roman might have a twin sister. The resident who examines her is a former student of Charles's, a young woman named Laurie Sturges. Lily recognizes her and tries to be helpful answering her questions. Dr. Sturges tells her she's very sorry about the pregnancy, and that they're going to do a D&C just to be safe. She smiles kindly and leaves Lily alone in an exam room. Lily looks at the ceiling and knows her secret is out, as well as over. A tear or two leak out of her eyes, but she doesn't sob. She knows she's mentally all right, because she passed the verbal protocol—the date, her name, the name of the President; all that is in place. But she had no name for the lost baby except "the pregnancy," which describes a set of physical sensations, not a person. Whatever the reason, those sensations are gone, replaced by emptiness, pain, and grief.

When Maureen gets home she hears a message from the Emergency Room about Mrs. Roman. She calls back immediately and learns that Lily is there, that her condition is stable, and that they have paged Charles, who is on his way from the airport.

The cast and crew of *Damn Yankees* have finished their pizza and are putting finishing touches on makeup and costumes, fussing over props, tweaking lighting cues, and itching with anticipation. Denny has jettisoned the ill-fitting red dress in favor of the tight black one. Once dressed, she hovers near the stage, occasionally peeking out into the audience to look for her parents. Some of the other parents arrived so early they were there for the pizza. Now many are seated in the auditorium and others have stopped to chat and visit in the aisles. Incongruously, the Stones' *Let It Bleed* plays on the PA system, courtesy of Rufus. "I laid a divorcee in New York City," sings Mick. No one seems to notice.

Since a half hour remains until curtain, Denny slips out to use the pay phone near the locker rooms. No game tonight. The hallways are dark and quiet, but Denny still feels exposed in her slinky dress. She's also pretty sure she's not supposed to be walking barefoot. Ordinarily, she might be enjoying this—exploring after hours—but her stomach has begun churning inside her, and her mouth is dry. She dials Maureen and waits impatiently for an answer.

Irving Flowers, one of the eighth-graders on the basketball team, emerges from the locker room as she waits. He doesn't see her—he's moving pretty fast, like he's trying to get away from something. Denny wonders what's going on in the locker room as Maureen's phone rings repeatedly in her ear. Denny knows Maureen doesn't go out, so she figures she's in the shower or emptying the trash down the hall or something. Denny's never encountered an answering machine before, but she grasps the concept immediately and simply tells the receiver, "Maureen? It's Denny!" She hangs up, but doesn't leave. She'll wait a bit and try again. Faith Jackson now emerges from the locker room and looks directly at Denny.

"How long have you been standing there?"

"Not long," says Denny.

"Oh," says Faith, taking in Denny's revised costume. "That came out pretty good, don't you think?"

"I guess," says Denny. Was Faith making out with Irving Flowers in the locker room? That's pretty weird.

Denny turns back to the phone and dials again. She hangs up when she hears the recorded announcement click in.

When Charles arrives at the hospital, Dr. Sturges gives him the rundown on Lily. He does a tiny double take when she mentions the miscarriage, and Sturges sees this. Both of them are embarrassed.

"Dr. Roman and I are divorced," Charles tells her and, for the first time, hears how extremely odd it sounds that despite their divorce Lily is known to her clients and colleagues as "Dr. Roman," just as he is.

He finds Lily still in her street clothes and smeared with makeup, lying curled up on a cot. When he walks in, she is both surprised and relieved.

"They paged me."

"Jesus, Charles, I'm such a mess," she says.

He scowls at her without realizing it, which is familiar to Lily and not even dismaying. Then he looks her in the eyes.

"Does Denny know?" he asks.

"Know what?"

"That you're here, that you've been in an accident."

"I don't think so. I haven't . . . I couldn't remember any-thing . . ."

"What about Maureen?"

Lily has not previously thought of Maureen. It's like discovering the missing link. "Yes! I spoke to Maureen!"

"When?" Before or after I did is what he's wondering, wanting to know if he's been protected, or at any rate kept in the dark.

"I can't remember."

Charles would never, under any circumstances, start the conversation about Lily's pregnancy—he knows it's none of his business in their current relationship. Lily, however, has lost all of her usual reserve and knows exactly what he will have heard from Dr. Sturges. Anyway, she needs to confide in someone.

"You must have heard I was pregnant," she says.

Charles is uncertain whether, or how, to react.

"I hadn't really decided to have it—" She breaks off. Talking about it to Charles feels altogether different from saying it to—who else did she talk to? Did she say something to a stranger? She can't remember.

"You don't have to talk about this," says Charles.

She looks up, meets his glance.

"I'm not your husband anymore."

"I know that," she insists, looking down again. She clasps her hands together on her belly and tries not to cry, but the more she looks at that part of her anatomy that is right in front of her, the more she feels just exactly how empty it now is.

Charles places his hand on her shoulder gently as he watches her body begin to shake with quiet sobs. After a few seconds, he says, "I'm sorry, Lily," and a while after that he adds, "I'm sorry about everything." It's no comfort, though.

Denny is acting her heart out in the school play. This is another drug that works. Lola has temporarily replaced Denny, and Lola is far too arrogant and self-sufficient to succumb to the need for mere parents. Even at the end, where she helps Joe leave in spite of what it means for her—instant transformation into an aged hag—Lola hangs tough. Denny as Lola is even tougher, because she is fending off not only romance, but abandonment and humiliation. There are some kids in the audience who, during her big number, see an opportunity to remind her of science class.

"Take it off!" yells Josh Walker.

"Oo wee!" add others—all cowards.

Denny only uses this as fuel, tossing a withering look into the audience as she sashays through her pantomime seduction of young Paul Rappaport. The rest of the audience is smitten. That evening, at Bexley Middle School, Denny is a siren. Only during the curtain calls, when the houselights are up, does she fully accept the fact that her parents aren't in the audience to witness this transformation. Who is there is Maureen, standing in the very back of the auditorium and clapping like mad.

BOOK TWO

THE CAMEL STOP
1990

For most of the flight, Denny watches the movie without renting the headset. Watching the performers without benefit of the dialogue makes it easier to assess their technique. If she can tell what's going on in the scene just from the actors' faces, they are doing their jobs well—unless, of course, they are overdoing it. Determining which is a test she likes to give herself since she moved to Hollywood—Silver Lake, actually—and declared herself an aspiring movie actress. She did that when she was twenty-four, just after the Berkeley Losers Theater Company broke up.

Today's in-flight movie has Linda Fiorentino portraying a screwed-up young woman with a penchant for vests, and although Denny can't figure out what the story is, she finds the actress convincing in her role. There appears to be a dark secret from the past that will deliver resolution of the sort found only in movies. This is the flavor of professional challenge that Denny longs for, though she thinks of her personal experience as fairly limited where dark secrets are concerned. She hasn't yet expanded her definition of "secret" to include all those things we *can't* know about ourselves or about the people we love. Today, for example, Denny is unaware that the sensation she is calling anticipation is really dread, and that the prospect of getting off the plane at Port Columbus International and returning to 2424 Sherwood Road has been sucking the life out of her for nearly two weeks. Even though she's not consciously aware of this condition, she will convincingly convey it to Lily and Phil with glance, tone, and gesture—all the tools of her craft.

Lily married Phil while Denny was a sophomore at Berkeley. It was a civil ceremony, and besides Maureen, who attended in the role of witness, there were no guests. They'd been involved in a long-distance love affair for almost seven years by then. It began six or eight months after Lily's miscarriage, when Phil called Lily at home one Saturday night.

"Hi, Phil," Lily had said uncertainly. She was more than a little surprised to hear from him.

"Hi, Lily. I wouldn't have called, because I thought you were married. But I happened to talk to Jerry Berg this afternoon, and he said that Charles was divorced. Which means you are, too. Right?"

"Charles and I are divorced."

"You're single, then?"

"Well, I've never really said that before, but I guess it's the case. I'm single." Lily was lying in bed during this conversation—in the bed she had once shared with Charles. At that moment, the bed was so littered with books, papers, magazines, notes, calendar pages, etc., that a partner could not have found a place for himself if he tried.

"Well, would you like to go out on a date?"

"What do you mean?" She knew what he meant, but she was stalling, hoping her sudden state of physical excitement would ebb enough so that she could respond with some dignity.

"Like a date. I buy you dinner, things like that."

"Where would that take place?"

"You don't sound like you really want to go."

"I'm just surprised. It's been a while since . . . I mean, how are you?"

"I'm great. I'm not nuts about Dallas, but I'm great. Why didn't you tell me you were divorced on the plane that night?"

Had she held it back? She must have. "You didn't ask?"

No, he didn't. But Phil had no idea he was about to become her lover when they were at that level of small talk. Afterward, it *had* occurred to him to find out more, but good manners (and the fact that Lily was asleep) had intervened.

"I'm not sure that's an answer."

"I don't know, Phil. It's just not the first thing I say about my life if I want to make a good impression."

"So you wanted to make a good impression?"

"Apparently."

Needless to say, they went on the date. In later years, it became a joke between them—they would have sex and, in lieu of "How was it for you?" Phil would say, "So, Lily, how's your marriage?"

Even after they were married to each other, Lily sometimes felt that her liaison with Phil was vaguely illicit—the difference in their ages was part of it, but the problem of how to present Phil to Denny had been a compounding factor. Lily's own mother had tried to pass off as uncles a series of seemingly well-meaning boyfriends after Lily's father had died. (Lily was seventeen!) Sure it was the '50s and Anne-Marie was a ladylike lady who went to church every Sunday, but teenage Lily had considered the uncle gambit the worst form of hypocrisy. There would be no "Uncle Phil" in Denny's life. Lily chose, instead, to lie by omission. While Denny was in high school, Lily went to conferences, to visit the labs of colleagues, and to meet with the editors of journals, and she also happened to see Phil on these occasions. There were no getaway weekends with nothing in them but sex and she confided the relationship to no one, not even Maureen.

This had been going on for a year or more when Denny confronted her mother one Sunday night. Lily had just returned from a weekend with Phil in it. Denny was almost fifteen. "So, who's your boyfriend?" she asked her mother. Lily shut the front door behind her and put her overnight bag down in the entryway. She looked at herself in the hall mirror to see if she looked like a woman who had a boyfriend. She just looked like herself.

"His name is Phil—he's a biochemist," she told Denny.

Denny, who had not really anticipated a straight answer, saw that her mother was now giving her full eye contact and beginning to suppress a goofy "I've got a boyfriend" smile.

Denny wanted to be mad, but, seeing the smile, she couldn't. (Denny had a boyfriend herself, at the time—her first head-over-heels, make-out-so-long-your-lips-get-numb boyfriend, Tim Duffy.) She put her hand up for a high-five, waiting patiently for Lily to catch on, which took a good five seconds. Then, she gently slapped her mother's palm. "Good for you, Mom."

Although she pressed for details that night, she never really got many. Phil was still living in Dallas then, and Lily's trysts with him were infrequent—there were no nonstop flights. Shortly before Denny left for college, Phil got a lab in Chicago, and that proximity plus Denny's absence from the house on Sherwood Road ushered in phase two of Phil and Lily's surprisingly durable relationship.

Now, in what Denny considers a ludicrous third-act twist, Lily and Phil are about to move to New York. Lily's early mockingbird research has finally been recognized as seminal, and she is getting the grant of a lifetime to work in the lab of the century. Denny plans to stay in Columbus for five days, during which Lily expects her to help them run a garage sale and to pack up or toss out her vast accumulation of unsorted childhood belongings.

Denny's own agenda for the trip includes eating her last Johnson's ice-cream cone, getting a memorial look at the bench in Franklin Park where she first made out with the aforementioned Duffy, and somehow finessing the facts of her life: she is a single, nearly thirty-year-old woman who lives in the balmy, palm-tree studded version of hell with virtually no income, a roommate who frightens her, and more solitude than any essentially social being should have to bear.

As the in-flight movie's end credits roll, Denny shuts her eyes and sees her house on Sherwood Road, the only place she has ever called home. She's learned that it's unusual to have had one house last so long in life, especially through divorce and remarriage. Knowing that only makes the idea of having to empty her stuff from said house all the more hateful. She pictures the denuded living-room floor—the once-gold carpet now a relief map of absent chair legs and forgotten stains. Though she learned to crawl, walk, skip, dance, and God knows what else right in that very room, it will soon look like she was never there. As for her bedroom, she has agreed to keep only what she can reasonably carry or ship back to L.A.

Before the movie, she'd tried to make a list in her journal of her most precious items, thinking she could spare herself the worst of the decision-making by doing some advance triage. It seemed logical that anything she could remember from 2,000 miles away would belong in the category "most important." This activity proved as impossible as that acting exercise where you're supposed to get to an emotion by recalling the smell in the air or the color of the dress. She has faked her way through enough of those. On the plane, all she could bring to mind were fragments: her closet, full of school clothes, when she was seven or eight; the cracks in the ceiling above her bed when she was fifteen; the smell of her mother's strange green perfume, worn infrequently; the bookshelves in the den; scrambled eggs on a blue-and-white china plate. Anyway, she doesn't need a party dress from first grade or a baseball glove to validate her identity. On the other hand, that dress *is* an amazing piece of '60s memorabilia, with its

Lazarus version of a Peter Max print. Stuff like that shouldn't be thrown away. She could still one day have a daughter who might appreciate a thing like that.

So she will go through the actual process of packing, in all its agonizing drudgery. She is pretty sure that Lily will be little or no help. Phil doesn't even figure in her equation—although he should. He's always on the lookout for a way to connect with Denny, and he's much better at helping with tangible projects than with idle conversation.

Phil and Denny have never found their footing with each other. After Lily admitted that he existed, she did invite him to Bexley for a few trial weekends, but Denny was in deep teenagerdom at the time. It seemed that whenever Phil showed up, she was panicked over schoolwork, lovesick, stoned, or hadn't slept the night before. During the one visit when she might have given him a chance, she was awakened in the middle of the night by the sound of her mother's low moaning during sex. Much as Denny wanted Lily to be happy and had endorsed the boyfriend concept in theory, that was just unacceptably gross and she blamed Phil. The next day, she could barely look at him.

Phil drives Lily's brand-new Toyota Cressida into short-term parking. Lily is in the passenger seat grimacing as they cruise for an empty space. They are in plenty of time for Denny's scheduled arrival, but whenever Denny is involved, Lily feels she is destined to be late. They by now have a long history of screwed-up arrivals and departures—most recently, Denny had somehow not seen her mother as Lily came out of Customs at LAX, returning from three weeks in Japan (Phil had stayed only two). Lily had taken a taxi to the address she had for Denny's apartment in Hollywood while Denny had waited at the Bradley Terminal, having her mother paged, phoning the house in Bexley to see if there'd been a change in plans, and fighting with the United customer service reps who wouldn't reveal to her whether or not her mother's name had been on the manifest. Since Lily was only staying overnight before continuing home, this missed approach was basically their whole visit.

So it's been more than a year since they've seen each other. Lily's afraid her daughter may look so different she won't recognize her. They talk on the phone fairly often but never about anything as mundane as appearance. Now that Denny is a working actress in Los Angeles, it today occurred to Lily, she will probably have dyed her hair and developed all kinds of strangely articulated muscles in her arms like that woman in *Terminator 2*. (Phil had insisted they see *T2*. It was time for her to start participating in the culture, he told her. And, to her amazement, she had liked it. She would even see it again, if the opportunity arose.)

"Do you think she'll look different?"

"Uh, no. Not really. Why?"

"Maybe she had to get her hair dyed, or her teeth straightened, or— She never used to look much like a movie actress. Did she?"

This is a trick question. If Phil agrees with Lily's statement, he's diminishing Denny—Lily's one-and-only daughter. If he disagrees, however, he's implicitly admitting the possibility that he might find Denny attractive. That can't be.

He's never felt any particular pull toward Denny in the few years that their paths have crossed. However, as time passes, the distance between Phil and Denny's ages seems to shrink, whereas the distance between Lily and Denny's ages seems to increase. So the answer's easy, really: "I don't know."

"I guess I'm exaggerating. I'm just afraid I won't recognize her."

"You'll recognize her. She's your daughter. You could probably pick her out by scent, if nothing else."

Denny walks down the jetway and straight through the gate area and hardly looks around. In a way, she doesn't want to see them, though she knows they're here somewhere. Heading for baggage claim, she stares openly at the presumed Ohioans, wondering whether they look different to her after such a long time away. Has she become an "Angeleno"? She sees a couple with small children—fat, colorless, dressed in Kmart casuals. The woman swoops up her unruly three-year-old like a sack of flour, then catches Denny staring and glares back. Denny's sure she has conveyed a look of pure contempt, despite feeling quite a bit of sympathy, or at least common cause. It's late on a Saturday afternoon in the dead of summer and Denny knows the drag of that in her every bone and sinew, even in the air-conditioned terminal—especially there, where the day looks molten through the super-thick partially soundproof glass. She is swimming unwillingly upstream toward a reunion with her mother and she feels like every bit as much of a grimy loser as the Kmart mom she has just cut down with one dark glance.

In the baggage concourse, Lily and Denny spot each other from a good way off. There is an awkward silence as mother and daughter take each other in. Obviously, no one has any difficulty recognizing anyone else, although at close range Denny can see that her mother *has* aged: her jaw and chin are soft, the skin under her eyes is glossy with moisturizer but nevertheless looks almost bruised.

"Hi, Mom," says Denny, projecting brightness for all she's worth.

"It's great to see you," Lily says, staring unabashedly at Denny's trim body in its Spandex mini-dress.

Phil watches them both with a bemused look. They are so polite with each other, but why? Denny looks up at Phil after pulling away from her mother's embrace. She's never gotten used to the idea that he is her stepfather. She's not sure whether it's the word *stepfather* or Phil's freckle-faced, wide-eyed, basically childlike appearance. She feels like she should call him "Sport."

"How was your trip?" he asks.

Denny smiles, shudders faintly, and says, "It's very weird to be here. I feel like a stranger."

Phil sees Lily look as though she is about to apologize for the whole state of Ohio.

"I mean the airport," Denny adds. "Did I leave from here? I don't even recognize it."

Lily frowns. "Maybe a different airline."

"You guys look great," tries Denny, glancing at the pager clipped to the strap of her shoulder bag, which has begun to vibrate. It displays a number in 310, the new area code for western Los Angeles. The number is not familiar, and this seems the wrong moment to start looking for a pay phone.

They detour for dinner at Tucson's Café, Columbus's lone attempt at a Mexican restaurant. It's Phil and Lily's favorite place to eat, just about the only thing they're really going to miss in Columbus, they claim—despite the fact that it's way the hell out on the Dublin-Granville Road. To Denny's eyes, it's just a Country-Western bar that serves food with salsa on it—there's one on every other corner in L.A., but for some reason it seems ridiculous to her in Columbus, or Dublin, or wherever they are. The piñata representations of Corona bottles that hang from the ceiling look like they were made by Pennsylvania Dutch schoolchildren, the hot sauce is almost indistinguishable from ketchup, and the fake sawdust on the floor smells vaguely like Pine-Sol.

When they are seated and looking at the menu (which Denny can predict to a tilde), she remembers how she did once see a tumbleweed, on La Cienega, late at night, when the Santa Anas were blowing. Despite the leveling effect of the Tucson Café's strong, salty margarita, she feels homesick. She wishes her car, her trusty Nissan, were here in the parking lot; then she could excuse herself after dinner and drive till she could see a body of water or an open space. The idea of home, which she assumes resides on Sherwood Road, in fact adheres to all kinds of places and experiences in her life at this point. In Los Angeles, in many ways, her true home is her car.

Phil has been watching Denny from the safe remove of his menu, trying to determine if she does or doesn't remind

him of Lily. The physical resemblance is not pronounced, but
there's something, a broken quality, that plucks at his memory. He never knew Lily at twenty-seven, and all evidence
points to her having been tied up tighter than a cord of fire-
wood back then, but he knew her at thirty-six, and he knew
her even better at forty-one. At forty-one, those ropes were
frayed to bursting. Will Denny find a more graceful and
gradual way through?

Denny gets up to look at the jukebox. It's loaded with
Johnny Cash, Merle Haggard, Willie Nelson, George Jones.
Her ex-boyfriend Zander used to try to get her to appreciate
this stuff, but her position was "If I'd cross the street to avoid
the guy, I don't *want* to like his music." Instead of the guys
with sideburns, she selects Patsy Cline singing "You Belong
to Me," a song that tends to make her sad.

"Do you want to see pictures?" asks Lily, when Denny returns to the table.

"Pictures?"

"Of the apartment in New York." Lily hands Denny a
photo envelope.

"Have I seen these?" Phil wants to know.

"They're the ones we took in April."

They are pictures of an empty apartment. It looks like a
pretty nice apartment: white walls, wood floors, and some
light coming in, but it's hard for Denny to make much of it.
She hands the first few off to Phil and goes to the next: a new
angle of the empty apartment. Apparently there are thirty-
six of these.

"Wow," says Denny without conviction, "so that's Central
Park out there?"

Phil leans in toward her. "You can only really see it when you stand at the window—we look down on the baseball fields," he says. "From where that one was taken, you just see the buildings on the other side of the park—Mount Sinai is right there." He points outside of the frame of the picture. There is no sense of nearby greenery in the photographs—all you can see outside the windows is a whitish sky. And here comes Patsy, with that catch in her voice,

Fly the ocean in a silver plane.
See the jungle when it's wet with rain.
Just remember, till you're home again,
You belong to me.

Denny looks down at her unmanicured nails—the flaw in her actress costume. Who do they belong to? Why couldn't *her* silver plane take her someplace better than this?

The pictures don't show the front of the building or anything about the neighborhood in which it resides. Instead, Denny sees disembodied corners, hallways, the eat-in kitchen. The two bedrooms are represented by doorways. There is even a photograph of an open closet.

"What's this about, Mom?"

"I took it to remind myself that whatever I thought I was taking with me, it was twice as much as could fit."

"I thought those prewar buildings usually have storage in the basement, too."

"How do you know that?" Lily looks at Denny a bit crossly.

"How do I know anything? There's a sitcom set in one."

"There is?" Phil is skeptical.

"Does anyone do anything out there but watch television?"

"I have to watch TV, Mom—it's part of my job. I have to be able to talk intelligently about the shows if I get called in. I know every show in prime time now. Names of characters, storylines, everything. Try me."

Phil and Lily both look equally appalled by this piece of news.

"There isn't really a sitcom set in the storage room of a prewar building in New York," Denny admits. "Maybe there should be, but there isn't."

"Note to self: Write sitcom about storage room, send to Hollywood." Phil mimes writing on a pad. No one laughs. He has also been known to make air quotes.

"My roommate sophomore year lived in one of those buildings," offers Denny, finally answering her mother's question. "Her mom wanted her to get rid of the stuff she had in their storage when she came home one winter. She spent her whole Christmas break in the basement. It was like a hundred and ten degrees and all she had brought with her were sweaters, so she had to strip down to her bra. So she's down there sweating like a pig and getting grimier and grimier, wearing nothing but jeans and a black brassiere and her stepfather shows up—he's this Park Avenue psychiatrist. She said she felt like she was the playboy pinup version of a painting by Thomas Hart Benton. You know, *The Pipe Fitter* or something."

"Well, they are pretty small, those lockers." Even with her memory intact, Lily is queen of the non sequitur.

"Don't worry, Mom, I said I'd clear out my stuff and I'm going to."

"First you have to help us finish the pricing. Those people are going to start showing up at the crack of dawn."

The food comes, and Lily requests a virgin margarita—with salt. It sounds to Denny like a fate worse than death.

"Tell us about your work. How's that going?"

"It's going pretty well, I guess. I got into a really excellent class with this old guy from the Neighborhood Playhouse, so that's good. And my agent thinks I'm going to start getting a lot of calls for commercials, after the one I did in May starts running. That's why I got my eyebrows shaped." Denny works her eyebrows. "They're more approachable."

"I didn't notice," says Lily, trying to see what's different. "What about intellectually? Are you finding anything to keep your mind engaged?"

Denny has to think about how to respond to this. Obviously the idea of an acting class being intellectually challenging is beyond her mother's ken. Surprisingly, Phil comes to her rescue.

"Oh, cut to the chase—have you met any movie stars?"

"Well, yeah. I mean here and there."

"Anyone we'd have heard of?"

Denny doesn't know why she hates this line of inquiry. Everyone wants to know about movie stars. If she's honest with herself, she's trying to become one, so what's she superciliating about? But it's depressing to think this is what passes for a common culture. It's no worse than OSU football, but that's not saying much.

"My friend Adam is Sally Field's assistant—he shops for

her, reads scripts, answers some of her fan mail, things like that. . . ."

Phil and Lily nod avidly.

"Do you think she can help your career?" asks Lily.

Why does that word *career* always sound so grating coming out of her mother? It's not as if Lily hasn't struggled with her own. Of course, now Lily's career is going like gangbusters. Denny's work is episodic, at best. It feels more like a condition than a career.

"Shit. I forgot. I have to return a phone call. Will you excuse me?"

Lily scowls involuntarily at any sentence that starts with *shit*. Phil assumes the question is not directed at him. To tell the truth, he has been just barely following the conversation, though he can fake along with alarming skill. Since their decision to move to New York, Phil has lost the thread of the conversation that used to be his marriage. For the first time, Lily has started to look old to him. Sometimes she even smells old. It's occurred to him that he has finally begun to admit the truth of Lily's age to offset the extent to which she has suddenly surpassed him professionally. The lab at Columbia is not a Nobel Prize, but it's definitely the top floor of research science, and Phil is pretty sure he will spend the rest of his life on the stairs. He is a stairs guy.

In the dank phone enclosure near the bathrooms, Denny taps out the unfamiliar phone number. It's Saturday evening at nearly 10 P.M. in Columbus. She hopes whoever she is calling in area code 310 doesn't have kids. There are few things she hates more than dialing into some nest of domesticity after its official dinner-to-bedtime routine has commenced.

She knows the rules, after all—she just doesn't happen to be a member of the club. To her immediate relief, the voice that answers the phone is male and gayish—or, at any rate, Valley.

"Hello?"

"Hi, it's Eden. You paged me earlier?"

"Eden? It's Seth!"

"Seth! Where are you?"

"I'm in Malibu and you'll be calling me 'Mister Seth' from here on in, or maybe even 'Mister Seth darling.' "

"Say it again?"

"Robert Altman wants to meet you."

"What? How? Seth! Robert Altman?"

"Yes, you may have heard of him."

"Well, yeah. But not in a while. I thought maybe he was dead."

"He's been doing TV. Remember the rule: We talk about movies, but we make television."

"But this is a movie?"

"Well, there's no script. But they say it's his comeback project."

"Oh my God, Seth. This is so amazing. When? Are there sides? No, you just said—"

"His assistant's supposed to get back to me tomorrow."

"Tomorrow's Sunday."

"They're in a hurry, what can I say?"

"How did they get my name?"

"Remember that A.D. from the deodorant ad?"

"Ned?"

"I don't know his name. But apparently he's an old friend of Altman's and you made an impression on him."

"I told him the 'feels great, looks terrible' joke."

"Jesus. Were you on drugs?"

"I guess so. But it worked, right?"

"I'll call you tomorrow. And return the page a little quicker next time, huh? I'm trying to have a romantic weekend at the beach here."

"Just call me at my mother's house. I'll be there."

When Denny returns to the table, Phil is reviewing the bill. She hadn't finished anything but her second margarita, but she's not sorry to see their visit to Tucson's drawing to a close. There's a chill between Phil and Lily, she thinks, but maybe her news will cheer them up. She resumes her seat and announces, "I have a meeting with Robert Altman."

"What, sweetheart?" Lily asks. She had been thinking about her new lab and if she will need to buy new clothes to convince her colleagues that she really is the big shot she is supposed to be.

"Robert Altman wants to meet me. You know who that is, right?"

"Of course I do. He made that movie where Lily Tomlin was deaf."

"Mom, he's a *legendary* director."

What is it about her mother that gives her the power to deflate Denny's successes so deftly and with so little apparent malice?

"I read that he was making a comeback," Phil says.

Denny nods appreciatively at him, wondering in what publication he could possibly have read this. Lily doesn't appear to have any follow-up questions at all. The waitress returns the check for Phil to sign.

"Did I tell you there was already a Denny Roman in SAG, Mom?"

"What does that mean?"

"People in L.A. call me Eden, now."

"You changed your name?"

"Well, Mom, it's the name you gave me. And I think it sounds better professionally, anyway."

As they walk to the car, Lily considers how, for Denny, "professionally" is still just a piece of who she is, not the whole identity. Eden Alice Roman. Charles had won that round. She'd thought Eden was tacky, and had favored Frances. But at that time she was anxious to please Charles, and there was no other name that appealed to him. The nickname "Denny" was what had made her assent. "Denny" sounded bright and resilient to her; she wanted her daughter to be tougher than she was. If the child had been a boy, they would have called him . . . This part of the memory is no longer retrievable. Anyway, it wasn't a boy, it was Denny. She has never called her daughter anything else. Not once.

Riding home in the backseat, Denny is a little bit drunk and morose. She blames the glucose-based sour mix, but the dehydration of flying is also at fault. There's also that feeling of having lost a whole day of your life in the non-world of airports and planes. And the crushing anonymity of being on the verge of something huge that no one knows about or, apparently, takes seriously. She feels off-balance: her shaped brows too arch all of a sudden; her little tank dress, which was perfectly comfortable on the plane, now binds like a bathing suit.

As they pull into the driveway, Denny waits for the feeling of home to wash over her. As she opens the car door, she draws a deep breath of the still, hot air. She smells lawn cuttings, dying barbecues, exhaust. Nothing happens. The way the eleventh stair creaks doesn't do it, either. Nor does the smell of the freshly laundered pillowcase on her childhood bed. No wonder she is not a Method actor.

Before going to sleep, she is supposed to select whatever items in her room are worth selling at tomorrow's garage sale, and to price them with the Sharpie pen and roll of masking tape that Lily has left on her night table (not exactly milk and cookies). It's the bulky evidence of her whole entire life. Well, except for a few things.

Charles had moved to Encinitas just around the time Denny had been packing for Berkeley, so he had agreed to adopt some of the childhood keepsakes she then felt she couldn't completely live without but was embarrassed to take with her to the dorm: a jewelry box containing a few evocative-smelling shreds of what was once "blankie"; her collection of punk bracelets from high school; and a pile of wretched Dr. Seuss books, battered and scribbled on but still capable of producing a few smiles. Poor Yertle. She didn't remember ever packing those things, but they'd been there in a drawer for her every time she'd been to see her dad. Maybe it was her own excitement about starting out at Berkeley that made Charles's move so benign compared to the way she feels about Lily moving to New York. Her father's dorky post-divorce apartment in Upper Arlington had never meant much to her, anyway; the house in Bexley is too full of memories to parse. What was the story with Yertle, anyway? Wasn't there something about a suitcase? And some prima donna bird that refuses to move from her perch atop the tower of turtles? Maisie?

So Denny's current task is pretty loathsome. After all, if something feels valuable enough to sell, isn't it valuable enough to keep? And would hoi polloi of Columbus really be worthy of any such item? (Lily had always forbidden the use of *the* with *hoi polloi,* because *hoi* means *the* in Greek, as any truly educated person knows.) Denny's old roller skates, tennis racket, ice skates, and briefcase are easy enough to imagine life without, but what about her gray-green Royal manual typewriter? When she was fourteen, she'd picked it out from among its brethren at the little office-machine repair store on High Street. She can't really imagine using it, but she believes it is "broken in" to her particular touch, somehow, like a nib pen or a baseball glove. Ten dollars? Two-fifty? Priced to sell or to imply value?

She reminds herself about her imminent meeting with Altman. A famous actress has no need for an aged manual typewriter. On the other hand, it would be a good thing to have around the house if/when the photographer from the L.A. *Times* Calendar section shows up someday. And in the short run, maybe not a bad thing to keep around in lieu of a boyfriend—it could make her single life look a little more intentional, less humiliating. She spends much of the night writing in her journal instead of pricing the priceless.

A few hours later, Denny wakes up unsure of where she is. The room is blurred with the residue of her dreams. She makes an effort to bring her mind to the surface—the strange not-strangeness of the place is scaring her. Then she hears noises from the other side of the wall: Charles and Lily having sex. Correction—that's Phil and Lily.

Burrowing into her pillow, she talks to herself in rational terms. She's happy her mother has found someone to love for as long as she has, but in the middle of the night, there's no point in lying. She would much prefer her mother to be asleep in the arms of her dad. There's nothing wrong with that, really. Maybe she's just been too good a sport about it for too long. She hopes that as she packs up this room, this part of her life, that feeling of resentment and anger, will ebb away at last. On the other hand, this week is her last chance to get it off her chest.

Phil has gone back to sleep, but at four-thirty, Lily opens her eyes and is fully alert. She has been up like this more and more since she made the decision to move to New York. It's anxiety (and not age), and it's appropriate, she assures herself. Until today, there has been no end of planning and preparation activities at which to throw herself. Today, however, the sale is ready to go. The vultures won't descend until eight and Phil has agreed to pick up the folding banquet tables and clothing racks they are renting at seven-thirty. As quietly as she can, she slips out of bed and into her clothes, then sets out for a morning walk through Bexley. She feels like she has spent her whole life in its square mile or so. Last night's bout of crepuscular lust makes her feel warm but also vulnerable. How many more years will Phil still want her? How will it be when the other women on the street are the glamorous lynxes of New York, New York?

Denny sleeps in. It's two hours earlier for her, anyway. When she wakes up at nine, the garage sale is going full tilt outside. She looks out her window, down at the maelstrom, and instantly sees a familiar-looking woman, probably an ex-classmate, cramming Denny's very own ten-speed bike into her Volvo. She feels violated. Lily never asked her about the bike—she could use a bike in L.A. She often wishes she had one.

After overcoming the problem of going outside, Maureen found that her life looked very different. On the one hand, she could choose her own produce. It's a small thing, but it was one of the most concrete ways she knew that life was worth living and that she was, in fact, living it. Still, you could spend a lot of time smelling the stem ends of cantaloupes and still not feel connected to other people the way Maureen knew she needed to feel. And that was the other hand. She knew she needed a reason, an excuse, to become involved with people and that her reason heretofore (because she paid the bills, kept the appointment books, etc.) was a bit of a stretch. She knew she was making things up, and she thought she knew why: insufficient raw material. So she applied to social work school and went to OSU, which has a pretty good program.

She entered the program picturing herself in the homes of the old, poor, angry, and disenfranchised of greater Columbus. In her second year, however, Maureen got waylaid by the astounding notion of transference. She had enrolled in the required course in clinical psychology begrudgingly, in part because she secretly blamed the practice of psychotherapy (in equal measure to the Catholic Church) for her father's wacky last years. However, reading how therapist after therapist would find him- or herself helplessly re-enacting each individual client's peculiar emotional dynamics—unwittingly playing the role of some unmet parent—she had a sense of being called home (her own transference with the therapist writing the textbook, no doubt). In each case history, whether the clinician believed the story to be about penis envy, breast withdrawal, toilet training, or the collective unconscious, they all seemed to get sucked into this same vortex. Maureen knew she had been in the vicinity of that place before, and that she had unfinished business to transact there.

Lily was Maureen's first private client. After Maureen had scaled back on Maureen, Inc., to make room for graduate school, Lily had missed her friend acutely. Denny was a teenager who no longer really seemed to need her mother, and Lily's relationship with Phil, which she was still carrying on mostly "on the road," was sweet but taxing. She needed a confidante, but she made an appointment with a clinical social worker. Self-knowledge was never Lily's strong suit.

Unfortunately for their friendship, Maureen proved remarkably good at her new job. After six months of weekly sessions, Lily had managed to discover the following:

1. She had been lying to Denny about Phil for four years, albeit by omission.
2. She had never mourned the loss of Phil's baby and was fundamentally averse to ever doing so.
3. She was morally opposed to (i.e., completely incapable of tolerating) any emotional situation in which she felt torn by competing demands. In other words, she had never really wanted a family.

At their final session (which Lily still—eleven years later—has not paid for), Maureen found herself filled with rage at Lily. She didn't express it, at least not in words, but just feeling it shocked her deeply. There was something in Lily, in Lily's character or past, that made Maureen murderously angry.

"I really do love him," said Lily, speaking of Phil, who had begun to heartily resent the fact that she never, ever seemed to want to bring him home.

"So why don't you think you want him around?" asked Maureen.

"What do you mean? I do want him around. I just don't like the idea of him in my house."

"Why not?"

"There's no room for him."

"Was there room for Charles?"

"That's different."

"Really?"

"Charles is Denny's father."

Lily had done her best to merge her own work into Charles's when they were younger—she had chosen neurosurgery in part because he was the resident. She was a good student and he enjoyed teaching her. But soon she was no longer a student. The roles of lover and colleague were not compatible in the same way that the roles of student and lover had been—not for either of them. Lily's next move—again, not entirely conscious but still strategic—was to shift her focus down to pediatric neurology: she could thus remain his colleague and yet not be his direct competitor. That hadn't really worked, either—she still had insights into his cases and she still spoke up like an eager student, instead of a deferential associate. Sometimes she believed Charles was envious of even the presumed disadvantage of her small hands. Finally, and most successfully for their marriage, Lily had produced Denny. When their twosome became a family, Lily's sense of Charles as an antagonist was temporarily muffled—stuffed in a closet with a sock in its mouth, but muffled nonetheless. For Charles, the appearance of Denny was a profound distraction—from work, from Lily, even from getting dressed in the morning. He was blindsided by her vulnerability—it was not a quality that he had ever really had to contend with in Lily.

"So you're saying there's no room in your house for someone who isn't Denny's father?"

"No. That's not the point. I don't want Charles back—you know that."

After all, Denny, Charles, and Lily as a threesome ultimately hadn't worked that well, either. Denny had turned out to be not a coefficient but a person, and Lily was ineluctably connected to that person, even before her tiny daughter could speak or smile. She vividly remembered the sense of failure it gave her to love Denny so desperately when Denny had really only been brought into being to rebalance her relationship with Charles. From this experience, Lily had deduced that she couldn't mix her love life with the job of being Denny's mother. Where on earth she got the idea that she could do both things if she just kept them separate was never explored.

"What *is* the point, Lily?"

"The point is, Denny and Phil will hate each other."

"Really?"

"Yes, really. I know them both very well, as it happens."

"I'm not criticizing your judgment, I'm just trying to get you to hear yourself."

"You just want me to dissolve in tears so you can feel like you've accomplished something."

"Lily?"

"What?"

"What was that about?"

Lily was silent after that. For the rest of the session—another five minutes, at least. She did not know what "that" was about but she also knew she *was* going to dissolve in tears if she said another word, and that was a completely unacceptable outcome. Not that she hadn't cried in her sessions with Maureen before. But those tears were like weather, passing squalls. The tears she held back during that last session were torrents, holocausts—she could feel them boiling up from the center of her chest, she could feel her esophagus blistering with them. As she willed them back down into her bowels, she pictured her diaphragm as a place where lava cooled and formed a crust and, gradually, a cratered moonlike surface that could tolerate motion. This image made it possible for her to stand, ever so carefully, and walk out the door. Then, in the tiny bathroom at the end of the hall, she threw up.

The worst part for Maureen was that, in a sense, Lily was right. Maureen did want her to fall apart. Not so that she could "win" as a therapist but because—well, because of the transference. She could feel the approach of Lily's demons the way her arthritic uncle Al could feel the approach of rain, and she wanted to kill them dead, as Raid would bugs. She could taste the adrenaline in the back of her throat.

The thing Maureen learned about herself that day was the thing all parents, all shrinks, all authors, and all lovers stumble on eventually: that the desire for resolution and closure comes not from any altruistic source but only from our pathetic human need to control.

Lily just felt she'd been tricked, somehow. She'd almost gone down a road that could lead only to shame and self-loathing. That was her view of what happened if one let oneself shed real tears. It was one thing at the movies, or in the face of a proximate blow—physical or mental—but never sitting in a furnished room facing an adult woman wearing lipstick and hose. She didn't really blame Maureen; she blamed biology, which had simply built her—like any woman (but notably, of course, her mother, Anne-Marie)—to be a histrionic fool. Fortunately, Lily thought, biology had also given her the brains to be extraordinarily vigilant about such outbursts. Still, Maureen had brought her much too close.

In the gathering morning heat, Lily watches a fortyish mother of toddlers examine her old copy of *Comprehensive Neurosurgery Board Review,* a book she is glad to leave behind—it has sat on the shelf judging her harshly for many years. When Lily first started to shift from practice to research, she had done well. Being an ex-pediatric neurosurgeon (and a woman) gave her enormous credibility as a researcher—more than she'd ever had as a practicing clinician. Then, after a dozen years of fairly steady grants—when Denny was fourteen or so—she'd finally published her research. Her assertion that new neurons were created and developed after birth, even in bird brains, was viewed by journal editors and peer reviewers with skeptical disdain. But she couldn't go back to practice because technologic advances had pushed neurosurgery into a whole new paradigm in the years she'd been away. With her ego battered by swipes at her research and no surgical practice to sustain her prestige, it was a bad time for Lily to realize that she'd also been entirely cast off by her daughter. Especially since Denny's life was hopelessly commingled with her own. She was always finding Denny's sweat socks clinging to her recently laundered underpants, Denny's T-shirts in the legs of her slacks. It had been a lousy time, on the whole, but for Lily the disinterest and ingratitude of her teenage daughter was the worst part. What had she done that was so wrong?

Lily has counted out seventy-five dollars in singles while her neighbors have been pointing out the scorch marks on her linens and the black gunk on the bottoms of her pots and pans. She takes the money inside to put in the freezer, a safe place. She finds Denny there, filling a plastic glass with ice water—the only thing in the fridge.

"Hi," says Lily. "How's it going?"

"I heard you guys fucking last night," says Denny.

Lily doesn't say anything, but she can't help wincing.

"No, it's great, Mom. I'm happy for you."

She looks at her daughter. Is Denny sincere? There is definitely something, some edge. She didn't have to say *fucking*.

"Am I still allowed to call you Denny?" Lily asks her daughter, sealing her plastic bag of loose cash.

"Of course—it's my name."

"I'm sorry I never really explained about me and Phil, about our relationship."

"You didn't do anything wrong, Mom."

"I don't think anyone can get to be my age, and a parent, and not have done anything wrong, but that's not the point."

If the phone hadn't started ringing just then, maybe Denny would have allowed Lily to say more, and even to feel better. Instead, she runs inside and pounces on the phone.

"Hello?" she demands of the handset.

"Monday, two P.M., in Malibu" is the answer. It's Seth, her agent. Denny turns her back on her mother, and Lily returns to the yard sale via the back door.

"Tomorrow?" Denny whispers. She was supposed to stay the week.

"American's got a seven-thirty flight that gets you to LAX before noon. Take a French bath in the lav. Bring your makeup."

Denny goes back upstairs in a trance, struggling to digest this latest information. By instinct, she opens the first big drawer of her dresser to choose a shirt—as though this were still her home and these her shirts and all she has to do is choose one and walk to school. Of course, the drawer is full of things she quite intentionally left behind, and, seeing that, she tries to act boldly. She opens a plastic trash bag from the pile Lily has supplied and dumps in a whole pile of T-shirts—maybe a dozen. As she scoops up a second pile, she sees a flash of red among them. And, before she can pick up pile three, she finds herself burrowing back into the trash bag to determine the identity of the red thing.

It's that cowboy shirt she borrowed from Maureen about a hundred years ago. A lucky shirt, in a way. She thought it was cool when she was twelve, retired it in ninth grade, and now it's cool again. Plus, it now fits; it's kind of sexy.

Maureen now lives in Clintonville (a once-new suburb about halfway between downtown and the current outer limits of Columbus) with her son, Luke, who is almost two years old and has the strength of ten men. It's not as bad as when he was an infant—at least now he can say most of what he wants and they have a relationship that she can understand, even if it is distinctly one-way. She hated being the mother of an infant. She hated it even more because no one had warned her about how badly it sucked. Maybe they thought that, at forty-seven, she must have known what she was getting into, but she hadn't. From the day she confirmed her pregnancy until the day Luke was able to walk unaided, she had felt simultaneously inadequate, exhausted, and responsible for every breath the kid drew, every particle of matter that entered his system. It gave new meaning to lose-

lose. But she did somehow know that if she could just survive the first year or so, it would get better. And, of course, she loves him.

This morning has not been a stellar example of better, however. They have a twelve o'clock doctor's appointment that must unfortunately include some inoculations, and Luke has gone into full-scale anticipatory terror. Maureen knows better than to announce a visit to Doctor Steve before it is absolutely necessary, but she is still trying to find that line between the too-early statement that allows time for an intractable tantrum and the too-late information that makes Mom a betrayer. Is it inevitable that you betray your nineteen-month-old? In any case, she has been erring on the side of too soon rather than too late and last night she read Luke a story with a nice doctor in it, tipping her hand.

At ten, she starts trying to get him to eat some of the wide array of colorful and nutritious snacks that are the approved fuel for two-year-olds these days: broccoli "trees," carrot "wheels," and the ever-popular cereal "O"s. Food is supposed to be a game. Luke isn't playing. He is obviously hungry (a.k.a. cranky), but he isn't buying anything that comes out of a Ziploc bag, even if you do put it on top of the fire engine and whiz it "across town" with the siren blaring. Maureen has read about other strategies for presenting food— beyond the cute names and shapes ploy—but she just can't bring herself to put carrot wheels in an ice-cube tray or broccoli trees in an ice-cream cone. Anyway, she doesn't have any ice-cream cones and the ice-cube trays are full of ice, and she suspects this morning's recalcitrance has nothing to do with presentation. Luke just knows he's being baited and switched.

It's so frustrating to recognize that you're being outpsyched by a not-even-two-year-old but still be unable to call him on it. She is exhausted, and the shower she took last night after he finally went to sleep was far too long ago because the T-shirt she's wearing has started to get damp under the arms and emanate a smell that, though not entirely bad, does not belong in the outside world of grown-ups, including Doctor Steve. Doctor Steve is gay, but—well, no buts: he is enormously important to Maureen. He "gets it" that what she's doing is almost impossibly difficult, he respects her for it, and he also makes jokes that she can laugh at.

She can't laugh at the jokes made by the married mothers in Tuttle Park, let alone at the jokes made by her own mother in Arizona—everything they say feels like criticism to her. Luke's father, Oumar, used to occasionally crack a joke that caught her off guard, but that was at least in part because Oumar making a joke was like the Red Sea parting. It seemed absolutely implausible, even as you stood there watching it happen. She remembers coming out of the kitchen with cups of tea when Luke was still relatively immobile. Oumar was sitting in her rocking chair holding Luke's sock monkey up on one of his knees and Raggedy Andy on the other, both facing Maureen like expectant children. He said, "I thought you didn't believe in demons."

Oumar never lived with them—he and Maureen never even really had an affair. They had spent one weekend together when she drove him across the Canadian border and back to re-enter the country with his official refugee status. She had helped him apply for and obtain this status, which would enable him—among other things—to return to Africa to visit or even retrieve his family. They spent the night in Niagara Falls and it was insanely cold outside and the desk clerk assumed they'd be sharing a room—so they did.

They got into bed chastely, pajama-clad and companionable after a very long day of driving. In the course of the night, the pajamas proved far too warm for even a king-sized bed with two people in it. When flesh touched flesh in the wee hours of the morning, neither of them wanted to think of a reason not to enjoy that blissful sensation and its various descendants. There was no condom on the premises, but Maureen was quite certain that Oumar had been faithful to his wife since coming to Columbus.

She had woken up with her back to Oumar, and even though they weren't yet touching, she sensed instantly that he was aroused—it was like there was a tangible third party filling the six inches or so between them, an astral body of desire. Maureen hesitated only briefly. No one gets pregnant at forty-seven without paying tens of thousands to a fertility specialist, she told herself. She knew this absolutely; she'd done the billing. Then, she had turned and taken Oumar's cock in her mouth, banishing all such thoughts and replacing them with pure sensation. Oumar, whose sexual experience had to this point consisted only of women who had undergone clitoridectomy, was not shocked (after all, this kind of profound sexual appetite is what the female circumcision is supposed to prevent), but he was still surprised. There was nothing whorish about Maureen's enthusiasm; in fact there was something wholesome—she wore her lust lightly. Maureen had been a new variety of female friend to him—he trusted her, and he considered her an equal, almost. Discovering that she was also someone he could have sex with was like finding out that a dog can talk: miraculous, amazing, but deeply unsettling when you get over the novelty. In the morning, they were both equally perplexed and apologetic and ultimately agreed to continue as they had before—as neighbors (though they lived nowhere near each other) who did each other small favors but stayed away from personal issues such as religious practice, financial strategy, and family entanglement.

Of course, Luke's arrival made quick work of that particular archipelago of forbidden territories. A talking dog was one thing, but a talking dog who gives birth to a son was just too much of a threat. Maureen asked for no financial help from Oumar, knowing he had none to offer, and when he told her he was moving to Louisiana to join a distant relative of his wife's in a motel-owning venture, she let him go without remonstrance. She served Luke as best she could—thinking that if she asked for nothing on Luke's behalf, Oumar could bear Luke no resentment. On the other hand, Oumar would never be there to play the role of father—he already had a son, and daughters, too, and soon they would all join him in Baton Rouge, and the hole in his life where Maureen had fit would heal up like an old incision.

In the front yard on Sherwood Road, Phil is negotiating with the prospective owner of their lawnmower—she drives a Miata and the mower doesn't fit. She has brown eyes you could move into with a family of five and still have room for pets. Lily is supervising the table of kitchen supplies, some of which are shockingly new-looking, despite having been received as wedding gifts in 1960. Lily has never mashed potatoes by hand, neither has she harped many hard-boiled eggs. A woman she mentally accuses of being a dealer is looking through the pile of (Irish?) linen napkins with feigned uninterest. Lily suspects these are worth something—that's why she never once used them. They have no sentimental value, but still, it's hard not to begrudge the professional her pantomime of casual scrutiny. Then Denny appears with an armful of vinyl records.

"Mom, I haven't gone through these, yet. You can't sell them."

"Well then, go through them."

"I don't have time right now."

"Sorry, but the garage sale is 'right now' and we advertised the records as part of it."

"And that's more important than my childhood memories? I mean, look at this, Mom. *Damn Yankees*. And *Jesus Christ Superstar* . . . What else is in here? All the Beatle records?"

"You can get all those on CD now, can't you?"

"That's not the point. Jesus, you don't have a sentimental bone in your body, do you?"

The Irish linen hunter has backed away, as have several other women browsing nearby. Denny's tone of voice is dangerously raw.

"All right," Lily says, trying to cauterize her daughter's rage—or her own. "Just put them upstairs, you can go through them later and then take the ones you don't want over to Goodwill at the end of the week."

Denny, who for one brief second thought she had won the war, now realizes she hasn't yet told Lily she'll be leaving at the crack of dawn tomorrow. There are two ways to play a hand like this. Denny attempts to inflict guilt but it probably would have been easier in the long run to simply deliver pain. "No, go ahead. Sell them. I've got no place for them in L.A. anyway."

She takes the small pile of records in her arms back to the larger pile near the Buckeye tree. A brother and sister, about twelve and fourteen, are busy accumulating their own pile of "treasures," which include various works by the Psychedelic Furs, Bananarama, etc., as well as Queen's *A Night at the Opera* and Sinatra's *In the Wee Small Hours*. The latter had once been Lily's and is now scratched beyond recognition. Great painting on the cover, though. The girl will tack it to her bedroom wall.

Denny returns to her own bedroom and surveys the scope of the problem: Though it may be something she can draw on later (the actor's rationale for any and all discomfort), it just feels grim and enervating right now. There are still considerable troves of clothing to sort through, and books and photographs (unbearable) and notebooks—what good are notebooks? She can hear David Byrne in her head. There's no foreseeable end to the stuff in her room. What she really wants is to go to the mall and find something to wear for the meeting with Altman, but it's Sunday and the stores won't open till noon or maybe even one. Until then, she figures she can at least finish the clothes, which are after all the bulkiest and maybe the least memory-laden category of item she faces. She will make it a game, like speed chess. She gives herself five seconds to decide the fate of each item: go or no-go. (This is a Maureen technique, but Denny has forgotten that.) She tells herself she will never question these decisions later, because they weren't a thousand stupid little sentimental decisions but one big, highly rational one. She takes as a precept that meeting Altman will one day turn out to have been far more important than any left-behind childhood artifact could possibly be. She rapidly tosses the cowl-necked sweater she wore the night she lost her virginity *and* the sad cardigan she used to don when she was depressed, then stops to test her assumption: Does this feel like a mistake or a relief?

Fifteen minutes later, telling herself it is just to retrieve that one snapshot of her father wearing two different shoes, she has attacked the photo box. This proves unproductive. She is yanked into a lopsided orbit of forgotten vacations, fifteen-minute friendships, parties, performances, even jobs: Denny at fifteen in her Kroger's cashier smock. There is an absolutely fissionable chunk of 1979 in the form of a picture of Tim Duffy, her first boyfriend, with his half-ironic Stetson hat cocked over one eye. He was death at sixteen. He played the banjo and sometimes even wore suspenders. She's not sure she has ever loved anyone that hard since, although it's difficult to understand why. When she'd seen Tim again a few years ago he was no more magically attuned to her than her then-current boyfriend, Zander, the playwright. He was just another arty guy in his twenties by then. When last heard from he was teaching English in Japan, and had fallen in love with one of his students, a graphic designer.

There are no pictures of Zander in this box; they are all back in L.A. She sealed them in a manila envelope in the back of a file drawer when they broke up last year. She had, for close to a year, believed Zander was "the one." Now she eschews the whole concept. There is no "one," there are only various boys who somehow represent what she herself would like to become but cannot pull together from the material at hand. Zander was Jewish. For some reason, she thought this made him a better candidate for love than others. Why? Was his particular form of self-involvement simply camouflaged to her because it was unfamiliar? There was no rancor in their separation, except that she knew he was on to someone else, another actress, within months of their breakup and she was . . . not.

At twelve-thirty, the garage sale is winding down and Lily and Phil are both sitting on folding chairs behind the cashier table, drinking juice (Lily) and beer (Phil) that Phil had set aside in a cooler on the porch. Denny bounds out of the house and cocks her head at the car parked at the curb.

"I'm borrowing the car. I need to go to the mall."

"Downtown?" asks Lily.

"I have to get something to wear to the Altman meeting."

"Right now?"

Denny comes closer but not all the way over to where a conversation can take place at a normal decibel level. She is not going to lie to her mother at close range—not even by omission.

"I need to get it taken care of—it's driving me crazy."

"Why don't you wear the dress you had on when we picked you up? That looked quite fetching on you."

The compliment, if it is one, sails by Denny.

"Every struggling young actress in L.A. has that dress. I might as well wear a T-shirt that says, 'Will give head for work'!"

Lily grimaces. Denny thinks to herself, Why do I say these things?

"They don't sell those in Columbus," says Phil to fill in the silence, but also because he appreciates Denny's bizarre approach to managing her mother. Matching wills with Lily is no minor task, and he knows it as well as anyone.

Lily is no longer really listening. She's remembering something Maureen once said back when she was counseling paroled sex offenders near Wheeling, collecting hours for her social work license. Lily had asked how bad it really was, and Maureen's answer was "Just never be a stepdaughter in West Virginia."

Lily laughed at the time—they both did—but it was the same type of "joke" as the one Denny had just made. Basically awful. Of course Lily does have a second husband, albeit in Ohio, and he has a stepdaughter who is beautiful, lively, and young. To rout this particular train of thought, Lily abruptly stands up and starts collecting unsold items for disposal.

Denny watches Phil take a long pull of his beer. He looks like some guy from the crew team or something. In spite of gray temples, he's good-looking. His baby face has finally developed edges. Denny thinks there should be another name for insanely young second husbands . . . something like "trophy wife." Arm Beef? Bat Boy? Sugar Buddy? ManSon?

"Sorry about that remark," she tells him. "Sometimes I just, I don't know . . ."

"Forget it," says Phil, quite sincerely. He reaches into his pants pocket and hands her his car keys. "Here you go, sport," he says.

"Sport?"

"What am I supposed to call you, 'dear?' 'sweetie?' "

"My friends call me Eden. . . ."

Phil rolls his eyes, "Wear your seat belt, sport."

"See you later," says Denny.

Phil watches Lily chatting with Mrs. Shaw, a late arrival who is obviously not shopping for anything. Mrs. Shaw is ten years older than Lily and has lived in Bexley as long as Lily has, but they were never really friends. Lily doesn't have many friends, as it turns out. The fantasy Phil had in graduate school is not the woman to whom he is now married. Then he thought her seemingly placid demeanor was ethereal and deeply calm. Now he knows it is an elaborate defense that, in her forties, she began at last to dismount. He likes to think he has helped her in that respect. He's pretty sure she has helped him.

It's not as if Phil set out to marry a woman twelve years his senior. Before he got involved with Lily, younger women had flirted with him—and alarmed him; they were so focused and certain about what they thought they wanted. He particularly remembers Melissa, a young resident in Dallas. On their first (and last) date, she stopped him from ordering dinner to suggest they go back to his place. (She had to be back at the hospital in two hours.) They went, but his place was a cavelike dwelling where the sheets were wadded at the base of the bed, the couch and coffee table were submerged under at least two weeks' worth of partially read professional journals, and there was a half-empty can of Diet Coke on the bathroom sink. It was relatively inoffensive compared to the apartments of his other single friends, Phil thought. Melissa excused herself, saying only, "I don't think I can go through with this." Then she wouldn't even look him in the eye for a month, as though *he'd* done something wrong.

Lily, in comparison to girls like Melissa, was wavering and uncertain and completely oblivious to his housekeeping. She also didn't particularly want to marry him, though he's pretty sure she's glad she did. He thinks she may be the smartest person he has ever met. Well, except for her two blind spots: her daughter and herself.

For Denny, it is beyond weird driving into downtown on a Sunday afternoon, not least because, as soon as she's behind the wheel, she forgets all about Lily and Phil and the insurmountable task she is leaving behind in her bedroom. The anesthetic of driving kicks in lusciously. Denny could be seventeen again, cruising along Main Street on her way to some adventure in the newer, fancier suburbs, where her cooler friends used to live. She passes the Camel Stop, a red-brick corner building, long abandoned, whose metal sign advertises a former cocktail lounge with a crude but evocative painting of a camel. It always seemed so poetically out of context as she drove this last stretch toward home, late on a Sat-

urday night. What is a camel stop? An oasis? A place where
you get a new camel? The place where old camels go to die?
(Coming in from the eastern suburbs, the sign for a bar called
The Silent Woman—perhaps the work of the same artist—
had a more sobering effect. That one is a painting of a fat
housewife with no head.)

When Lily's career got its current jolt, she had been off in
her own world for so long she was almost happy to be doing
work everyone else thought was crazy. With patchy grants
and shared post-docs, she had nevertheless shored up the evidence for neurogenesis rather well. Luckily, she had tenure.
Once in a while, someone would try to validate, or disprove,
her latest experiment using different species and different
nuances of technique, but the answers never came out the
same way twice. Eventually, Lily's work was no longer part
of the real discourse.

Then, in 1987, this brilliant Persian kid at Rockefeller
found Lily's mockingbird paper—she's not sure how. He,
Ghafarpour, used her data to support his own very striking
work on primates, using a radically new, persuasive, and
better-funded technique. So, rather suddenly for the world
of science, Lily became someone who had done ground-
breaking primary research instead of an addled crackpot
somewhere near Appalachia.

She has long been both those people, really, and feels
more comfortable with the combination than she expects to
feel as the marquee name at her new lab in New York. Or
perhaps she will just be the crackpot, all over again: Dr.

Rothman (Ghafarpour's current rival in the neurogenesis wars) could as easily be bringing her to Columbia to keep her away from Ghafarpour as to have the actual benefit of her thinking. Finding and using her work had been clever of Ghafarpour (she was no threat, and his extraordinarily thorough review of the existing research distinguished him as a respectful and diligent newcomer), so it wouldn't be surprising if Rothman was bringing her there as some kind of counterstrategy.

Strangely, Lily is old enough not to care. She is happy just doing the work, and it will be a joy to leave the grant writing to someone else. And she knows she is not going to live forever. At least sometimes she knows this.

Denny has entered the ultimate furnace of souls: the cosmetics floor at Marshall Field's. It is a realm of more mirrors, lights, sounds, colors, and smells than most humans would tolerate voluntarily, but it seems to be the price you pay for going to the mall. Denny is confused and distracted by the miasma of fragrance—there is a new one that may have even more clobbering power than the dreaded Obsession. It's been fouling Denny's air for months, often as an accessory to another young blond actress with better boobs or cooler shoes than her own. Denny glares at the brilliantly made up Hispanic teenager wielding the spritzer and, in return or out of sheer boredom, Matilda releases a cloud of the stuff more or less in Denny's face. In Denny's current state of guilty anxiety, this could be cause for tears, or violence, but it is also the moment when she hears her name called from somewhere across the floor. Scanning the chaos, she spots a vaguely familiar face amid a head of shaggy grayish brown hair. The head is attached to a white woman wheeling a sleeping two-year-old African American boy in a stroller. The woman is smiling at Denny. It's Maureen.

They hug and kiss and stare in amazement. "What are you doing here?" and "Who is that?" volley through the air and go unanswered. There is a slight pause before Denny says, "Maureen, you look beautiful!"

Because she does. She has grown into herself in a way that makes faint wrinkles and a bit of extra weight brilliant assets. This allure is even stronger when she smiles.

"So do you, but you smell like a whorehouse. And you're wearing my shirt."

There is so much to say.

Lily is standing in Denny's nearly empty bedroom. She came in for some reason, as she used to when Denny was a teenager—on some vague errand that provides her the right to enter and to scan the domain for disruptions. When Denny was in high school, Lily was like a searchlight, not knowing what was wrong but scanning slowly, taking the time to see whatever could be seen. Now there is little remaining habitat for her to examine, and the signals she used to pick up, with her exquisite maternal antennae, are now much harder to read. The sight of the plump black trash bags in the corner disturb her. She had wanted Denny to get through most of her packing this afternoon so they could have time to spend together more companionably later in the week, but now she wonders what, exactly, Denny has thrown away because she was just too impatient to sort through it. Impetuousness is part of Denny's character; this is no news, but there has never before been such an opportunity to jettison so much of her past. Lily is Denny's past, and underneath everything else, she knows this.

Lily is never nostalgic. She thinks of herself as a person who moves on with a quick step and considers retrospection a form of self-indulgence that requires far too much time. But, as is often the case with people who legislate away vast emotional territories, Lily also has an enormous, almost bottomless, capacity for regret.

Open on Denny's bed, although facedown, is the blue lab notebook in which she now keeps her journal. It's the sort of notebook Lily has been writing in all her life, and it looks unfamiliar to her in the context of Denny's bedroom—like something Lily herself might have left behind. (She doesn't stop to think of the tribute it represents—that Denny chooses to record her thoughts in the type of notebook uniquely associated with her mother. There were shelves and shelves of them in the lab where she sometimes visited—they represented all that was unknowable about her mother's other world.) To Lily, a lab notebook is no more personal than a paper towel.

She knows the book is Denny's diary but, fighting back the urge to open and examine the contents of the black garbage bags, she somehow persuades herself that it is permissible to turn over the open book instead. Just for a glance. Inevitably, the glance supplies several instances of her own name scattered across the two visible pages and, feeling instant remorse, Lily replaces the book as she found it. Though she did not read a single sentence, her brain has recorded not only the pattern of "Lily"s on the page but also certain other words that would jump out of the jumble to anyone's eye. Words like "death," "rage," and "bitch," for example.

11

Denny gazes down into the eyes of Luke, who has thrown himself around her waist with gleeful adoration. His look is so purely what it is. She can't remember the last time anyone looked at her like that, even when they were acting. It pulls on her like gravity, and in reaction, she scoots him up onto her lap to play patty-cake. Maureen watches this all take place, wondering who Denny has become or if she has become at all. The three of them trade hand claps, sitting on the rim of the empty fountainlike thing near the mall elevator. Denny and Maureen show Luke the basic pattern for "Miss Lucy," a.k.a. "The Lady with the Alligator Purse," which Maureen taught Denny when Denny was about eight. Luke giggles in a deranged fashion every time they get to the refrain. What does he think of when he hears the words "Alligator Purse"? Eventually they run out of verses. Denny is aware that she's running out of time for her shopping expedition, but she finds it hard to tear herself away.

"So what else?" Maureen asks, "Do you still see anyone from Bexley?"

"Sort of," says Denny. "Faith Jackson opened a muffin store in West Hollywood that I go to sometimes."

"A muffin store?"

"Yeah, it's a thing there—muffins. Don't ask me why."

"How did Faith of all people wind up in retail?"

"Faith is complicated, as it turns out." Luke clambers down from Denny's lap and leans his head on her thigh. "She was trying to be an actress. She and I have become pals, sort of. Anyway, there's this idiotic acting exercise where you think what kind of food you would be?"

Luke rotates. It appears he intends to use Denny as some type of gymnastics prop.

"And she realized she was a muffin?" Maureen supplies.

Denny can't help but laugh. It's a ridiculous story.

"She admits that to people?"

"Dump truck?" Luke approximately asks. Denny does a double take.

"Did he say 'dumb fuck'?"

Maureen now hears her son's query as Denny heard it, and laughs as she arranges a dump truck and fire engine for Luke on the floor beside them. She apparently has a small city stored in her handbag.

"Do you remember how you hated Faith in grade school?"

"Yeah. She was a priss."

"A muffin, you might say."

"Exactly."

Luke makes zooming noises. They watch him, smiling.

"So, what food would you be?" Maureen asks Denny.

"Probably something pretentious like an oyster or an artichoke."

They grin at each other. Maureen gets it. She nods.

"I'm going to audition for Robert Altman tomorrow afternoon. I have to buy a shirt."

It takes Maureen a second to understand what Denny has just said. The name Robert Altman conjures up the names and faces of actresses she once admired but who seem to have vanished—Shelley Duvall, Ronee Blakely, Geraldine Chaplin. And Denny Roman? Well, why not?

"At his house in Malibu. He wants to meet me."

The way Denny sets her jaw is more like some poet or ideologue than any ingenue or leading lady. Denny is a very specific person, a character—well, yes, she's Altmanesque!

"Go on."

Denny shrugs.

"What does that *mean*—he wants to meet you at his house in Malibu?"

"Who the hell knows, Maureen? It probably just means that my picture reminds him of someone, or that he somehow fast-forwarded through all the pathetic parts of my reel."

"You have a 'reel'?"

"You have to. It's just a student film somebody did—I play a vampire. Then there's a monologue from *Medea,* and this deodorant ad where I dance around in a white chiffon dress."

"Aren't you afraid you'll be typecast as a blood-sucking child murderess with B.O.?"

"Ha-ha."

Luke is getting bored with zooming and is starting to rub his eyes. Maureen knows he's about fifteen minutes from a total meltdown, and in the event of a meltdown, she always loses—patience, sleep, something. It's a must to avoid, as Herman's Hermits used to say.

"Come on, that was funny. Maybe not one of my best, but . . ."

"You've been hanging around with toddlers for too long, Maureen. Real grown-ups don't say 'B.O.' "

Maureen feels so relieved to be with someone who can take the piss out of her that she just grins.

"So, what are you going to do for him at this 'meeting'? Will you read?" She starts picking up Luke's various toys and stuffing them back into their appointed places in the stroller.

"I doubt it. Maybe. I can't seem to get past what to wear . . ."

"Are you crazy? Wear that shirt. You look like Ingrid Bergman in a Western."

"Was Ingrid Bergman ever in a Western?"

"If she wasn't, she should have been. Not everyone who gets famous gets famous for the right thing."

"What does that mean?"

"I'm not sure. Didn't it sound wise?"

Denny smiles. Maureen always sounds wise to her, "Like Ish Kabibble himself." Maureen had forgotten the imaginary talking Sugar Daddy. "You really think it looks good?"

Maureen nods vigorously. Denny sniffs her own armpits. "I guess I could wash it out tonight if worse comes to worst."

"Will you call me and tell me how it goes?"

"Sure." Denny can see that Maureen is getting ready to leave, and suddenly she feels panicky about letting her.

"You know we're—my mother's moving to New York—"

"Really?"

"Next week."

Maureen stops herself from saying, "Does that mean I'm never going to see you again?"

"Why?" she asks, instead.

"She got a job at Columbia. Her own lab."

That makes sense. "Phil, too?"

"Phil, too."

"They're going to make a fucking fortune on that house."

Denny hadn't even thought about that. Is Lily now rich?

"She's so brave, your mother, in her way. Marrying young Phil, going back to research . . ."

"Selling my record collection to the idiot kids from down the street . . ."

After getting Luke into the stroller, Maureen writes her address and phone number on an ATM receipt and hands it to Denny.

"Next week's my birthday, you know," she says. "You have to call me. It's my birthday wish."

Denny accepts the slip of paper solemnly and nods. "You have to send me pictures. Of him."

Denny wheels Luke to Maureen's car—an old dark blue Volvo station wagon. When they get to the parking space, he is utterly and deeply asleep. Maureen transfers him into the

straps and bindings of the child seat, then installs herself in
front. Denny stands by the car, watching.

"Maureen?"

Maureen looks up.

"Who's the dad? Do you see him?"

Maureen thinks back; her face shifts as she tries to recall
whether Denny and Oumar have ever really met.

"Remember Oumar?"

"The cabbie?" Denny smiles, picturing Maureen arm in
arm with polite, towering, midnight-blue Oumar.

Maureen nods.

"Wow. Does he live with you?"

"No. He moved down to Baton Rouge. He brought his
family over about a year ago."

"Where from?"

"A refugee camp in Mali."

Denny looks blank and nods.

"That's in West Africa, right next to Mauritania, where
they're from."

"Far away," says Denny. She can't even begin to picture it.

"He writes to us once in a while," says Maureen, turning
the key in the ignition. "It wasn't really a love affair. Just a
good idea."

Yes, it was.

Lily has now read about thirty pages of Denny's journal and
is feeling guilty, miserable, and sick. Denny has never even
mentioned her apparently completely desolating breakup
with Zander, nor that her roommate Janie is a junkie, nor

that one of her closest girlfriends was held hostage and raped in her luxury apartment in Brentwood just that spring. She has not mentioned that she spends days at a time not leaving her bedroom except for peanut butter sandwiches and trips to the bathroom. In what could have been an encouraging development, Lauren's rape drove Denny to take a self-defense class, but the entries about that activity are perhaps the most disturbing of all. Lily has finally had enough after Denny's description of the "final exam."

You were supposed to pretend to be asleep in your bed and the "assailant" sneaks up and sits on top of you, whispering and stroking and giving orders like a pro. I could smell his breath. Waiting for an opportunity to strike while pretending to go along with the guy's whispered suggestions was like waiting to die. Several things happened that I had been taught to recognize as good opportunities to attack, but I couldn't move. I was frozen.

After a while, it started to seem like the guy was actually going to rape me right there in the class. I just lunged at him practically at random. I aimed half-assedly at his neck and was not at all sure my first blow even connected. All I can remember clearly is the noise that came up out of my chest. It was a hideous primal sound I probably hadn't made since I was a baby. I can still hear it in my head, but I try not to.

Anyway, they had to pull me away. I had freed my-self and knocked the guy down, and I was trying to kick him to death with all my might. I don't remember this, but I saw it on the tape. Everyone clapped afterward, but I just felt like a monster. If I could pay to go back in time and basically vomit back the whole experience, I would be so grateful.

In Denny's mind's eye there is a shirt: jade green or maybe lavender and made of some special cloth she has read about but never owned. . . . Knitted silk? Ramie? What is ramie? At Jacobsen's, there is no such shirt. Nor does it exist at Marshall Field's, or Casual Corner (duh!), or even at Lillie Rubin. Denny is tired, hungry, and increasingly lost. She should have gone to Lazarus—the department store that won't stay dead. On her second circuit of the mall, she tries on all kinds of things that are *not* the shirt: trendy things from the teenage girl stores, theoretically louche things from Gucci men's wear. Dresses, skirts, harem pants, halters. Anything that could possibly make her look like she should—like a real actress, embodying some unknowable combination of intelligence, opacity, and magnetic allure. It's a lot to ask from an article of clothing.

The mall closes at seven on Sunday. At six-thirty, Denny is folded up like a collapsed marionette in a dressing stall at The Limited. (The Limited, like Wendy's, is an Ur-mall business that originated in Columbus and remains headquartered there.) She has just torn a size-four dress that she never had any chance of fitting into and that looked like something a streetwalker would wear even before she had ripped it. She is sobbing but trying to do so silently and also without ruining any more merchandise with her tears and mucus. Wiping her nose on the red sleeve of the diehard cowboy shirt, she gets a nauseating whiff of the perfume bomb lobbed at her earlier, which makes her want to tear up the red shirt—her only hope of sartorial salvation at the moment. She knows she has to get herself upright and out of the dressing room, but it's hard to imagine how. If she can stop crying, she can leave the dressing room, and if she can get herself out of the mall, and through the parking structure, and find Phil's car, she can go home, which isn't home anymore, and try to explain to her mother that she's going to be getting on a plane in something like twelve hours.

Trying to muffle her sobs, she retches involuntarily and a gulp of something very much like vomit arrives in her mouth. Given the choice of swallowing it, spitting it on the dressing room floor, or into the torn dress, she tries to spit carefully into the corner of the dressing room least likely to be seen by surveillance cameras. Then, humiliated and ashamed, she grabs the dress and leaves the cubicle, walking as quickly and purposefully as she knows how. She tosses the torn dress over the rack of unwanted items and tells herself she will come back and pay for it some other time.

To get herself the rest of the way to the car, she tries to imagine writing a letter to Leslie Wexner, CEO of The Limited, that would somehow explain the series of events that led her to send "the enclosed check for $125." By the time she passes the Camel Stop on her way back to Bexley, she is smiling ruefully over the line "In my haste to find the proper combination of saucy elegance and tarty dishabille, I found that I had torn and vomited on an otherwise saleable teenage fashion garment."

"Listen to this," says Lily, with Denny's lab notebook in hand. Phil is sitting in the denuded kitchen drinking ice water after struggling with the fucking lawnmower in the hundred-degree heat for the last hour. He's not sure what Lily's doing with a lab notebook but he also doesn't particularly care. Lily reads:

Tonight we talked about limits. Lotus asked us to say how far we thought we would let things go before we felt compelled to fight. She reminded us that purses and wallets are just "things," and we should let them go right off. (Thieves, motivated by money, may shoot rather than struggle with you, but rapists tend to like their prey alive. This is one of the "advantages" of being attacked by a rapist, she told us. I wanted to punch her.) One girl, who had once been dragged into a van at gunpoint, said she was determined never to find herself trapped in a car again. Even if the guy was armed, she said, she would fight to avoid that. Frieda, who's at least fifty, said, "I guess I draw the line at penetration." Then there was a silence and I realized "penetration" is not a word anyone had said in class before.

Thinking of the attachment to "things" Lotus had nixed five minutes earlier, I started convincing myself that the distinction between the inside and the outside of the vagina was really just academic—a construct, like virginity, created by men to commodify and degrade women. I interrupted Lotus to ask if the smartest thing wouldn't be to just wait for the guy to ejaculate and *then* counterattack. She looked at me like I had missed the whole point. Obviously, I had.

"What the hell are you reading?" asks Phil as Lily looks at him imploringly.

"It's Denny's notebook," Lily says. "Her diary."

Phil looks at Lily without comprehension, trying to re-play the passage in his head, using the young woman to whom he has loaned his car as the protagonist. Somehow he'd managed to avoid that conclusion while Lily was read-ing it. Denny knows someone named Lotus?

"It's my fault," says Lily.

"What? That there are rapists? That your daughter lives in the world? Why would you say that?"

"That sense of helplessness, that loneliness, that's my fault. I made her that way."

"She doesn't sound helpless to me."

"No, but that's the thing—it doesn't look like what it is. When she's afraid, she acts out. I mean, that question she asks the teacher—that's it exactly. You see her—she does it with me all the time. Like earlier, that remark about the T-shirt?"

"Will give head for—" He stops himself. Even just re-peating that much of it seems unnecessary.

Lily nods but keeps talking—it's all tumbling out of her now. She sensed that Denny's urgent need to go to the mall today was part of some larger lie, and her readings in the blue notebook have made clear just how little her daughter chooses to confide in her. Lily's brain is working overtime to sew all this up into something manageable.

"It's learned behavior. When I was all wrapped up in surgery she had to be so inventive to get my attention, and then inventive wasn't enough, she had to be outrageous. And then it stopped having anything to do with getting my attention and just became the way she relates to me."

"I don't know, Lily. I mean, yes, it's horrible to read about your daughter imagining her own rape. But, aside from the fact that you shouldn't be reading it at all, I don't understand why you want to make it all your fault."

"I don't want to make it my fault, she does."

"I'm missing a step here."

"She blames me for everything that's wrong with her life. I'm the source of it all. The bad guy."

"Why you any more than her father?"

Lily's not listening; she's still casting around for a theory to account for all these loose, disturbing feelings.

"That's how it is. It was just the two of us. It could have been different if she'd had a sibling—"

"She had you to herself—what little kid wants to share Mommy?" Phil is a champion problem solver, but he's focusing on the wrong problem.

"Of course, Maureen knew," Lily says to herself.

"Knew what?"

Lily looks at Phil and takes in where she's just gotten herself. She has never lied to him directly about the child she lost. Not directly. But her sudden silence has caught his attention. That, and the look in her eye. His brain begins to replay her last few remarks.

"What?" he asks again, his tone already uncertain. Phil has always had the impression that Denny's birth was so complicated it left Lily infertile (and that the pills she took were for endometriosis, not birth control).

"I got pregnant that time in the airplane." Lily watches Phil's eyes abandon concern for sorrow and then, out of sorrow, start to find rage. She speeds up her story. "And then I miscarried. It was too soon to tell you about it beforehand, and afterward . . . It would have ruined the 'how's your marriage?' joke . . . It would have ruined everything. It was just too much of a mess." She smiles winningly, but he's not buying.

"What about the next time we talked about it, and the time after that?"

"Well, I guess I sort of believed it—that I was just physically infertile."

"And were you or weren't you?"

"Well, I was pregnant for three months, so maybe not."

"But you just said you miscarried. So there was a physical problem of some kind, right?"

"No. No, there wasn't. I got into a stupid car accident. I wasn't looking. I was mad at Denny, or mad at life, I don't know. I wanted everything to be different—and everything could have been different— Oh, Phil—" She reaches a hand out toward him, but he retracts violently.

"Don't touch me."

"God, I'm so sorry."

"You lied to me for fifteen years, Lily? What the hell is wrong with you?"

"But there's more to it. I mean, I didn't just make up my mind to lie to you for fifteen years, it got complicated—"

"Really?"

"I never said I couldn't conceive . . ."

"You said there was too much scar tissue—"

"There *was* lots of scar tissue . . . the placenta was attached."

"But you weren't infertile?"

"I thought I was, for a long time."

"But that long time was over before you ever met me, wasn't it? Come on, Lily. You can't have it both ways."

Lily loves Phil. She never intended to hurt him this way, and now she feels sick.

"Can we go lie down . . . ?"

At some point in their marriage, Lily and Phil developed the ritual of lying on top of their neatly made bed, with their clothes on, matched up like parentheses, to have a painful talk. Sometimes they even hold hands. It's a terrible habit, creating a neural pathway that sluices pain right into the delta of sex and sleep; Lily always tells insomniacs not to read, eat, or watch TV in bed, to avoid clouding the commandment: bed = sleep. (Sex is excepted, of course, because of its eventual sedative effect.) But in her own life, she has made bed the place where everything gets sorted out.

The routine is, they each speak their piece, and then they lie there and just breathe together for a while and usually, nine times out of ten, they wind up making love. Usually.

This time, although Phil dutifully follows Lily up the stairs and into the bedroom, he hesitates at the foot of the bed when Lily lies down. Then, tentatively, he sits—even just lying beside her is an act of trust he's not sure he can muster. Seeing him hesitate, Lily trails her foot up over his calf. She would give anything to avoid the talking part right now.

Then, looking into his eyes, she sees them verge with tears. She sits up, reaching to test this observation with her index finger. Phil pulls back involuntarily, which jostles the tears onto his cheeks where they roll downward like the tears of a child. This has never happened. Lily takes a deep breath. She feels the loss of that baby all over again, seeing it through Phil's eyes as well as her own. Awful.

"I was a coward. That's all. I was afraid."

Phil rolls onto his side, away from her, as a sob starts to silently convulse him.

Lily hadn't even realized she'd been keeping a secret; now, on the other side of it, she can't believe she was ever that stupid. It's only when the damage is done that she can ever deduce the heft of her own blows. What can she do to make this better? Nothing. Tears fall out of her right eye and she feels them wearing a groove in her temple, but she doesn't sob or sniffle. She just turns her head to gaze at the shoulders of her dear ex-friend Phil, three feet away but entirely inapproachable.

"I'm so sorry," she tells his back.

He half turns to look at her, with utter contempt.

"The worst part, Lily—" Phil collects himself and sits up—"is that you would have let me go on believing that crap forever if Denny hadn't pushed you off balance this morning." Phil wipes his eyes impatiently and scans the room for a box of tissues. "I mean, this isn't even about me, it's about your ongoing drama with your only child. We've been married for ten years and I'm like a fucking extra in your movie."

Lily is stung. She shuts her eyes in self-defense.

"I'm going to take a shower," Phil continues, "and after

that I'm going to take a walk, or a drive, or—in any case—
I don't want to talk to you. I want you to leave me alone. Can
you do that?"

"Of course I can," says Lily.

But what will I do? she thinks. Just lie here hating myself? Is that all I can do?

After Phil has closed the bathroom door and the shower
is running, she realizes that her first action must be to put
Denny's notebook back where she found it, before Denny
gets home. And that's exactly what she does. Then, she takes
off her clothes, turns off the light, swallows one sleeping pill,
and gets into bed. The blood pounds in her ears.

12

Turning off of Main Street into the leafy dusk of Bexley, Denny tries to plan the rest of her night. If she were home in L.A., she'd drive over to Silver Lake video and rent all the Altman films she could find. Then, since she wouldn't be able to sleep anyway, she'd stay up all night watching videos and trying on clothes. She wouldn't try to remember dialogue or camera moves or anything like that. She doesn't want to appear sycophantic. She just believes that if she has recently immersed herself in a director's work, she can subconsciously prepare to connect with him or affect him in some way. She'd seen most of Altman's films in college; there was a retrospective one winter. Maybe in bed tonight she can try to replay them in her head.

When she gets back to the house, she finds a freshly show-ered Phil sitting on the couch doing the crossword puzzle. He is drinking a glass of milk. This guy is beyond belief, she thinks. The house is eerily quiet.

"Hi," she says, placing his car keys on the coffee table in front of him.

He looks up. "Did you find what you needed?"

"No, I found Maureen, and she told me I should wear this."

Phil frowns in mock evaluation, then nods at her. "Good shirt," he says, and returns to his puzzle.

"Is Mom asleep?"

"I think so."

"Is she sick? It's awfully early."

"Something like that."

Now Denny can smell the lingering presence of a fight. Phil's not just quiet, he's shut down. "I'm going to do some hand-wash in the bathroom. Do you think we have any Woolite, or anything like that, that's not packed?"

"Maybe under the sink in our bathroom." Phil makes no move to get up. Denny waits another second.

"I don't want to disturb her," says Denny.

Phil nods and tries a group of letters, printing carefully. Go ahead and fucking disturb her, he thinks. Disturb her all you want.

"Maybe I'll just use soap, then."

He looks up. "You know you can just use soap. That's what I do."

The red shirt dyes the water profoundly pink, as though its redness—pent up during its years of disuse in the back of Denny's dresser—has been waiting for this moment. Denny has never hand-washed a cloth shirt before—it becomes remarkably heavy and hard to maneuver, and she feels like she is skinning her knuckles on the fabric every time she has to pull it up from the water to move it around. She feels so twisted inside that this additional abrasion is almost unbearable, but she persists because if nothing else she needs this shirt, tomorrow, clean. The red water reminds her of that weird chocolate cake with the red food coloring in it—it seems wrong. Denny flashes for a moment on Luke, how he looked at her so thoroughly and hopefully. Does he look at everyone that way? She can't imagine living with a child that age—the sheer exhaustion of reflecting back that smile, let alone providing the right toy, playing the desired game.

When the shirt is on a hanger on the shower rod, dripping pink onto the rail of the tub, Denny again hears how silent the house has become. It can't be more than eight-thirty or so. She feels like they are all trying to separate from this place by keeping themselves quiet. Like they are letting the house die quietly, or it is letting them. If she goes to bed now, she will be up for hours thinking thoughts like this.

Phil is where she left him, on the couch.

"Do you want to go get an ice-cream cone?" Denny asks. "I think Johnson's stays open pretty late."

He puts down the crossword and stands up, checks his back pocket for his wallet, and crosses the room to hold the front door open for Denny.

"Best idea I've heard all day," says Phil.

They walk the first hundred feet or so in silence, or what passes for silence behind the deafening roar of cicadas. Denny, aware that Phil has been trying his best with her so far, brushes off her conversational skills.

"So what are you going to do in New York, Phil?"

"I got a job," he answers. "I'm eminently employable."

"You don't sound too excited. What kind of job?"

"It's a biotech start-up in New Jersey. They're paying me a disgusting amount of money."

"I'm sure you could get them to pay you less if you'd feel better about that."

"Yeah, I know. It's just that I can feel Brother Thaddeus shaking his head at me from beyond the grave."

"Who's Brother Thaddeus?"

"My chemistry teacher at Loyola."

"Those Jesuit schools do good work," says Denny, sincerely, sensing that Phil is not quite fully defended just at the moment.

"Yeah, that's the whole idea." Phil smiles to himself in the dark. It is, after all: good work. This makes him sad.

Johnson's is set back from Main Street at the edge of the neighborhood. Its green metal parasols become visible as they round the corner of Cassingham onto Main. It's one of the few businesses that remain unchanged from Denny's childhood. She is not nostalgic, just surprised. She's never noticed before how the little store can look almost enchanted, in its haze of fluorescent lights and gnats. There's hardly anyone there, despite the hot summer night.

"I'm leaving tomorrow morning," she tells Phil.

"I'm sorry?"

"Taxi comes at six. My meeting with Altman's at two. At his house."

"Does your mother know?"

"No."

Phil is in no mood to look out for Lily's feelings at this particular moment, but he has to shake off the instinct. He sees Denny waiting for a response.

"Well, Stan, this is a fine kettle of fish you've gotten us into." It's a strand of humor he hasn't pulled out since high school, which makes sense: High school is about how sure of himself he feels after today's shredding.

Denny grins. "It's okay, Phil. It's not 'us.' It's between me and my mother."

Is it ever, he thinks, for that is certainly today's lesson. But he also feels how Denny has just made much more room for his feelings than Lily has, anytime lately.

Inside Johnson's, Phil orders a Nutty Buddy; it looks funny in his hand, like a toy. Denny gets a float: orange soda and vanilla ice cream. She hasn't had a float since she can remember. It tastes like Chernobyl.

"Was orange soda always this nasty?" She angles the cup toward Phil, offering a sample.

Phil smiles at her, amused at this combination of remark and gesture. "So you're trying to poison me?"

"Hey, I'm drinking it. I just don't remember it tasting this bad."

Phil pays for them both, then turns back in the direction of the house, holding the door of the ice-cream parlor open for Denny.

"C'mon, let's sit here for a minute. It's not too hot out anymore," says Denny.

"Yeah, must be down to, what, ninety-two?"

They settle themselves at the farthest table, sitting together on the tabletop with their feet on the bench, looking east across Main Street.

"Your mother says you used to work over here."

"Here?"

"There," he points up the street.

"Oh, at Ling's. My God, is it still there?"

"Sure. What else is going to move into that crazy building?"

"I don't know. It might make a good day spa or something . . . kind of a seraglio, you know?"

Phil is stopped by the word *seraglio*. It's pretty funny applied to the faintly Orientalized stucco box up the street.

Denny is quiet for a bit, then nods directly across the street at a real estate office.

"Was the Town & Country Shop still there when you first moved here?"

"I have no idea."

"They had clothing from the fifties, I'm not kidding. Once I went in there to buy underwear, and the lady got up on this ten-foot ladder and picked a cardboard box off the top shelf. When I looked up there, there were like hundreds and hundreds of identical boxes. Like the government warehouse at the end of *Raiders*."

Phil laughs, which endears him to Denny in a new way. Everything feels so different since she and Phil went out on this errand. It's so much easier to remember who she is when her mother's not around. She gets down off the metal table and brushes off the back of her shorts.

"Let's go."

"What was in the box?"

"It was full of unopened plastic bags of cotton underwear, sorted by color and size, and there was a picture of a pixie on each package. Sometimes I still think about that pixie when I put on my underwear. I thought she was going to come see me someday."

"What is a pixie, anyway?"

"It's a type of fairy. With short hair and like a Robin Hood outfit."

Phil nods. "I had similar feelings about Boog Powell at one point."

Denny shakes her head—she's never heard of the Oriole All-Star.

"He batted cleanup for my home team."

"And they had his picture on packets of underwear?"

"No, I thought he might come and visit me someday."

"Why does that sound so sad?"

Phil grins at Denny's gentle irony. He has for the most part dispatched his ice cream. All that remains is a portion of the empty cone, which he has been nibbling at absentmind-edly. It's now slimy and half-dissolved, but he continues holding it upright.

"Are you going to eat that or not?" asks Denny.

"What?"

"The pathetic-looking remains of your ice-cream cone."

"Ah, the hat," he says, as though naming a solemn and holy object. He balances the thing on his index finger and raises it to more or less eye level. Then he nods at it and tosses it into his mouth.

Denny laughs. "Looks terrible, feels great," she says. She suddenly really likes Phil.

They turn back onto Sherwood a block earlier on the way home. It's much darker now, and the trees make a canopy overhead. It feels like the end of summer and, for Denny, the mix of loss and hopefulness is as strong as it ever was in childhood. She longs for something but not just a part in a movie—something bigger and much more vague. The feeling is heavy, hard to distinguish from the rhythm of walking beside a man, of almost touching his arm in the dark, of knowing he is feeling the same breeze on his face that she is. The lawn and flower smells that still hang in the damp air are part of it, the soft pat of their feet on the macadam is, too.

"What is that?" Phil asks, breaking her reverie. " 'Looks terrible, feels great'?"

"Oh, just a stupid joke," says Denny.

Phil looks at her expectantly.

She hates herself for bringing it up. As their block comes into view, she thinks, Tomorrow, you will get in a car, and on a plane, and go. And all this will be over. And you don't even know what it is that you're leaving behind.

"So what's the joke?"

There's no getting around it.

"Guy wakes up one morning and he feels *amazing,* better than he ever has in his life. But his wife takes one look at him and she's like, 'Jesus, you look terrible! What's wrong with you?' 'Nothing,' he says, 'never felt better in my life.' So this goes on all week, you know, people at the office, guys at the corner bar, everybody's saying, 'Dude, you look terrible!' and he keeps telling 'em, 'But I feel great!' Yada yada yada. Finally, the guy goes to the doctor. 'Doc, I think there's something the matter with me.' 'Well, what are your symptoms?' And he tells him. So the doctor looks up the symptoms in this big fat book, 'Let's see now, feels great, looks great; looks great, feels terrible; feels terrible, looks terrible; ah, yes, here we go: looks terrible, feels great. Yup, okay, well . . . it says here that you're a penis.' "

Phil laughs, of course, but the joke also makes him faintly uncomfortable. "Do you tell that one a lot?"

Denny shrugs. "It's part of my repertoire."

"Why?"

"That's a good question." In a way it's a relief that he's asked this question, not that she knows the answer. "I guess it's so I can be one of the guys."

"Really?"

"Well, not one of the guys, exactly, but it's—it just puts me over the boundary of girlfriend material, I guess."

Needless to say, this still makes little sense to Phil, and she can see that on his face, so she blunders on. "When I feel like it's dangerous, like when I'm getting attention that I can feel is threatening to someone else. One of the other girls."

"What other girls?" They are alone, as far as he can tell.

"Lily," Denny finally answers, recognizing that Lily is not another girl and the other girls have never been Lily. "Can you see how that is? Sometimes I feel like I can't get far enough back to avoid making her mad at me, or thwarting her somehow."

"So stop backing up," Phil tells her with an authority that surprises them both.

"Easy for you to say."

"Not really."

Phil's gait slows. They are both reluctant to step into the pool of light that shines out over the driveway.

"But I mean it, Denny. You can't make yourself small if you're not. And you're not."

She puts her hand on Phil's forearm to stop him walking any farther, and, filled equally with loss and hopefulness, ambivalence and desire, he kisses her. The kiss is simple but nonetheless passionate. Sometimes lips are so soft, and so unguarded, they let you into the other person almost instantly. That's how it feels to Denny.

Phil, looking worried, whispers, "Sorry," but Denny shakes her head, shrugging it off. She is weighing whether this act of trespass makes it even harder for her to leave, or possibly easier. Phil is in equal measures appalled with himself and drawn to Denny—but he's pretty sure the attraction is not for any of the right reasons. No doubt she's fertile, he thinks, recognizing the caddishness of the thought even as he thinks it. The Jesuits may do good work, but they don't prepare you for this kind of thing.

Denny sees the conflict on Phil's face. If I were a food, I would be dirt, she thinks.

In the morning, Denny creeps down from the third floor, wearing the still-damp cowboy shirt. She is planning to be outside before her taxi pulls up and has left a note upstairs for Lily.

> Dear Mom,
>   I'm so sorry to sneak off like this. I couldn't face telling you, but I also couldn't pass up this meeting, and they wanted to do it today. I think it could really change my life.
>   Love, Denny
>
> P.S. Please don't throw out the box of photos. I'll get it next time I see you.

She's also left everything she could fit crammed into the plastic garbage bags by her bed—she was up most of the night doing this, and doing her damnedest not to think about kissing Phil. She'd set aside the box of photos, just hoping her mother would cut her some slack under the circumstances of her hasty departure.

The first bad sign is that Phil is asleep on the couch. The second is that Lily is sitting at the kitchen table, wide awake, and has been listening to Denny's movements for the last twenty-five minutes. When Denny gets to the bottom of the stairs, she hears her mother call, "Denny?"

Denny's chest constricts with fear. She sets her bag down gently at the foot of the stairs before entering the kitchen. She's trying not to wake Phil, even though she suspects that Lily's voice has already done that.

"What's going on?" Lily asks her.

"I'm going back to L.A."

"Right now?"

"For that meeting. With Robert Altman."

"Are you coming back?"

"To Columbus? No. C'mon, Mom. I can't afford to fly across country again. Besides, what if I get the part?"

"How likely is that, really?"

"Mom!"

"You're just leaving me with a lot of shit, here, Denny. You're acting like a teenager."

This hurts. It's something she accuses herself of in dark hours.

"Mom, I have to go." She moves toward Lily to give her a hug and Lily can only relent, standing to receive it. "I'm sorry," Denny chokes into her mother's shoulder, which is so familiar even now. Lily strokes and pats her back.

"I know," Lily says. "This is a terrible way to leave your childhood home, isn't it?"

Denny doesn't think so. She thinks it's the best way she can think of to leave this house—with the hope of transformation so palpably close. Just the simple prospect of stepping out the front door seems luxurious from the perspective of the barren kitchen and this anachronistic hug.

The meeting with Altman is delightful—like a reunion with a long-lost friend. "Two in one week!" Denny tells Maureen when she calls the next day. They also talk a few days later on Maureen's birthday, and the next week, and hundreds of times after that. That's the good news. Bad news is, Seth is still waiting for Altman's office to "get back to him" about their interest in Denny. He will still be waiting when chicken have teeth.

Phil hoards the details of his nighttime walk with Denny. It's not much of a secret, but it gives him some ballast against the secret Lily held from him for so long—enough to counterbalance his very strong urge to make the move out of Bexley the end of the marriage. Phil is not a burner of bridges, he's a family man. Unfortunately, he just didn't get everything he wanted in a family. Who does?

When it comes out, Denny sees *Short Cuts* in a movie house with amphitheater seating. Everyone in the whole place is on eye level with Julianne Moore's cooze during the beautiful and talented actress's monologue, which may or may not have been about ironing. All anyone can remember is that she is a natural redhead.

BOOK THREE

FUNNY CRY HAPPY
2000

Some mornings, Denny wakes up feeling hollow. Howl-ingly empty, she says to herself. It's not exactly a new phenomenon in her life, but lately it feels worse. When did lately start? She hasn't figured this out yet, but it started the morning she got the phone call. The voice was unfamiliar.

"Is this Denny?"

"Yes. Who's that?"

"Naomi Furst? We met at Maureen's fifty-fifth birthday."

Denny vaguely recalled a tall woman with green eyes. They'd talked about the preponderance of peachy, quasi-flesh-colored buildings in L.A. and wondered what sublimi-nal effect they might have on the people driving by them. Naomi had just come back from visiting her in-laws in Tarzana. She and Denny had agreed that buildings should not be the color of fruit.

"Hi, Naomi. What's going on?"

"I'm sorry to tell you this. It's very bad news."

"Okay."

"Maureen died last night. She had a stroke."

Denny tried to put together the arc of a swimmer's arm with Maureen's face, expressionless and colorless. It was Maureen's face circa 1975. It didn't work.

"Denny? Are you all right?"

Who was talking? Some woman? Some stranger? Tears were running down Denny's face, and her cheeks were aching. Her stomach was folding in half. "Uh-huh," she managed to say.

"We haven't figured out what to do about a service yet, but I'll let you know when I know."

No one had ever died on Denny before. Her father's father went when she was very young and though Lily's mother had died when Denny was a teenager, that was after a heart attack and several hospitalizations. Besides, Anne-Marie was old. Maureen was not supposed to die.

"Did you see her?"

"At the— What do you mean?"

"Recently, any time. I mean, was she happy?"

"Oh, Denny, I can't answer that."

She could hear that Naomi had also begun to cry.

"What about Luke?"

"His grandmother's on her way. He'll go with her, I guess."

"To Arizona?"

"It looks that way."

Though Denny had lived in California for close to twenty years, Arizona sounded much too far away.

"Where was she?"

"In her office."

"With a client?"

"Alone."

"Like Eleanor Rigby." Denny didn't mean it in the maudlin way it sounded, but as a reference to Maureen's version of the song, where she "gets over" all the lonely people. She pictured Maureen flying away from her consulting room, from all the sad stories told there. Maureen would have gotten it. If she had still been around.

This was almost a year ago. Denny had provisionally moved to New York because her first full-length play was being given a workshop production by Brooklyn's small but promising Truculent Theater Company. When Naomi called, Denny was living in a tiny furnished sublet, a studio. No one lived in a studio in L.A., and the adjustment was tough for Denny. The place was so dark, and it was filled with hideous '70s artifacts (orangey-brown shag rug; white molded-plastic bookshelves; tragically grimy, once-olive burlap curtains). There was a sticker inside the medicine cabinet advertising a formerly nearby pharmacy with a phone number that began "JUdson 6." She joked that the apartment had turned her into a bachelor—someone who ate all her meals out and even went up and down the five flights of stairs first thing in the morning for a cup of coffee.

In June, she finally moved into her own, bigger, brighter apartment in lower Manhattan, and, at first, the new place seemed to banish the haunted mornings. But they came back after a few months. It seems as if the busier she is, and the more new people she meets, the more bottomless the pit feels when her eyes first open.

This morning, Denny has a rehearsal at ten at the Second Stage in Midtown. Her play, *Gray Matter Theater,* will begin its new, improved off-Broadway run in less than a week. The action takes place before, during, and after a bypass operation that eventually kills the patient. It's not something doctors usually say in so many words but: the trick to bypass surgery is that your blood is chilled and your metabolism slowed to a point that looks—and no doubt feels—an awful lot like death.

For the most part, the play is about Beatrice, a brilliant and successful American Studies professor with a brain full of arcana. She has gathered vast stores of seemingly "fun" knowledge in a fruitless attempt to compensate for her basic humorlessness. Her husband, Arthur, the cardiac surgeon, is a linear problem-solver and basically a stand-up guy. And then there is Sam, who was Beatrice's ex-husband and is now Arthur's patient. At the beginning of the play, Sam is a wit and a screw-up and Beatrice hasn't seen him in years. ("If you know a world-class cardiac surgeon," he explains, "even if he *is* married to your ex, that's the guy you want.") Sam comes out from under Art's knife with a functional heart but an intractable loss of spirit. Beatrice, who probably still loves him, takes it upon herself to talk him out of his funk. She starts out cheering, cajoling, storytelling, and reminiscing as hard as she can, but Sam's depression is real, and frustrating, and she winds up hectoring, deploring, and demanding instead. He kills himself shortly after she leaves his apartment. It's a comedy, of sorts.

At Truculent, there had been months of rehearsals and rewrites. The director (a lesbian barely out of her teens) and the implausibly tattooed guy playing Arthur-the-cardiac-surgeon were always crossing each other, and the actress playing Beatrice was a kook of major proportions. It was, as people have begun saying about almost any group, "a dysfunctional family." At Truculent, Denny sometimes felt like the only adult on the premises.

At Second Stage, there are real actors and a "name" director. Sandy Lindstrom, one of America's many former sweethearts, plays Beatrice; and Sean Dowd, a post-post-rehab ex–Brat Packer, has reemerged to direct. The presence of even forgotten movie stars is a mixed blessing for Denny: They are famous enough to draw an audience if the initial reviews are strong but damaged enough to make the whole enterprise appear fatuous and pathetic if the play itself doesn't hold together.

Sean had seen the play at Truculent in January and then invited Denny out to lunch at the Odeon to talk about moving it into town. It was a brilliant winter day and the light in the restaurant raked across Sean's face in a way that both dramatized his bone structure and picked out the intense color of his dark blue eyes. Denny looked at his face and told herself, You can't possibly trust anyone that handsome. Nevertheless, she agreed to let him see what he could do to get an off-Broadway production together, and he had pulled it off. She shrugs off his pleasant greetings and polite inquiries on the assumption that they are nearly involuntary on his part—that it's somehow part of the genetic package "dreamboat" to be uncommonly nice. That first day at the Odeon, he had stood aside at the doorway for her, and pulled out her chair, and waited for her to finish her sentences before he began his. He behaved like a really excellent waiter, Denny thought. Maybe, as a struggling actor, that had been his métier.

Sean's ideas for the play had struck Denny as so benign she wasn't even sure they were real ideas. He wanted the visual design—the costumes, lighting, etc.—to mirror the ten stages of the experience of being a bypass-surgery patient:

1. Diagnosis
2. Resistance
3. Preparation
4. Anesthesia
5. Chilling
6. Death
7. Recovery
8. Recognition of loss
9. Rehabilitation
10. Acceptance

He wrote this list for her on a white index card that day at the Odeon. He kept a stack of these cards in a special leather wallet in his jacket pocket—a sort of anti–Palm Pilot. The idea of making these "stages of experience" some kind of thematic backbone for the play seemed very literal-minded to Denny that afternoon, but also inoffensive. She couldn't really see how far he planned to take it. Then, as he began to work with the actors, she noticed that even his most offhand notes often employed metaphors associated with the stage of the play they were in, according to his surgical breakdown: "Remember, we're still diagnosing the problem at this point. Isn't there some way you can make these gestures more exploratory, more hypothetical?" When he rejected a paint color for one set (an apartment) as "too somber for a recovery room," Denny called him up at home that night to ask him if he wasn't taking the whole metaphor thing a little too far.

"Too far for what?"

"Just . . . I don't know—forced? I mean, the play is about the characters, Sean. I don't think I even put this surgical metaphor in there on purpose."

"It's business, Denny."

"You think a warmer backdrop color in scene six is going to increase box office?"

Sean laughed. "I thought you used to be an actress."

"What?"

"You know, 'business'—the stuff you do to keep your conscious mind off How To Say The Words."

"The scenic artist needs business?"

"The play as a whole needs it. That's my theory of drama: Keep your eye off the ball."

"Huh," said Denny, still unsure whether anyone as handsome as this guy could possibly also be smart. Later, she realized that Sean's theory of drama was the necessary by-product of his cheekbones. She'd once read that Paul Newman wore brown-tinted eyeglasses because otherwise people he was trying to talk to would fall into a blue-struck trance. Sean's playmaking strategy was a version of the same thing: Don't look at this, look at *that*. It was also allied to a whole category of schoolyard taunts she has always held near and dear. In her mind's ear, she can hear Irving Flowers taking this piss out of Josh Walker: "Yo, Walker, I think I hear your mama calling you," he'd comment as Josh went on endlessly about some football play he thought was interesting. It meant, "If you really believe anyone is taking you seriously right now, you are a self-deluding jerk." As a playwright, Denny is testing herself against this possibility just about every time she opens her mouth.

It's not a big shock when, pretty much right off the bat on this morning in September, La Lindstrom declares a "major" problem. When she first brought up this particular quibble several weeks ago, Denny had nodded and ignored the comment, telling herself Lindstrom was just being a diva. But today the actress still can't find her way into the line on which Act Two turns. She pronounces it "unactable." The little-known stage actor playing her husband gamely offers a variety of behaviors and attitudes for her to play against. "What if I . . . ?" is his refrain. Similarly, Sean has exhausted his supply of technical suggestions, which all begin, "Why don't you . . . ?" Finally, Denny intercedes.

"You have to take a breath in the middle. And get to the 'moment' later. Much later."

Lindstrom looks at her. At first it seems as though Denny's suggestion appeals to her. But she is an actress, and she's only "taking a beat."

"You know what? I *don't* 'have to.' I've done my best and so has everyone else. It's your turn. *You* fix it."

Suddenly, sickeningly, Denny sees that the actress is right. When she thinks how many performances Truculent went through with this piece hanging loose, she feels humiliated. It would be as if Thornton Wilder never told the audience that Emily was already dead in the third act of *Our Town*. Well, that's how Denny goads herself, but she knows it's not nearly that bad (and is pretty sure that her play isn't that good, either).

At the turning point in Denny's play, both Lindstrom's character, Beatrice, and the audience are supposed to recognize that she—who at first seems to be the emotionally healthy one in the marriage—is just as rigid as her husband, Arthur. That moment of realization is supposed to carom off her repeated use of the phrase "You can't have it both ways."

She first says it early in the play, talking about her husband's work. In performing bypass surgery, Arthur both kills people and brings them back to life. Then, after they recover, he takes credit for their renewed health—but there is a huge gap between what "health" means to his patients before surgery and the fabric of compromise they are ultimately forced to wear. This bugs Beatrice. Later, when she repeats the phrase, she is talking to Sam about their alleged "good old days" as a couple, trying to talk him down from his ledge of post-op despair. When she hears herself, she is supposed to experience a little hiccup of self-revelation—*she's* the one who wants things both ways: both marriages, both lifestyles, past and present, all at the same time. In other words, it's "unactable."

Denny knows that finding the right new phrase is not the

answer. There is something she needs to fix elsewhere in the play, something that will prepare the audience to "get" this idea without portentous breathing or gesturing from Lindstrom. She pledges to have new pages for everyone by the following morning and sets out for home.

Since moving to New York, Denny feels like she has never stopped walking. She decided that she was a real New Yorker when she found herself walking twenty blocks in a sleet storm and not minding in the least. She walks because she is anxious and she walks to think. Today, she walks with a deadline, which seems like a bad idea, but speeding home on the subway just to sit stagnant at her keyboard is no good either—she's tried it. She knows that if she walks home, by the time she gets to Chelsea she will at least no longer be thinking about Sean's look of despair and exasperation.

In California, she used to drive for the same purpose as she walks in New York. It alarms her when she looks back on all those empty miles. On many occasions, she had struck out with no particular destination from her place in Silver Lake and found herself, two or more hours later, at her father's house in Encinitas. It wasn't even a nice drive, and half the time she found neither Charles nor his wife, Ellen, at home. She would park under the riotous bougainvillea that decked their carport and walk down the beach to watch the surfers. Sometimes she'd even spot a pod of whales. In spite of boyfriends, auditions, jobs, apartments, dinners in nice restaurants, etc., this is what she most often remembers when someone says "L.A.": sitting on the beach alone, watching the waves and the whales and the boylike men in black rubber suits.

In 1992, Charles developed a condition called essential tremor—shaky hands. No longer able to perform surgery, he now continues to teach and consult but has also taken up a number of unlikely occupations, including gardening and knitting (like stutterers whose affliction is calmed when they sing, Charles finds that his hands work almost fluidly with needles and wool). He doesn't give a damn what anyone else thinks about it, either. He met his second wife at the yarn store. Ellen is a retired Jungian therapist and was—until her coronary bypass in 1997—a bit of a mystic. Now she is just depressed. Early in their relationship, they often pursued friendly arguments about the possible existence of a collective unconscious. Charles had almost stopped resisting Ellen's belief in the concept of synchronicity. Of course, he does not believe there is any intelligent force causing him to meet someone named Cress on the same day he is offered a Toyota Cressida as a rental car and a watercress salad at lunch, but he has given up trying not to notice that these things happen. Then Ellen had her surgery.

Just as Charles had truly begun adjusting to being a man

of wealth and leisure, his sardonic and witty companion of close to five years was transformed into a fragile, weepy wraith. Depression is a frequent consequence of bypass surgery. Some say the sadness comes from the physical experience of having another human hold your heart in his hands, another theory maintains that it is the result of having been—for sometimes as long as half an hour—clinically dead. Ellen's depression, unrelieved by all known SSRIs, tricyclics, and even lithium, is one of the cruelest and most ironic things that ever happened to Charles. He spends his whole life fixing brains, only to fall in love with a woman whose faulty heart seems to have had the last word.

Denny witnessed the four-year rise and fall of her father's partnership with Ellen firsthand and, needless to say, some of the things she saw wound up in her play. She also knew that the innovations in neurosurgery on which her father had built his career were made possible only by incorporating coronary bypass into the procedure. Charles regularly stopped people's hearts in order to get more time inside their brains.

Shortly after setting up her temporary quarters at the New York bachelor pad, Denny got a call from Charles and Ellen. They were talking about moving to Hawaii. Denny heard herself say "But who will take care of me?" into the phone, quite without meaning to. She's not sure if anyone heard her, since no one provided an answer, and she quickly rephrased her question to sound like a reasonable one, meaning more like "Whose name will I put in the box that says 'contact in case of emergency'?" Still, it wasn't long after that when she found herself signing a lease in Manhattan, where her mother (and Phil) still live. Since Denny moved east, however, Charles is newly garrulous and prone to spontaneous calls just to say "I love you." Denny finds that she reacts to such calls with dismay. Where was this fountain of affection when she was eighteen, let alone twelve?

Recently, all over town, Denny keeps seeing the same fuzzy brown plaid couch put out on the street for trash. It's like some kind of omen. The thing is hideously ugly, not to mention scratchy and synthetic-looking. She can't imagine why so many New Yorkers once bought them, let alone when: the shape is basic and the fabric could as easily reflect a 1960s vision of rugged manliness as a '70s take on warm and rustic, or even a bad week at Target in the early '90s. (And about what else can you say *that*?) In the late summer of 2000, it seems like a whole Macy's warehouse full of these couches has been abandoned in the course of a few short hot weeks. Denny wonders if her next play could be about the couches. Three one-acts set around the same couch? She can see the different casts: fornicating teenagers; hipster artists with ironic furnishings; divorced math teacher dad somewhere in the East 30s, correcting homework with the ball game on. But she doesn't know what these stories would be about. The couch itself tells her nothing. She is supposed to be thinking about how to fix *Gray Matter Theater*.

She started writing the play one night in L.A. when, after almost-but-not-quite getting another part, she finally realized she was never going to become any form of the oddball girlfriend on a sitcom, and moreover that she probably didn't really want to. This revelation came not long after Phil had told her to "stop backing off," but Denny has never connected the two things.

Waiting for the light to change on 32nd Street, Denny notices a slender, extremely dark-skinned man driving a cab. His left arm, propped on the window ledge, makes a perfect V on the yellow car door. It makes her think of Oumar. When the taxi pulls away, her eyes follow the yellow until it is out of sight. It seems that this is always happening to her: little things she sees and hears remind her of Maureen. She wonders if the same associations have always fired in her mind but never got her attention because there was no accompanying pain to make them stand out. Now, things as generic and common as hearing a Beatles song on the radio or seeing someone eating mint chip ice cream (the green kind) have this terrible halo effect.

Maureen, after all, had been lighting the way. Not in any manner that Denny was consciously tracking, let alone trying to emulate, but when Denny got scared that she was just too weird or sensitive or selfish to thrive in the world, she would think of Maureen and know that Maureen lived just as erratically and that Maureen was just fine. It was a perfectly good rationale, except she should never have told Maureen about it.

She called on a particularly grim Sunday when she had just broken up with David, the last of the L.A. boyfriends. David loved her, but he was one of those people who created chaos. She'd tried to tolerate it—his tendency to lose anything she ever lent him (umbrellas, socks, books, keys); to break and leave unrepaired all the machinery in his apartment (oven, answering machine, alarm clock); to forget her birthday; and to refer to outdated movie listings when making plans for the evening—but she ultimately could not. Recognizing this inability made her feel like she was never going to get it right, because as flaws go, David's were about as superficial as it gets. She reassured herself that Maureen had never "got it right," either, and *she* was living a full and happy life.

"This is insulting, Denny. Can you hear yourself?"

"No, you don't understand what I'm saying. It's . . . you let people be who they are."

"Who? You? Luke?"

"Sure, yes. Who else?"

"Denny, have you ever noticed that I've been single for as long as you've known me?"

"You had Jean-Claude . . ."

Wrong answer. Jean-Claude was a Frenchman, a bisexual Frenchman as it turned out, and Maureen had married him in a moment of panic when Luke was four. Luke and Maureen had even moved to Paris briefly. It was an unmitigated disaster and over in something like six months.

"You never met Jean-Claude and, moreover, you never really endorsed Jean-Claude, so shut up."

"What?"

Maureen had never told Denny to shut up before.

"Look, Denny, I'm sorry, but you have a big fantasy about who I am and I wish you'd get over it. You're not twelve anymore."

"I'm sorry."

"It's not easy being the much-older single mother of a boy

who looks nothing like me and shares almost none of my interests or abilities."

"Don't diminish your relationship with Luke."

"Don't presume you understand anything about parenthood, Denny."

The phone call ended awkwardly, with both of their apologies left unendorsed. Maybe it could have been the beginning of a new chapter in their friendship, but in the few times they talked after that, they did not find a new place to start. Denny was in the midst of moving east and working with Truculent, and she was distracted. Maureen was parenting an increasingly opinionated and aggressive boy who was nothing like Denny had been at his age. It was an awful place to leave things, but who knew?

On the western edge of Chelsea, near where the Ladies' Garment Workers' Union seems to have several housing projects of its own, Denny often sees couples of aged New Yorkers making their unsteady way through intersections, resting on benches, exposing their pale cheeks to the elusive sun. She admires them, but they frighten her. They look frightened themselves—each partner the other's only mirror and only form of defense against thugs, vermin, ice, falling cornices, dank demolition bridges, and various kinds of invisible toxin. New York is no place to be rickety and infirm. To Denny, the city's old people seem intensely committed, determined. But when one partner dies, the one left behind will be shipped off to live in a residence, or with a relative, even at some obscene age like ninety. To be turned away from New York City after all that bravery, only to live out your sentence in an extended ranch house that smells of Lysol and Glade, seems hideously unfair. Denny hopes she will be in a position to kill herself in such an event. But she is only thirty-seven, and she has no partner to lose.

She feels like she's become morbid since Maureen's death. She sees that she is aging, physically, and will continue to do so. Being wiser—or, at any rate, more accustomed to being exactly who she is—is not such great succor most of the time. She wants to be this wise and comfortable *and* young and beautiful. She has never been beautiful. She might have been, if she had not spent so many of her best years trying to be pretty. Denny is going gray and not doing anything about it. Her hair is still long, and her eyes are still large and dark, but they now have a distinctly bruised quality—"eyes put in with dirty thumbs" is what a guy in an elevator had once told her they were called. Denny still has a shot at being beautiful, of adopting the canny, noble version of beauty she sometimes sees in the city's older women—the beauty she saw in Maureen that first time she saw her with Luke. She just doesn't know how to aim. It's one of those things you can't really come at head on.

Lily was supposed to have retired last year. Her birthday came and went, as did the anniversary of her start date, but she chose to ignore these milestones and the significance she seemed to be alone in recognizing. None of her colleagues in the department appeared to be keeping track—God knows she had ignored that kind of thing when she had been chairperson a few years earlier. She certainly had enemies in the department—or opponents, at any rate—but they had always attacked her research, not her right to do it. She didn't even know where the human resources office was or who worked there; surely it was their job to find her if her time was up. She hadn't really looked at her interoffice mail in months; most of it was usually flyers and campus-wide policy pronouncements that didn't affect her lab anyway. (They managed to come up with a new policy on sexual harassment every other year, but students continued to have affairs with their professors, and professors continued to have emotional reactions to certain students, whether or not they went to bed with them.)

Periodically, a post-doc would show up in Lily's lab who would rapidly and completely take over her fantasy life. She assumed Phil had the same experience, and sometimes she would even guess who his focal point might be, just by the way a new name would casually float to the surface when he talked about work. There is such a man in Lily's lab now. His name is Greg, and he does flirt with her sometimes. He "gets" her style of thinking, her way of circling back to significant ideas but not drilling down until a pattern starts to emerge. Lately, she sees fewer patterns, or, to tell the truth, the pattern she sees is that the battle she's been fighting for the last thirty years never much changes. Every few years, someone identifies a new lab technique that will prove things once and for all and, every few years, someone else finds a flaw in the new lab technique, or in the species under study, and proves the opposite. Kids like Greg follow it all much more ardently than she does, and she lets them; she is grateful, in fact. When research by colleagues in California showed that mice with "enriched environments" produced more new neurons than those living in standard cages, Greg assembled what he called a "lab rat rec room," complete with black-light posters and a matchbox-and-tinfoil stereo system. It was a teenage boy's vision of an enriched environment, and the sight of it gives Lily a twinge of pride and pleasure every time she passes through that corner of the lab. Sometimes just the sound of the exercise wheel in motion makes her grin and think of Greg.

Phil is well aware of the fact that Lily's sixty-fifth birthday has come and gone. They had talked about it quite a bit in her late fifties, and then, radio silence. She had talked about starting a second career, some small business. She'd even gone as far as joining some entrepreneurs' association that still sends them its godawful magazine. After she was unable to find a specific business she wanted to start (heritage seed dealer, antique photo restorer, and freelance genetic counselor were some thoughts), this idea faded and was not replaced. Phil had considered throwing her a surprise birthday party, but after a few vague hints he recognized her profound lack of interest in the celebration of age sixty-five. He thought she would at least want to take advantage of the reduced-fare Metrocard, but she was still swiping her way through the transit system at full tariff.

In the streets of SoHo, Denny sees throngs of young women in the cool heart of being pretty, their salad days. (Their salad years, more like, since they seem to live on little else.) In TriBeCa, the stroller set start to appear. She doesn't like them, either. During her twenties, Denny's girlfriends from college had all been single, the way she was—without any apparent agenda. She didn't realize that the others were all covertly playing the odds of finding a suitable guy against the certainty of running out of viable eggs. Then five of them married the summer Denny was thirty, producing children and moving into houses shortly thereafter. Now she gets photos of these kids in the mail but can barely remember talking to their mothers. At age thirty-five, her remaining single friends suddenly started putting their diaphragms in wrong, forgetting their pills, and insisting on AIDS tests so their more promising boyfriends could ride bareback. Denny, without thinking about it, just stopped looking into the eyes of children on the street. Now she looks at old people and dogs instead.

Denny's apartment is in lower Manhattan, on Gold Street. Across from her building and down the block, there is a vestigial street called Eden's Alley. If she had not already fallen in love with the Victorian-looking former power plant at 29 Gold, the sight of this tiny ex-thoroughfare would certainly have closed the deal. Even though it is a cul-de-sac, she never reads the sign without feeling as if—in spite of the dark mornings—she has finally started to be in the right place at the right time.

As she trudges up the third flight of stairs to her quasi-loft (it wasn't zoned residential, and so lacks certain niceties, such as a bathroom with a sink in it), she sees a gangly, dark-skinned boy sitting with his back against her apartment door. At first she is scared and considers turning to run. But the boy looks scared, too.

"Denny?" he says.

Denny nods back, still keeping her distance.

"It's Luke."

"Luke? Holy shit."

She stares at him as she fumbles to find her keys and un-
lock the door. The last time she saw him, at the funeral, he
was still unmistakably a child. Now, he's that other thing,
that thing in between.

"How did you get here?"

"I took the bus."

"From Phoenix?"

"Carefree," he shrugs. Denny thinks this is some new
slang expression, but in fact it's the name of the town where
his grandmother lives.

Denny holds open the door to the apartment, still staring
at Luke, forgetting that Bingo the cat will take this opportunity to shoot out and down the stairs—which he does. It's a
game, of sorts, though Denny has never actually found it to
be any fun.

"Shit," she says. "Here, throw your stuff over there—
bathroom's on the left. Bingo! Here, kitty."

"Bingo? Like 'was a farmer had a dog'?"

Denny is already two flights down.

Luke raises his voice to offer some advice: "You shouldn't
chase him."

Denny has stopped within view of the cat, who is eyeing
her warily. "Why not?"

"Well, he'll hide, won't he?"

"So?"

"If you ignore him, he'll have to come back. I mean, he's
going to want you to feed him at some point."

It has never occurred to Denny not to chase the cat, and

she is surprised at herself for never having come to the same conclusion she has just been led to by Luke. This is why people live with other people, she thinks. We don't even know when we're being really stupid. She starts back upstairs.

"I'm not much of a farmer and he's not much of a dog. I thought it was funny."

Luke nods, standing in the doorway of Denny's apartment. "Is it okay if I stay here for a few days?"

Denny prepares her favorite meal for Luke while he calls his grandmother to tell her he is okay. Alice gives him unshirted hell. After many apologies on Luke's part, they make a deal: He can stay in New York till the end of the week, as long as he catches up on homework within two weeks of coming back. Luke doesn't tell Alice that his real plan is to stay in New York for good. He has sworn to himself that he will not be in Phoenix or anywhere near it on Saturday, the day he officially becomes a teenager.

Phoenix was like death. His grandmother is a sweet lady, but she didn't have the energy to be in the same house with him—she went to bed at eight. He felt like he was living on tiptoe. The house was an old lady's house, with photos of his mom as a kid on the dresser and an upright piano that hadn't been tuned since—since before hip-hop. He had to ride his bike for miles in the blistering sun to get to a 7-Eleven, and there was nothing going on there, either. The streets were silent and empty—because of the heat, everyone said, but Columbus got pretty wicked in the summer, and there were always people on the street. A few, anyway. His mom would say hello to them; his mom said hello to everyone. He said hello to everyone. But that was in Columbus. Phoenix was like death.

Maureen used to e-mail Denny about Luke's progress when he was little. It always seemed miraculous to her, in light of the number of things she felt she'd gotten not quite right (starting with failing to supply a viable father). Luke was good at math and sports, and by the time he was seven had started to show signs of perceiving irony, or something like it. Maureen first noticed this after a visit to her mother in Carefree. She had sped and screeched to the Phoenix airport in a state of intense anxiety about missing their flight, only to discover that their reservations were for the following day. They spent the night in the airport Marriott so that Maureen wouldn't have to confess her error to her mother. The next day, when they were at last settled in their assigned seats on the correct plane, seven-year-old Luke looked at her with a twisted grin and said, "Now, *this* is what I call visiting Grandma." Denny wrote back to ask if Luke had been watching a lot of Bugs Bunny.

By the time he was four, Luke had become Denny's unofficial nephew. She even spent a few vacations with Luke and Maureen—memorably, for Denny, a trip to the Yucatán when Luke was eight and they discovered a shared fascination with human sacrifice. At Chichén Itzá, the "sound and light" show described a gory and melodramatic Mayan ritual. For the rest of the trip, the heavily Sylvester-accented greeting "Hail, el Sacred Jaguar de la Cenote" ("sthah-cred hag-yu-ar day lah sthay-note-ay") could be used to amuse Luke and appall Maureen. Later, as a casual greeting, it was

shortened to either "Hey, El Hag" or "Yo, C-note-ay," and finally just "Hag" or "C-note."

Denny intends to question Luke on the exact nature of
his plan when they sit down to eat, but, seeing his plate, he
looks at her with such alarm that she is waylaid.

"What?"

"This is what you eat for dinner?"

"This" is a steamed artichoke and a baked potato. They
sit next to each other on the large white plate like a still-
life—the mirror image of the pair on Denny's plate across
the table.

"Haven't you ever had an artichoke?"

"Yeah, I've had an artichoke. Next to something that was
actually food—like a piece of chicken, maybe, or even a
steak."

"You won't be eating much steak at this house, El Hag. I
no longer perform the sacred human sacrifice."

Luke laughs—he had forgotten their old joke. "Yeah, but
that"—he points at his plate—"is still weird."

"I'm weird."

It really is her favorite meal, and it saddens her that Luke
doesn't appreciate its peculiar virtue, but that is the least of
her problems. She savors a few artichoke leaves, watching
Luke out of the corner of her eye as he prepares his baked
potato with several forkfuls of butter.

"So, Luke? You really thought you could come stay here
for a week without telling me first?"

"Uh, sorry."

"Well, don't be sorry, but it was kind of stupid, don't you
think? I mean, what if I was away or something?"

Luke doesn't respond. She thinks he is trying to think of a witty comeback at first, but then she realizes he is hurt because she called him stupid.

It's already after eight. She will probably not get to work on the play until at least nine-thirty, when she will be exhausted. She watches him chug his glass of water. She had only enough milk for coffee in the morning, so she served water, thinking, He's twelve. He doesn't have to drink milk at every meal. Does he?

"Luke?"

His eyes roll up to see her.

"When you're finished, will you make me a list of things you like to eat?"

He nods, then speaks at last. "I'm sorry I showed up unannounced."

"It's okay, I'm glad you came."

Denny wants to reassure him that he is—and will always be—welcome here, that she is essentially his godmother and she loves him, but to say all that would imply that he can stay at her place indefinitely, and he can't. Luke hasn't told her about his secret plan, either, but she can sense that he is on a mission. She tells herself why he can't stay: he has to go to school; he has to have a bicycle, and piano lessons, and a Little League team, and a war on drugs, and God knows what else.

"What grade are you in?"

"I'm still on summer vacation."

Although she's pretty sure yesterday was Labor Day, Denny's willing to back off. "In the fall?"

"Eighth."

Where do kids go to eighth grade in New York? Do you have to try out for one of those special schools like Stuyvesant, or is it still just plain public school? Middle school? She doesn't think she's ever heard anyone use the words *middle school* in New York.

"How was the school in Phoenix?"

"It was okay."

"So you just needed a vacation from your grandmother?"

"My grandma's okay, too."

"Well, something must have made you get on a bus for three days, besides wanting to see New York City."

"Not really." His mother always used to say, "Tell the truth—it's the easiest thing to remember." "I guess I wanted to come and live somewhere where I wasn't the only spot on the block."

"Spot?"

"The only black one."

It's about race? thinks Denny. I don't know *anything* about race. But she answers, "You might be the only kid, period, on this block. Well, except for the Korean grocer's kids."

Luke nods, wondering why he went down this road. It wasn't really the right truth—it just came out.

"Is Arizona the place where they banned Martin Luther King Day?"

"Yup."

"Well, you know, I'm not going to be much help to you with all that. . . ."

"Why would you be?"

"Yeah, why would I be?"

Luke likes this response. He grins at her as he takes his plate to the sink and, without asking for directions, finds the garbage, the dishwashing liquid, and even the dish pad in its little wire-mesh holder inside the cabinet. He gathers the pot and the colander, and her plate and fork, too, and quietly begins the job of cleaning up the meal. Denny watches in awe. Can I keep him? she asks herself. And then she remembers Maureen, a few years ago, saying she thought Denny would one day have a family of her own, that it was her destiny to share the kid part of herself with another kid. Denny didn't believe in destiny, and still doesn't, but she had believed utterly in Maureen.

Denny is up for hours trying to repair the play. The audience is supposed to leave the show having laughed at Arthur and Beatrice and at their pain, and then, later, feel chastened as they realize they have also been laughing at themselves. After hundreds of rehearsals and God knows how many rewrites, it's no longer possible for Denny to tell whether anyone will laugh at anything. This afternoon, she had left the theater with the conviction that the unactable line could be fixed by changing how Beatrice gets to it, but her conviction wavers as the night wears on. At one A.M., she decides that Lindstrom just can't act and, at two-thirty, that the difficulty has something to do with meter rather than meaning. She winds up changing four sentences in an earlier scene and reconstructing the last "can't have it both ways" speech to scan more fluidly. Both of these fixes strike her as pretty weak, but at least she will be able to deliver new pages at rehearsal the next morning, as promised.

She sleeps soundly in the first night of bosky September air, but when she wakes up there's that awful feeling, again—which is really only the renewed realization that there is no Maureen anymore—that she is the grown-up now.

Lily sits in her office gazing out the window at the George Washington Bridge. She is supposed to be reading the notes posted each Tuesday night on her lab's Intranet site, but instead she is trying to invent an excuse to have lunch with Greg Handt, the charming post-doc from Idaho. It's a stupendously beautiful, clear day. She doesn't really suppose she could engage in a romance with this young man; that's not the point. She just likes to listen to him, and look at him, and feel good about the fact that he is her protégé and no one else's. The pleasure of his company helps her believe that she is actually interested in the work of the lab to the extent that she is supposed to be.

She finds herself walking over to the part of the lab where Greg's team is working. She can hear the timbre of his voice in their far-off conversation before she recognizes anyone else's, let alone the subject of the debate. There are often fairly inane conversations in the lab while routine chores are being completed, and this is one of them. Greg is describing the plot of a movie he saw on television as a child but never knew the name of. He is hoping one of his co-workers will know what he's describing.

"He's like facedown in the swimming pool, and he's talking at the same time about all the things that got him to that point. It's in black and white."

"Who's the actor? Would that help us?" asks Sunil, a post-doc from New Delhi.

"No, I don't think so. Pretty normal-looking guy."

"Humphrey Bogart?" This from Tatiana, who is from New York City and should know better.

"No, no, no one famous. Anyway, he's living in this like haunted mansion with this overbearing has-been actress."

"I thought you said he was facedown in the pool."

"It's a flashback, Sunil, Jeez!"

"Is it a horror movie?"

"Not really. No. Well, there's this dead monkey, but no monsters or knives or anything."

"Is the actress famous?"

"You mean the actress playing the actress? I don't know. She's like a hundred years old in the movie, so maybe she really was famous in the twenties or something."

Lily has stopped in the hallway, uncertain whether or not to reveal herself and put an end to their misery. She is no great movie buff, but she knows *Sunset Boulevard*. She and Phil just watched it again on tape a couple of years ago. The idea that they don't know who Gloria Swanson is doesn't trouble her, but not knowing William Holden? Everyone knows Bill Holden. Don't they?

"Anyway, it just scared me to death. I can't explain it, really. There's like this suffocating quality and she's sooo creepy. Like she has no idea the world has gone on without her. She's always making these grand entrances—even though they're basically alone in the house. Maybe there's a butler or something . . ."

Lily can't stand it anymore, so she rounds the corner to confront the little group.

"It's *Sunset Boulevard,* and he's William Holden. You should really rent it sometime. It stands up pretty well."

They all look a little bit surprised. Even though Lily makes every effort to be approachable and friendly with the young people in the lab, her appearance in their midst is always somewhat disconcerting. She can barely keep the kids straight in recent years—especially the damn Indians with their impossible names. Sunil is terrified of Lily; Tatiana just thinks she's kind of a bore. Greg likes her almost as much as she thinks he does, but he is also entirely aware of the fact that she is as old as his grandmother.

"*Sunset Boulevard?* Really?" says Greg. "I've heard of that. Are you sure?"

"You have no idea how depressing it is that you have to ask. It should be like *Great Expectations* or *Catcher in the Rye* at this point. You shouldn't be allowed out of school without seeing it."

"But we're scientists," says Tatiana, looking at Lily's feet in their high-heeled sandals. Expensive shoes, she can tell, and much too sexy for someone Lily's age. Is she vain about her ankles?

"There was a graduate student here a few years ago who used to have movie nights. Maybe we should reinstitute that." It was ten years ago—but never mind.

"I can organize that," offers Sunil, ever hopeful of being noticed.

Lily nods at him, having now entirely forgotten her excuse for coming over. "How's the new PET scanner?"

The PET scanner is not all that new.

"Fine," says Sunil, tentatively.

"Better than ever," says Greg. Lily smiles gratefully at him and looks at her watch as if remembering something.

"Wow, time for lunch," she says.

Not knowing what else to do with him, Denny takes Luke along to the theater. They ride the subway. Luke has never seen the subway and compulsively reads every shred of information he can find, including the weathered handbills describing service changes that have, at this point, become standard operating procedures.

"What do N and R stand for?"

"I'm not sure if they stand for anything." Luke has no reaction to this information. Denny is not accustomed to conversations in which her statements have no apparent impact.

"People sometimes say they stand for *never* and *rarely,* because they're both so slow."

This gets her the fleeting corner of a smile.

Once seated on the train, Denny observes Luke in the context of the other people in their car—few of whom are black, but at least there are five or six other kids of his general age. She can see that he is also scanning them, trying to see where and how he might fit. She can't discern any apparent reasons for him to be scorned and rejected, were he to go to school with these kids. But can adults even see these things? Denny tries to recall the "losers" in her seventh-grade class. Henry Goldblum? Denny Roman? She can remember worrying about what to wear as she stood in front of her closet in the house on Sherwood Road; she can remember the "bad" kids, all three of them, with their rudimentary punk look. One kid, Michael Something, had adopted a grungy denim jacket as his cool prop. Because of his small size and the age of the jacket, it was obvious—to Denny at least—that the item had belonged to his mother, which more than undid any of the effect he was trying to achieve. In seventh grade, you are still very much the child of your parents. This makes her heart ache suddenly for Luke, and she puts a hand on his shoulder, which he interprets to mean it's time to get off the train—and it is.

As they walk west on 42nd Street, Luke's attention is compelled by the signs and people. Summer tourists are still in full force. Oblivious to the scene, Denny starts to talk.

"I hope rehearsal isn't too boring for you. It should only be a couple of hours. I don't think anyone could stand it if we got into another thing like yesterday. But listen, if you start going crazy just give me the high sign." She pinches her neck, demonstrating.

Luke is not listening. She finally realizes this. They are a block from the theater, but they're way early.

"Do you want to come with me to get a coffee?"

They sit down in a glass-walled mock café, each with a

cup of coffee: Denny's second and Luke's first. Ever. Maureen was convinced that coffee predisposed your brain to debilitating levels of anxiety, but Luke's not about to remind Denny of that. Although not much like a normal adult, she does occasionally flash some parental types of behavior. Being with this dry-witted, hip-looking older woman, in the middle of New York City, drinking coffee, makes him feel distinctly brave.

"Hey, I made that list," he tells her, pulling a page out of a spiral notebook she did not previously notice he was carrying. She has forgotten what list, but reads the following:

Chilli
Spanish Rice
Chicken Frickasee
Lamb stew (with peas)
Western omlet
Macaroni and cheese
Meat Loaf

"Wow," she says, meaning "Wow, I have never cooked a single one of these things in my entire life." Her kitchen repertory revolves around grains and legumes, things she learned to prepare in shared houses in Berkeley. "This is really . . . hearty food."

"My mom was a good cook."

"I had no idea."

Luke nods, endorsing this fact.

"I'm a vegetarian," she adds, wondering why she suddenly feels like she is on a bad blind date. "Luke, you know you can't stay here permanently."

"I know that."

"I mean, you don't necessarily have to go back to your grandmother's, but you probably do need to be somewhere where there's a real family. You know, two parents, other kids . . ."

Luke looks up quizzically at this statement. "You're saying my mom and I weren't a real family?" He says this in the tone of voice that tends to preface a schoolyard fight.

"No, of course not. Of course not."

"Better not be." Now he's kidding.

Denny's new pages appease Lindstrom, but Sean examines them skeptically. The fact that she has a good excuse is not going to do anything for anyone in this room, so Denny just stands pat. At this point, the value of keeping things moving far outweighs the value of having a perfect line reading. She suspects Sean will see this, too.

She thinks about the head of steam she had the day before—she was going to take the play apart and rebuild it. Or was she? What she really wants is to start something else . . . she has to start something else. None of her ideas is anywhere near coherent, and she knows it will take a long time—years, probably—to get where she is with this play with a new one. Where she is with this play, in Denny's mind, has little to do with the state of the production or the level of the cast, but with the degree of her own involvement.

The play has been the focus of her life for three years, maybe longer. During that time she sometimes met other writer-artist types who had children, and she would marvel at their capacity to do both things. She could barely buy groceries or do laundry for herself when she was caught up with writing, and had more or less given up on trying. Periodically, she would invite a few people over for dinner, which would induce her to clean the apartment and cook a meal. She will have to buy groceries today for Luke. When?

Luke sits quietly in rehearsal, drawing pictures of the actors and the set in his notebook. No one pays any attention to him and he barely listens to what is going on, but he is happy to stay in the theater where it's cool and dark. The city is overwhelming. The subway, the streets near the theater, the variety of people, and the way they don't even look at you when you walk down the street—these things all surprise him. Of course, what else would a city be? He's seen it on television, in the movies, and in comic books, and he's been to D.C. a few times to meet his mother's cousins and be in a protest march about some bombing somewhere. But that was nothing like this. It's definitely better than Phoenix, greener and older-looking, and you don't need a ride to go places. That's huge. But it makes him miss his mother even more than Phoenix did, if that's possible. And that is not what was supposed to happen.

Denny is different than he remembered, more serious and distracted. When she visited them, she was fun. One summer they had all spent a week at the beach together and she had built castles with him, and gone on bike rides, and caught fish, and made up songs about the other people on the beach. His favorite was one about a mother and daughter with matching bathing suits. It had rhymes like "We sure think we're really cute./They're small but they cost lots of loot."

Denny's mind is not on the play. She is making lists and schedules and doing arithmetic, as though the question of whether or not Luke can stay can be determined by some formula. How much money would be enough? There is always someone living on less. How much time would she need to set aside? How many new things would she have to learn to do? Watch football? Keep track of vitamins? Explain sex? Of course he knows about sex, he's almost thirteen—his birthday's really soon. She reminds herself to check the date. But sex isn't just one conversation—he's about to be an adolescent. He's supposed to rebel and run away. Or is that what's happening now? He sits in the audience so placidly, drawing and smiling to himself, but maybe he's just on good behavior. Maybe he can make me another list, of all the things he likes to do, and then I can really evaluate whether it's going to work. What is it with these lists, she asks herself? Since when do lists make decisions?

"What about that, Denny? Can we make that change?"

She has no idea what they've been discussing.

"Sure, that makes sense to me."

Even though they're only changing an *our* to a *my,* Denny's response is so entirely out of character that Sean takes an extra moment of eye contact to make sure she doesn't want to reconsider. Denny shrugs, which is even more out of character. He suspects the sudden appearance in the house of an adolescent African American boy has something to do with this, but Denny has not asked for his help. Does she know that Matthew is more or less the same age? Does she even remember that his son lives with him?

At the first break, Denny calls Alice in Arizona. What Denny wants to learn is whether Alice really wants Luke with her. And if he were to stay with Denny, how would that work? What, if any, money is there for him? Maureen's father was a doctor—as is her brother—so there should be something set aside. Denny's not sure if it's right to ask about money at this point, but she's gotten into trouble before by avoiding that conversation.

"I don't understand—you want him to stay with you?" asks Alice.

"I'm not sure yet. I'm just trying to find out if it's even possible before I disappoint him."

"Seems to me there ought to be some consequences for Luke. For running away like that. You don't want to go through what I just did, let me tell you."

"But there's nothing to run away from here."

Alice has lived long enough not to take this personally. She lets it pass before saying, "You think that's what he really wants, to stay in New York?"

"Don't you?"

"Well, no. I mean, why would he want to move to New York City all of a sudden?"

Why indeed?

"How's he doing in school?"

"Fair enough. Mostly B's. I don't think it's much of a school, though."

Denny writes down the books on Luke's summer reading

list and is surprised to find that it includes both *Catcher in the Rye* and *To Kill a Mockingbird*. Is *that* the age that Luke is? She felt so rescued by those books, as if they had found her in her suburban wilderness and made it okay to be the child she was. Will Luke even have to feel weird in New York City? Every third kid in his class will be mixed race and/or adopted, living with a single parent, in a walk-up apartment. But she knows that is not the point. The discomfort is inside, and it starts before seventh grade. Moreover, it never goes away.

Denny knows that she needs help with the problem of Luke. What she doesn't know is who to ask, or even what to ask for. Her friend Anna is a wise parent, but she has girls and they're young. Michael and Danny's son Gabe is about the same age as Luke, but he lives with his mother for the most part. Anyway, if she called them up she'd have to be entertaining and bright for much longer than she currently feels able. And what would she do with Luke while she was grilling her friends about whether or not to let him stay? He's too old for a babysitter. Anyway, she doesn't know any. She winds up doing what she knows she shouldn't—she calls her mother at the lab. Lily doesn't answer, and Denny leaves a message asking if they'll be home tonight and can she come over. She plans to hand Luke over to Phil at the earliest opportunity. They can go to the park and play ball or something.

Lily has taken the day off for the first time in living memory, but that doesn't stop her from checking her voicemail hourly.

The idea that Denny wants her advice on something flatters her deeply but also frightens her. She can't imagine what it could possibly be. An affair? Denny hasn't mentioned being involved with anyone lately. She realizes she could spend her day shopping and cooking instead of worrying, but instead she sends Phil an e-mail telling him about Denny's visit, and he writes back to say he will be happy to cook, which is what she knew he would say.

Yesterday, Lily received a meeting request with the subject line: "Retirement plans?" To buy time, she'd refused the request, saying she had planned to take vacation time on the suggested day, but Dean Rothman is going to a conference next week, and then he's going to get "very tied up in budget meetings," and he needs to sort this out before he approves staffing plans for next semester. So Lily was backed into setting a meeting on Thursday, which is tomorrow. Today, she's working on a rationale for the continued existence of her lab. She's written so many grants over the years, she should be able to tell this story in her sleep. This morning, however, she woke up not so sure how it goes.

By late afternoon, the play rehearsal has begun to deteriorate. The actors know that at this point they either have it or they don't. New information will come from playing in front of an audience, and they may make some adjustments in the first week or so, but lines, cues, blocking, lighting—it's got to be solid by now. Luke is clearly bored, and if Denny is honest with herself, she is, too. She joins him in his row at the back of the house.

"We're having dinner at my parents' tonight."

"Your parents live here?"

"My mother and my stepfather. My dad's in California."

"Did you grow up with your dad?" He thinks of Denny as a Californian.

"Not really. He moved out when I was nine."

"What about your stepdad?"

"They got together when I was in high school, but he didn't move in till after I left."

Luke nods, having concluded that Denny is another person from the fatherless universe, like himself, like his mother. It's a common enough thing, but it's still something that marks him. Since the blackness of his appearance comes from his father's side, he figures that his lack of other blacknesses—certain figures of speech, beliefs, and interests that he notices among other African American kids—are just more side effects of having no dad. Does someone like Denny, for example, wonder what she's missing in the same way he has, since he was very young? He used to ask himself the same question about the little Chinese girls. There were two on his school bus in Columbus, Meimei and Ally, but there were no "real" Chinese kids in the entire school. Maybe those two had yet another version of the missing feeling. Or maybe they didn't even know.

"You have to tell me what you like to do, Luke. I'm afraid I'm just going to drag you around with me all day and it's going to be hellish for you. You know, maybe we can find you a basketball game to play in, or, I don't know . . ."

"Soccer."

"Okay, soccer. There's probably soccer in Central Park."

Luke nods. "And the Internet."

"Do you have a computer?"

"Not in Phoenix. I had to use the ones at the library. . . ."

Denny wonders if she is going to have to buy him a computer.

"I was on a waiting list for a charity one."

Denny takes a new look at Luke. Are those clothes from Goodwill? How poor *were* they? Luke reads the look.

"What kind of place were you living in, in Arizona?"

"A house. Like a bungalow. It was okay."

"Suddenly I thought you were, I don't know, poverty-stricken."

"Nah. My mom had some insurance for me anyway."

"That's good."

"Yeah, it's supposed to pay for college."

"There must be a lot of it."

"It's supposed to build on the interest, you know what I mean?"

Luke has investments.

At the lunch break, Denny calls her father, counting on Charles to counteract the criticism she fears getting later on from Lily. She still plays them off each other that way. But Charles and Ellen are not at home. Their message, which hasn't changed in years, is in Ellen's voice and, to Denny's mind, is persistent evidence that the father she had as a child was body-snatched at some point, and the guy in Encinitas is a pod person: "There's no answer, but please don't feel you've missed us, we're with you right now. Bye!"

Denny's never asked what it's supposed to mean, and she's also never heard it without feeling the need to make some kind of rebuttal. "Look, you can't be in two places at once, I don't care how enlightened you are!" Once, she found herself reciting garbled fragments of "The Second Coming" into their machine: " 'Things fall apart; the centre cannot hold; Mere anarchy is loosed upon the world . . . The falcon cannot hear the falconer.' " Today, there's too much to explain, so all she says is "Hi, it's Denny."

When Phil gets home from work, Lily is sitting on their bed, completely surrounded by piles of paper. She has apparently gone down to storage and brought back the contents of several file drawers.

"I thought Denny was coming over for dinner."

"Not till seven-thirty."

"It's seven."

Lily nods. Looking down, she scowls at a nearby article, then picks it up to scan it.

"So what's going on here?"

"I think they want me to retire."

"I see." But he doesn't, and his tone says as much. It's highly unlikely that Columbia would ask a scientist of Lily's stature to leave before she was ready. "How much longer do you want to stay?"

This question sounds like a non sequitur to Lily. She looks at her husband, who is standing awkwardly in front of her. There's no place for him to sit on the bed because of the piles of journals, papers, notebooks, and folders she has been sorting through.

"Never negotiate without a goal," he says.

Ah, yes. Phil's rules. All absolutely correct and all equally pat and annoying when introduced into Lily's actual life. "I'm just not ready to retire." She senses his disapproval and adds, "What would you do?"

"Interesting question," says Phil. "I always pictured it being easy, because you'd already have led the way."

"And we'd move up to the lake."

"Well, that's what we said."

"I don't want to move up to the lake."

Phil nods. "No, neither do I."

After rehearsal, Denny and Luke take the A train to 59th Street; this time the train is well populated by black people, some of whom stare unabashedly at the white woman and the black boy. Luke doesn't look like most of the other African Americans in New York, and the possibility that Denny is a relative, though highly unlikely, cannot be entirely ruled out. Across the car, two teenage girls with elaborate manicures whisper and giggle, keeping their eyes on Luke. Denny sees and feels Luke's discomfort. She is used to the scrutiny of the subway, and although this may be a new slant, it's all really just human curiosity and she can't knock it. She, too, likes to know what the other people in the city look like, what they're wearing, and reading, and listening to. If she never rode the subway, she might drift away into abstraction like her mother, and she has made a lifelong study of paying attention, if only to avoid that. Luke stands up and turns his back to the teenage girls, taking hold of the bar above Denny's seat. She gives him what she hopes looks like an encouraging smile—it's not a familiar expression for her face. What would she think their relationship was if she saw the two of them on the train? Big Sister? Tutor? But why couldn't she be his mother? She's old enough.

Phil and Lily's doorman, Hector, knows Denny and greets her by name. She introduces Luke as "Luke" for now, avoiding the problem of who Luke may be to herself or to the people upstairs—"Mr. and Mrs. Coughlin," Hector calls them.

Luke wonders momentarily why he has no last name in Denny's introduction. Of course, neither did Hector. If he moved to New York would he be expected to take Denny's last name? "Luke Roman" sounds like a comic-book charac-ter, but "Luke Coughlin" might be all right. Close enough to his real name (Kelsey), not that he would give *that* up. On the other hand, that was really just his mother's father's name, and that guy left Alice when Maureen was nine. The eleva-tor has a mirror in it. While thinking all this, Luke makes faces in the mirror that make Denny laugh. He can turn his eyelids inside out, which makes her squeal just like the girls back in Columbus used to.

When they get to the tenth floor, Denny stops him.

"Do you remember the high sign?"

"What high sign?"

She pinches her neck. "They're sucking my very life's blood?"

"That's not the high sign, that's the *distress* signal."

"Glad we got that straight," she says, ringing the bell.

Phil opens the door.

"Hi," he says automatically, without even really looking at Denny. Then, spotting Luke, he says "Hi" again, more intentionally, and holds open the door that he would have let Denny catch for herself.

"This is Luke," says Denny. "Maureen's son. Did you know Maureen?"

She leads Luke into the living room, indicates that he can dump his knapsack on a table in the hall.

"Just through your mom—I mean, I know who she is."

"Was."

"Right. I'm sorry, Luke."

"That's okay, Mr. Coughlin."

The only people who call Phil "Mr. Coughlin" are the kids at the community center in Queens where he volunteers. He looks hard at Luke, trying to determine whether he is the good kind of polite thirteen-year-old boy, or the scary Eddie Haskell kind. It's hard to know.

"Can I get anybody a drink? Denny, glass of wine? I have a nice Sancerre. Luke, is Coke okay with you?"

"Do you have seltzer?"

Phil nods and steps into the kitchen. Luke examines the room from his position on the couch, trying to figure out exactly what kind of place this is. Downstairs, seeing the doorman in his uniform and the furniture in the lobby, it seemed like they must be rich, but now he's not sure. Everything looks old, nothing matches, and it seems smaller and darker than Denny's place. On the other hand, there could be mad rooms down that hallway.

"Where's Mom?"

"In the bedroom. She'll be out in a minute."

They hear the fridge open and close. Denny catches Luke's eye and mouths the words "Phil's okay." Luke nods, wondering if this means Denny's mother isn't.

Phil returns with the drinks, then sits forward in his easy chair and waits for Denny to sip her wine. Since their kiss, for which each of them blames only him- or herself, Phil and Denny have a strange loyalty to each other, a conspiratorial, though chaste, alliance. Denny sent him a note when she got back to L.A., although it took her a month to do it. It was the first time she'd ever written to him personally. She'd described her meeting with Altman, treating her seemingly instant camaraderie with the director with an appropriate—and prescient—level of skepticism. After the paragraph of news, she tried to address that moment on the threshold.

> I know we weren't supposed to kiss each other, but I also know we didn't hurt anyone and that it made me feel close to you in a good way, believe it or not. I hope you feel something similar, or at any rate that you don't feel like you crossed any uncrossable lines with me. I don't really have very many uncrossable lines, as it turns out.

Phil had eventually confessed the whole thing to Lily and was no longer guilty when he received this letter, but he had still cherished Denny's offhanded offer of forgiveness. He *had* crossed a line—in his own book of lines, anyway. In so doing, he had also—somehow—become Denny's real parent.

"So, I thought you'd be up till all hours tonight, getting ready for Friday," Phil says to Denny.

"If my part isn't done at this point, I don't know—there's not much hope. You guys are coming, right?"

"Of course we're coming."

"Good."

"What's good?" Lily asks, pulling down her pushed-up right sleeve. Luke is surprised to see an old lady enter the room. Not a frail old lady like his grandmother, but a woman with jowls and deep lines in her forehead. Lily is equally surprised to see him.

"Hello?" she says, looking curiously at Luke.

"Mom, this is Luke Kelsey. Maureen's son."

"Maureen's son?" She continues to stare at him, and after a moment she smiles.

"Sure, I can see that. Wow. Pleased to meet you, Luke."

"Another seltzer drinker," says Phil, handing Lily her glass. Lily clinks glasses with Luke, then sits down beside him.

"What brings you to New York?"

Denny feels she must have asked Luke this question herself, but she has no idea what he will say. Everyone turns their attention to Luke.

"Phoenix," answers Luke.

As Lily and Phil chuckle, they both turn inquiringly toward Denny.

"His grandmother lives in Phoenix," she offers, as though that might answer their implied question.

"In Carefree, actually, is what it's called."

Now everyone looks at Luke.

"And my mother told me that when she was at a cross-roads, Denny always helped her figure out what to do."

"Wow, that's ironic," says Denny. Then, "Are you at a crossroads?"

"No. I mean, that's not what I meant. Just that Mom said that you were like family."

"Did something happen?" It's a Lily kind of question.

"What do you mean?"

"Did something bad happen in Phoenix—I mean, Care-free?"

"Something besides my mother being dead?"

There is an awkward silence while Phil and Denny both furiously try to figure out a good segue.

"It's nice that your mother said that," offers Lily.

Denny starts to say "Thanks," and then stops herself.

"Lord knows we trusted Maureen," Lily adds.

Luke looks across the room at the bookshelves, trying to change the subject with his glance. Phil and Lily use this opportunity to shoot Denny more demanding looks. She shrugs and shakes her head lightly.

"Do you like books, Luke?" asks Phil.

"Sure, some of them. I like adventures. My mom read me *Treasure Island* back in the day," he says, spotting the title on their shelf.

Phil smiles at Luke's expression. "You're welcome to borrow anything that looks interesting to you."

Luke gets up and goes to the bookshelves to look more closely—not that he has any interest in borrowing a book. Denny gestures to Phil that she wants him to take Luke out, though whether out of the room, out of the apartment, or out of the country is not clear. While Phil draws a blank, Lily has a moment of inspiration.

"Luke, would you like to play Quake? Phil has a really fast computer."

Luke turns, surprised. "Sure."

Phil and Denny are now both staring at Lily—she knows about Quake?

"The kids in the lab play sometimes," she explains. "I heard them yelling these terrible things and got Greg to explain to me what was going on."

Phil stands up. "C'mon, I'll get you set up."

As soon as they are out of earshot, Denny says to Lily, "I really don't know what to do."

"Listen, my love, he's adorable, but you have to send him home. You can't suddenly make room in your life for a teenage boy. You don't even have a door that closes in that apartment!"

Although this—right down to the awkward endearment—is exactly what Denny would have expected her mother to say and, in fact, what she has come to hear her say, hearing it has an unexpected effect. It makes her want to prove that she *can* suddenly make room for Luke, in spite of her life and her apartment and whatever other defects these things imply. She has a sudden fantasy of her life as Luke's mom—talking to his teachers, helping with his homework, taking him to ball games, being a forty-year-old woman at the movies with an African American teenage boy companion. Her play will be over, but it won't matter if she can't write another—she will have a life—which is better than a play. Her mother watches Denny's face and intuits some, if not all, of what she is thinking. Lily has her own hidden fantasy about being a grandmother and her own proximate fear of running out of work. In this rare moment, she can clearly see the impact her comment has had on her daughter and she can also see that further comments will only make things worse. Denny catches her mother staring at her and winces.

"I don't know, Mom" is all she can say. She reaches forward to pick up her wineglass, hoping to deflect Lily's scrutiny. She takes a sip and says something she didn't expect to: "I'm getting tired of living alone."

As soon as the words are out of her mouth, she feels tears start in her eyes. Her mother looks at her quizzically and Denny shakes her head, as if to deny that the tears belong to her.

"You know he's not going to be around for long. As soon as he makes friends he'll be out all the time—he's an adolescent."

"He's not even thirteen."

"When you're thirteen, fourteen and fifteen seem like a long way off, but when you're the parent of a kid that age, it's . . . very, very fast."

"But it's a few years," Denny says, hearing herself sound pathetic. "I can't just send him back. He spent all his money to get here."

"That was his choice."

"Yeah—"

"And you can still show him New York."

The idea of "showing" New York to Luke in anything less than the twenty years or so she plans to spend finding it herself seems absurd to Denny.

"I miss Maureen," she says.

Phil comes back into the room and takes a look at the two women. "More wine?"

"All the time," she adds, wiping her eyes with her hand.

"I know you do," says Lily, looking down. "She took good care of you."

This admission surprises Denny. Lily had stopped speaking to Maureen after that day in the consulting room, and though Denny didn't know the details, she had correctly deduced that her friend had told her mother some truth that Lily didn't want to hear. Lily had pointedly ignored Denny's occasional references to Maureen and Maureen's life in the years since. Is Lily fishing for reassurance, now, after all this time?

"He's a good kid," says Phil, returning with the wine bottle and a glass for Lily.

"Yeah," says Denny.

Lily waits to see if Phil will venture a further opinion; she's betting he will.

He finishes pouring and again surveys what he can of the damage from their faces.

"Have you been arguing?"

"No," says Lily.

"Just with myself," Denny adds.

"It's a tough one to call," he says, meaning he can't decide who came down on what side, between Denny and Lily. They both think he means he can't pin down his own opinion, which disarms them.

"Can you afford a kid?" he asks Denny.

"Can anyone in New York City?"

"We could help you out . . ."

Lily's head turns. That's her fixed income he's spending.

"You mean you think I should keep him? God, why does it keep sounding like I found a stray dog?"

"He found you," says Phil.

"You didn't answer her question."

Phil nods, considering. "There's always boarding school," he says. Phil went to boarding school; he knows it's not the worst thing that could happen.

"Die! Die! Die!" Luke shouts, from the study down the hall. They are all caught off guard and even a little bit frightened at first. Then they laugh.

Denny lies awake that night, her brain flooded with emotions. She prefers to treat them as problems to solve in her play. When she first started writing it, it was like a puzzle. The characters were all real to her, and the ways in which they interacted and triggered one another's worst behavior seemed to come out of nowhere, only to snap together like machined parts once she had worked them around enough. But now she too clearly sees the polemical nature of their twists and turns, and she fears that her offspring the play has all along been too easy for her to manipulate—as have, for that matter, most of her boyfriends. If Luke comes to live with her, she's afraid she will be unable to stop herself from trying to rewrite him as well.

Lily, in her bed, also lies awake. She will never stop being Denny's mother, or lose the need to fix whatever she's presently deemed wrong with her daughter's life. Even though on the rare occasion when she attempts to *do* something for—or to—Denny, she usually succeeds only in pissing her daughter off. Though Lily is most in favor of sending the boy back to his grandmother, she tries to think through a scenario where Luke could stay and she and Phil could somehow shoulder enough of him for Denny to continue her career, which is soon-to-be-careerless Lily's prime concern. All she comes up with is a weekly trip to the Museum of Natural History, assuming Luke even likes such things. And dinner—they could make dinner once a week. Then she realizes that she will soon have more free time than she is used to contending with. In Luke, she and Phil could at last have a child, at least for a while. Soon Luke is a Ph.D. candidate in biology and the owner of a large house with a flower-filled garden where Lily plays with *his* baby. Lily falls asleep before she can see that this infant, and not Luke, is the heart of her fantasy—a second chance to soothe the always still raw place in her life with Phil.

Phil has already blinked through his version of the same dream—that was the first thirty seconds for him. He has made peace with the fact that Luke is Denny's problem and, insofar as it's really okay with the grandmother, Denny's decision. A thirteen-year-old boy, not an infant, is what Phil has always wanted, but he's seen enough of his friends' kids to know that they rarely turn out like your fantasy—and when they do, you really have to worry. Basically, Phil is lonely. He knows it. He also knows that, short of divorcing Lily and starting all over again on that campaign, there's nothing he can really do about it. Luke seems like a good kid, but he's not going to fill the hole. Everybody has an unfilled hole, somewhere, Phil figures. That's why we get out of bed in the morning.

At 2 A.M., Denny crawls out of her bed and takes the phone with her to the toilet—the only room in her apartment with a door that closes. She calls Sean. She knows he will be up, because they often talked at this hour in the early days of rehearsal. Still, he's a little surprised to hear from her.

"I can't sleep," she says.

"The play is fine. The actors are just anxious. It's always like this right before an opening."

"Thanks."

"So now you can sleep, right?"

"You give yourself a lot of credit."

"I was kidding. It's not really about the play, is it?"

"Not really." Denny wonders where she got the idea that she wanted to talk to Sean about this. But it's too late. "It's about Luke. Well, really it's about me, of course."

"Goes without saying."

"Shut up."

"Go on."

"I can't talk to you about this."

"Why not?"

"I don't know. This is a conversation for someone who knows me much better than you do. This is a conversation for Maureen."

"Who's Maureen?"

"My oldest friend." Her voice cracks.

"Oh."

"And Luke's mother. She died last year—stroke."

Denny tries picturing Sean in his huge 5th Avenue apartment, which she's never seen. Is he in a bedroom? The living room? A study of some kind? Is there decor? Using her mind's eye keeps the tears back.

"Jesus, you're tough. I had no idea you'd just lost someone close."

"I think I better go, now," says Denny. Her chest feels like pulp.

"It's a good show, Denny," he says, trying to be reassuring. All this remark does is remind her that even if Sean isn't the self-referential monster she had expected him to be at first, he's still an actor at heart and therefore it's all about him. At the moment, she suspects he can't distinguish between her play and his own ego, but she also secretly hopes that will change.

Luke wakes up at six to the crash of garbage cans. It amazes him that people sleep through this, but they must. He has very mixed feelings about his adventure at this point. Nothing is what he expected it to be—he feels constrained in Denny's life and afraid that staying in New York will offer no relief. In Arizona, he may have had to take a bus to get to school, but at least he had friends to hang out with, places to skateboard, stuff happening at school, even girls to tease.

He can't imagine just stepping out into the city to find other kids, other things to do. He barely saw any other kids yesterday, except in the subway. Would he have to ride aimlessly on the subway all day?

Maybe that would be kind of cool. There are parts that are aboveground, Denny said. He could probably spend a

month making sure he rode to every stop on that whole mul-
ticolored map. There were beaches and ballparks and piers
and bridges and cemeteries that looked massive. He creeps
out of bed to find the subway map he got yesterday, which he
left on the table near the front door. He spreads it out on the
floor right there and gets down on his knees to consider possible routes.

By the time Denny opens her eyes at 8:30, Luke has plun-
dered her supply of colored highlighters, pens, and index
cards and is deeply engrossed. She observes this on her way
to the bathroom but doesn't walk over to take a real look
until she's got a hot cup of coffee for herself and a glass of O.J.
for him.

"Whatcha doing?"

"Figuring out what to do while you're at the theater all
day."

"Uh-huh. So tell me."

"It's not finished yet."

"Is this one of those things where it takes longer to plan it
out than it does to actually do it?"

"You mean, like your play?" asks Luke, without irony.

"Good point," says Denny. She decides to watch what he's
doing for a while instead of kibbitzing. He's scored the map
off into nine boxes, and is following the D line with his green
highlighter, periodically circling a stop—for example, Prospect Park. Other train lines have already been so treated. A
much-abused wallet card with the year's calendar printed on
it is marooned near Randalls Island.

"So you're going to tour the five boroughs by subway?"

Luke counts off the landmasses on the map to himself. "Is
that a subway on Staten Island? I wasn't sure."

"I have no idea—I've never been there."

Luke looks up at her to see if maybe she is joking. Nope. "That's the idea. What do you think?"

"And you're going to get off the train once in a while, in these places you've circled, but mostly just ride?"

"Yeah, I think so. How long do you think it would take to go from, say, here to here, Inwood to Far Rockaway? That seems like maybe the longest one."

"Uh, all day?"

"Nah, come on. It's only . . . there's no scale on this map . . . but what, maybe fifteen, twenty miles? And those trains definitely go at least forty when they're really clocking. It can't be more than a couple of hours."

"Okay, a couple of hours."

"So, if I get off two places a day, and have lunch and stuff, I figure I can do two train lines a week, three of the shorter ones."

"How many trains are there?"

"Twenty-five."

"You'd really want to do that? For twelve weeks?"

"Why not?"

"I can think of lots of reasons. The first one is, I don't think kids your age ride on the trains alone."

"We saw those kids yesterday, remember, the brother and sister?"

"Well, yeah, but they were . . ." She was going to say "black kids from the ghetto," though of course she has no idea where they live or anything else about them.

"They were poor," she tries, lamely.

"Said the lady who can't even afford an elevator."

She decides not to address this misimpression. "And for

another thing, we don't even know if you're going to be here for two weeks, let alone twelve."

"I can do it in segments, every time I visit."

Denny goes from being irritated at the prospect of watching over him to feeling horribly rejected in a matter of seconds. She'd been assuming that Luke was dying to stay with her, thought she was the coolest thing on earth. She now sees that he is evaluating her every bit as intensely as she is him, and she has apparently failed some initial tests.

"I better get dressed," she says. "Did you wash and all that?"

"Flossed and everything."

"Jesus. You flossed?"

"The Dude abides," says Luke, quoting his mother quoting *The Big Lebowski*. He's never seen the movie, but it was an expression Maureen sometimes used to mean "things are as they should be," and he always liked the way it sounded.

Denny has seen the movie. She just grins.

On the way to the theater, Luke asks Denny if he can spend the day by himself. She's not sure. She tries to remember herself at his age. Would it have been okay for her? All that comes back to her are times she took refuge in Maureen's office—when she was mortified because Jack Boyd had overheard her talking about the way his jeans fit; when she got her first period; and when the school janitor had invited her to sit in his office with him and listen to the radio and she got creeped out.

"You can't go anywhere with anyone you meet, okay?"

"Of course not."

"And no subways for now, okay?"

She gives him five dollars and her cell phone and he promises to return in three hours. She watches him walk back up 42nd Street, toward the madness. Maybe he'll explore Grand Central, or the library. There are good things out there. Turning back toward the theater, she remembers shopping with Lily when she was eleven or twelve. She would sit on the dressing room floor and tell her mother what looked good on her, while Lily gazed halfheartedly at her own reflection. Too brilliant to bother noticing about clothes, Denny used to think when she was a little bit older. But maybe just too adept at getting other people to manage the details is how she sees it now. And maybe Denny, even then, was too good at taking that on.

Lily looks at David Rothman, who is the dean of Biological Sciences, her department. He is among the most charming people she has ever met—his eyes are immense wells of sympathy.

"Does this mean I can stay, but I have to give up my lab?" she asks him.

"I wouldn't do that, Lily. Besides, you've got yourself funded through when, next year at least?"

She suspects that his utterly sincere assurance of support is without substance, but he can't ask her to leave as long as she keeps her work funded, she's sure of that. At this point her name is worth something on a grant application, though there is less funding every year, and the sheer effort of putting together the applications is more and more tedious. Nevertheless, she has a distinguished reputation. Why would he even want her to leave?

"I'm confused, David. What is this meeting about?"

"I'm trying to find out if you really want to keep working."

Lily blinks. Rothman is never this real; what's his game? She looks across at his hands on the desk, the wiry gray hairs choking his battered wedding ring. She remembers seeing her own bony, spotted hand through Greg's eyes, just this morning, as she tapped at the glial cells displayed on his computer screen. It had occurred to her, then, that it might really be time for the owner of that particular claw to retract it and go. Now Rothman seems to be treating her as a peer—a fellow, as the academic convention would have it; another member of the pterodactyl clan, as her own imagination had cast it earlier that day. Staring at his bright Ashkenazic blue eyes, she becomes aware of her heart as a sore lump of muscle, alone in her chest, pumping ardently but without any real goal. Tears approach her eyes and she looks down again, at her own hands, folded now.

"It might, in fact, be time for me to go," she says.

"I'm sorry," says Rothman.

Luke has found his way to the north reading room of the New York Public Library's main branch, at 42nd and 5th. At first he thought he was in a museum. Two little old ladies, perched like birds at the information desk, had steered him upstairs after drawing a blank at his initial question, "Where should I go to look up information about Mauritanians in the U.S.?"

He wanders up the gargantuan marble stairs in a state of amazement. It's like a palace of snow, like something from Jules Verne, like a marble birthday cake. The catalog area and reading rooms are at a slightly more normal scale, or perhaps he is adjusting. The online index turns up books in French and books kept elsewhere (The Schomburg Collection?), but he finally identifies one call number, completes a little slip of paper, and submits it to the clerk, who seems not much older than he is. He sits on the bench facing the "Even Numbers" display, waiting patiently for his digits, 184, to tell him *Mauritania's Campaign of Terror* has arrived. He feels as if he is inside some virtual world, like a game where you have to explore an environment, picking up clues, acquiring powers, and gaining access to new levels, and it takes like a month to get to the end.

On the streets of New York, Luke has seen people that look like his father—just a few, but that's a few more than he's seen anywhere else he's been. He figured the library could tell him more: How many Mauritanians are there in New York? When did they come and why? Do they live in that place on the map called Morrisania? (By analogy to the Acadians who became "Cajuns" when they got to Louisiana, sort of.) Climbing the library's grand front steps, passing the lions, the European tourists, the massive doors, he was quite convinced that all answers were contained within, but now he is not so sure. In Columbus, he would have asked a librarian for help, but these librarians are nothing like those librarians, or even like the nice ladies downstairs. They don't even make eye contact with the members of the public, except for the sexily clad black girl dispensing books from the pickup desk, and she only does so for some tiny fragment of a second.

His book appears in a library binding—never a good sign, but he carries it back to his seat as though it were a Christmas present he had wished for. As he works his way up the aisle toward an empty seat, he sees the freaky array of other library users doing all kinds of things: Some have piles and piles of books, some no books at all. Others are dozing, tapping away at laptops, avidly completing index cards, picking their noses, eating covertly, yawning, even appearing to weep. Walking among them he feels like he has advanced to a new level of the game. It's so satisfying to crack the binding and smell the particular smell of a new hardbound book. Maybe he's the first one to read it—it's like a discovery. But, leafing through the pages, as his mother taught him, "to get a sense of it," he finds no pictures and very few summary paragraphs. When he tries to start at the beginning, he is lost within a page or two.

"Looks like a pretty serious book."

The man next to Luke has been watching him. Simon Alves is a skinny, light-skinned black man. His eyes are blue, or, not blue but gray with a bluish edge. And the visible tips of his hair, shaved nearly clean, are almost white. He's not really an old man—well, it's hard to tell: "Black don't crack." But he's upright and smooth-skinned, dressed in jeans and a black-and-white-checked overshirt that seems to match his eyes in some way it would be hard to explain.

"It's not what I wanted."

"I see that. Why not?"

"Well, this is about a bunch of Arabs. They're all barefoot and traveling around on camels and living in tribes."

"Sounds interesting to me."

"I guess so. I wanted to find out more about the Mauritanians now, like the ones here in New York. They're not Arabs, they're black folks."

The man nods, examining Luke's face for signs of his heritage, which start to make sense to him. At first the Roman nose and loosely curled hair had made the boy hard to place, as did his skin color, the purplish brown of chocolate milk. Now he can see the Berber mien, probably mixed with some kind of white mother. Of course—a white mother.

He picks up Luke's discarded book. "May I?"

"Sure. I guess I'm just going to give it back."

The man examines the book's front matter and table of contents. It is, of course, about contemporary conditions in Mauritania, despite the camels and the bare feet. The Maur underclass, who Luke thinks of as "Arabs," are, in fact, Luke's black-skinned people, but it seems unnecessary to browbeat the boy with this fact.

"Did you try periodicals?"

"Uh, no."

"It has a different catalog than books. Maybe you'd find more of what you're looking for in a New York paper, like the *Times*. Or the *Amsterdam News*."

Denny, embroiled in a debate between Sean and Mace—the actor playing Sam, the bypass patient—is feeling an unfamiliar combination of anxiety and rage. Much to her chagrin, Mace has a point. He *is* a plot device. His point of view *is* inconsistent. If they had had an actor as intelligent as this one in the original production, she certainly would have done something about this, but she was lulled into believing it was okay as long as no one pointed out that it wasn't. How many other sinkholes like this one are still lurking in this one lousy play? Every time one turns up she feels as if she knew it was there all along, or should have. But later, when she tries to find them by herself, they disappear. The bitter part is, the reviewers never know what you rewrote the night before, what you changed fifty times, or how open you were to other people's suggestions and readings. They just call you an idiot if something doesn't work.

Mace has described an alternate ending, just a few line changes and different emphases that leave things more open to interpretation: What if Sam gets Arthur as his surgeon because he wants to be reunited with Beatrice? Or perhaps his real reason for choosing death is because he can't have her. After all, Denny named her Beatrice. Isn't this a reference to Dante? These are all interesting ideas, and ordinarily Denny would listen wholeheartedly. Instead, she interrupts.

"Sam doesn't die of a broken heart and there is no inferno. It's supposed to be a comedy. In any case, it's not a romance. Actual people are coming to see a performance in about twenty-four hours, and that's how it is. Your job is to act in the play, to the best of your ability. My job is to write it, and that job is done, as of right now."

"Yeah, but—"

Denny stands up. She has never read Dante and she's not

starting tonight. "You've never seen me get mad, but that doesn't mean I won't. If I gave you half the crap about your performance as an actor that you give me about mine as a writer, you'd go home in tears every night. So shut the fuck up! All right?"

She can't believe she said, "All right?" But she has accomplished her aim. Sean is nodding gravely and Mace is staring at his knees. She sits back down awkwardly. Why did she stand?

Sandy Lindstrom, who has only recently drifted back from lunch, has been watching from an aisle seat a few rows behind Denny. She now glides forward, takes the adjoining seat, and whispers "Hell, yeah!," giving Denny a not so gentle rap on the arm. Denny looks at the actress with a twisted expression—she wants to beam, but she also feels embarrassed by her own outburst; the result: She looks like a hopeful prune.

"They're just nervous," says Lindstrom, in a silvery whisper. "He's never been out of New Haven," she says of Mace.

Denny laughs nervously, then remembers Luke, who has never been out of Columbus, except that he has—but only to another maze of cul-de-sacs. Now he is somewhere in Midtown Manhattan and she let him go. What was she thinking? The prune look converts into one of obvious panic.

Then, in one of those weird coincidences that really isn't so weird, Sean's assistant approaches with a pink phone message for Denny. It says, "Luke's on hold."

"Excuse me, I've gotta take a call," Denny tells Lindstrom.

She threads her way to the backstage phone, an old black

desk model with colored push-buttons along the base. She punches the flashing one.

"Luke, are you okay?"

"Yeah, I'm at the library. I thought you could help me with something."

"Sure," says Denny, still ratcheting down from the anxiety that overtook her a moment ago. "What?"

"Do you know when my dad came over from Mauritania? Like, what year?"

"No, I don't. I'm sorry."

"Do you think it was in the eighties?"

"That sounds right. . . . Are you finding stuff about that?"

"Not yet, but this man is helping me. He really seems to know a lot."

"You mean the librarian?"

"No, he's just a guy I met. He's pretty cool. His name's Simon."

"Oh." Denny's antennae are up again, but she cannot form a question that will get to the root of her discomfort.

"Okay, well, we're going to periodicals now," Luke says. "Simon thinks we'll do better there."

We? "Wait, Luke. Tell me more about Simon."

"What do you mean?"

"How old is he, what does he look like, what does he do for a living?"

"I don't know. He's normal-looking, I guess. His head is shaved. . . ."

Shaved head is never good. Greek fisherman's hat would have been worse, but not much.

"I don't like the way he sounds, Luke. Can't you get the librarian to help you?"

"Why?"

"Because. He might be bad."

"Oh, come on, Denny. He's just a guy who's helping me. I swear on my mother's grave." The expression stops them both. It was out of Luke's mouth before he realized that his mother actually has a grave these days. "Look, I'll be back there in an hour, okay? Don't worry about me."

"Okay," says Denny, not at all sure that it is.

"Bye," says Luke, and hangs up.

Denny stares at the phone, feeling all wrong. Then she remembers that she has given Luke her cell phone and she punches in a fresh line to dial that number. It rings and rings. There's no cell reception at the building on 42nd and 5th—it's a fortress.

Denny resumes her seat in the theater next to Lindstrom.

"What's wrong?" asks the actress.

"That kid?" False start, there's no point in explaining.

"I'm worried about my kid."

Lindstrom nods, sympathetically. "How old is he?"

"Thirteen," Denny lies.

Lindstrom winces.

"Some bald-headed guy named Simon made friends with him at the New York Public Library. Should I be worried?"

To Luke's chagrin and the mild amazement of his new friend, the periodicals have little to say about Mauritania or Mauritanians. A week of rioting in the capital in 1989 merits two inches in the *Atlanta Constitution.* Occasional sentences in news summaries report the expulsion of "tens of thousands of blacks," an election, and a trade agreement, but nothing more extensive. The racial murder of a Mauritanian man in Denver in 1998 gets slightly more attention, but the stories do not discuss the man's background or life in the United States; they are, instead, mostly about his murderer and about a white woman who was also shot and may have tried to help the victim. Simon suspects the "expulsion" is what started the first wave of Mauritanians who came to New York. He can remember one summer in the eighties when, suddenly, these tall purple-skinned men were the ones selling umbrellas when it rained, but without more than the sentence or two in the news summary there's not much point in sending the boy down that road. And they're not the ones selling umbrellas anymore, either.

Denny bolts across town with a metallic taste in her mouth. She knows she is reacting to an irrational belief, she knows Luke is perfectly capable of defending himself from any possible molestation without her help, she knows she is not his mother or anything close, but there is also something inside her that makes her feet run all the way up the massive front stairs of the library.

When she tears into the cool gloom of the periodicals section, it doesn't take her eyes long to find Luke and Simon hunched side by side in the quasi-shelter of a single microfilm reader. They are reading a 1997 article in *The New York Times Magazine,* "God Created Me to Be a Slave," which shows a Mauritania of bare feet and camels and is set in the present. The woman in the story speaks of being "bred" when her owners came in the night to rape her, and Luke is uncomfortable reading these words while sitting next to Simon. He jumps when he hears Denny's voice.

"Back off, right now!" she says, her hand on Simon's shoulder.

Simon shoves his chair back noisily and glares at Denny. Anyone who wasn't previously watching this interaction has tuned in at this point. "Excuse me," drawls Simon, delicately shaking off Denny's hand. When he gets a good look at her he is more amused than insulted. This small, blond dervish is Luke's defender?

Luke stands up and looks at Denny with a combination of disgust and disbelief. "I told you I'd be back in an hour," he tells her.

Denny, looking from Luke to Simon, can tell she has interrupted nothing more sinister than the joint consumption of a magazine article—a form of intimacy, possibly, but not a dangerous one. "Let's go," she says to Luke, but still looking at Simon, who shrugs at her.

"Luke?" he says, softly.

"Yeah?"

"Well, when you're a little older, you may want to look into an organization called the Association of Multi-Ethnic Americans. They have a convention every year. They talk about issues that affect the mixed-race people in this country."

Luke carefully writes down the name of the organization in the open notebook on his lap. Denny is silent, humiliated by her whiteness. "You've been to it?" Luke asks.

"Once or twice."

"I'll check it out. Thanks for your help." He shakes the older man's hand, then sidles past Denny and heads out of the room.

"See you around, Luke," says Simon, still watching Denny.

Denny catches up with Luke in the middle of Bryant Park.

"I'm sorry," she says.

"I don't want to talk about it," says Luke.

"I don't know how to act like a mother," continues Denny.

"Who asked you to?"

"No one."

"Look, I'm not going back to that theater with you right now."

She digs into her bag to give him her apartment keys. "Here—" she starts to say, but Luke isn't interested.

"No, I need some time off. I'll see you later." He turns and walks away from her, heading south and west across the park—heading toward her place, if you want to look at it that way—which Denny does, fervently.

She goes back to rehearsal but cannot really concentrate. When she gets back to the apartment in the early evening, Luke is sitting outside her apartment door, as he was the day he arrived. This time, however, he looks away when she greets him.

"I'm taking you to dinner in Chinatown," she says, hoping to reclaim some lost ground by leading him to a cool new place. Luke would prefer to sulk alone, but he's hungry, so he follows her silently over to Pearl Street, under the bridge, up St. James Place, and through Chatham Plaza. The Vietnam Restaurant is in the elbow of a dark street that is quiet, full of bad smells, and deserted. Luke would be pretty impressed if he wasn't still mad. Downstairs, in the underground warren of rooms that make up the dining area, Denny orders him an incredibly sweet drink that is a mixture of lemonade and soda. He thinks they could put it in cans and make a million dollars. After scarfing up half his dinner, he realizes that that's what Sprite is, only they screwed it up along the way somehow. When he looks up at her, she is staring at him.

"Do you forgive me?"

"Not really. You acted like an idiot."

This hurts Denny in a whole new way. She looks down at her vermicelli, which has lost all appeal. If she starts talking again, her voice will break, so she doesn't. Anyway, what's she supposed to say? She's not even sure what was going on there in the library this afternoon. She didn't even recognize that voice that came out of her mouth. "Back off" was one of the things she'd been taught to say in that stupid self-defense class she took in L.A. She hadn't used the expression since, at least not without some ironic detachment.

Luke knows he shouldn't have come back at her so harshly, but he is tired of being on good behavior. If she doesn't trust him to take care of himself in a public library, of all places, she obviously doesn't think very much of his judgment. He knew the guy was probably gay, but it wasn't like he was going to jump him or anything.

Denny puts thirty dollars on the table.

"Do you want to take the rest of that home?" she says, nodding at his pile of barbecued pork.

He shakes his head no.

"Let's go, then. I'm tired. I've got a show tomorrow." Her voice is nearly affectless. The waiter comes over to scribble a check—Denny just shoves the money at him, knowing it's more than enough.

"Thank you, miss," he says. She smiles back at him and shrugs. In some ways, this guy is her oldest friend in New York, and she doesn't even know his name.

That night, Denny falls asleep on her bed while watching Conan. Luke, who has never even seen Conan before, sits on the floor at the foot of the bed, out of her line of sight. Eventually, he turns off the television and falls asleep too, relocating to his sleeping-bag nest on the rug, twenty feet away.

When they wake up the next morning, it's awkward. In the course of the night Denny has managed to undress herself and get under the covers and now she has to pee. Bingo the cat has slept with Luke, which Denny recognizes as an act of defiant betrayal. Even the cat knows she's the bad guy. Luke blinks his eyes and stares at her without expression. Behind him, the clock tells her it's nearly noon.

"Luke, could you do me a favor and look the other way while I put some clothes on?"

He nods.

"Like, now?"

He gets up and wanders toward the refrigerator while she makes a break for a nearby T-shirt and, at least partially clad, dashes to the bathroom to pee. When she comes out, Luke is dressed.

"I'll see you at the theater," he says.

"Where are you going?"

"I can take care of myself."

"I know that."

"Later, then."

"What if you called me?"

"Yeah?"

"In an hour or so, just so I know you're okay."

Luke shrugs.

"Please? You have my cell phone number—I wrote it on your notebook cover. I just don't want to spazz out like I did yesterday."

"Okay, okay. I'll call you later," he says, his dignity preserved by Denny's plea of spazziness.

Phil comes home from work a little early. Although he could never articulate it to himself, let alone to Lily, he is anxious on Denny's behalf and has come home early to somehow prepare. He is surprised by what he finds when he walks into the living room: various items are missing—not like there's been a theft, but more like a practical joke of some kind. What's gone are various throw pillows, an ottoman, a lamp, and a rug they bought in Turkey—it had always looked awful but had also cost a fortune. Lily's piles of paper are gone from the bedroom, as is the green bedspread that Phil had picked out and was always proud of as an example of his little-utilized visual taste. Lily, herself, is also missing but soon returns, red-faced, from a final trek to the basement—where her subtractions have been divided between the bulky trash area and the storage room.

"What's going on?" asks Phil, stretched out on their newly clutterless couch.

"I'm making space," yells Lily, pouring herself a glass of water in the kitchen.

"You're saying you need more space?" Phil is being arch.

Lily carries her water back into the living room.

"Don't you ever feel cramped here? There's just too much . . . decor."

"Uh-huh. Where are you going with this?"

"Not sure." She sits down. "Tuscany?"

"I'm pretty sure they have throw pillows in Tuscany."

"Yes, in a villa, I suppose you can have throw pillows."

Phil looks skeptically at Lily, but a new idea has clearly landed. She smiles at him, implacable. He reaches for her water glass and takes a gulp.

"Isn't Tuscany a cliché?"

Lily shrugs. "How about Morocco?"

Luke, wandering uptown aimlessly, finds himself at the Film Forum, where a matinee of *A Hard Day's Night* is about to begin. He's never seen it, it's in black and white, and it beckons him. There are about five other people in the theater.

Luke is surprised by how much he starts to enjoy the movie. There are shots and shots of hysterical teenagers—kids slightly older than he is and therefore fascinating. He also particularly likes the character of Paul's grandfather, "a very clean old man" but also "a right mixer." Between the four lads from Liverpool, the grandfather, and the band's manager and assistant manager—Norm and Shake—they form a kind of all-male family. Each member has adopted a characteristic role: sensitive artist, team player, sly observer, worrywart, etc., and much of the movie's humor and energy come from watching them bait one another with the stupidest of ploys.

The movie is a goldmine of no doubt antiquated British slang, some of which Luke finds vaguely familiar. His mother was prone to speaking in Beatle-ese from time to time. Afterward, walking up Varick Street, Luke tries out bits and pieces of recollected dialogue in his head: "She's a well-known drag, is Susan." In the back of his mind there's a fantasy about living somewhere else entirely, somewhere where the people speak English, but things are in black and white. His mother took him to Ireland when he was five, but all he can remember is throwing up in a car with the driver on the wrong side.

Meanwhile, in a taxi hurtling across the Triboro Bridge are Denny's father, Charles, and his wife, Ellen, coming from JFK. They are dressed as though winter weather began on September first and therefore have begun to wilt. Living in California eventually does make people stupid, in some respects. Although Charles was born in New York, he has not been back since his mother died, eighteen years ago. He has not seen the spiffed-up version of the city, with its primary-color-clad neighborhood improvement squads, its super-stores, and its taxicabs that natter at you about seat belts and receipts. Apropos of her recorded announcement, Charles is trying to explain to Ellen who Eartha Kitt is, and he is getting nowhere. Didn't she play Batwoman or something? Or was that Leslie Uggams? Vicki Carr? Ellen, at first ashamed of her ignorance, has begun to laugh at Charles's befuddlement. Why would he even expect himself to have kept track of anyone in the category "early '60s chanteuse"? Was he running with the Rat Pack before he went to med school and met Lily? This is an encouraging reappearance of the old Ellen—maybe they just needed to get out of town?

Before her surgery, Ellen had been teaching Charles how to take a joke at his own expense. This requires him to wholeheartedly disobey deeply ingrained instincts— "abandoning my nature," he calls it. It turned out he was directing a great deal of effort on this front: staying serious when others got punchy, examining every joke for the veiled message it necessarily contained. It was Charles's idea to surprise Denny at her opening, and he has even called the manager to arrange for good house seats and to make certain their surprise will really be one. Until this moment in the taxi, he wasn't even sure Ellen was really there with him.

Her father is truly the last thing Denny expects to see tonight, although he is no more surprising than the sheer volume of familiar faces that ultimately appear. Denny lurks at the back of the theater, watching people enter before their eyes adjust to the light—which she has specified be kept low. Luke showed up half an hour early and is seated in the third row next to Lily, who has arrived ahead of Phil. Denny spots her friends Michael and Danny from college; her dear friend Anna along with her husband, Bill; some of the people from Truculent; and even a few students from NYU—young actors still utterly reverent about visiting a "real" theater, with plush seats and a proscenium. Someone must have posted something on a bulletin board.

A bit later, her friends who have young children show up—still guilty about going out for the night. In this group

she spots her ex-boyfriend, former-playwright Zander, who
is now some kind of network executive. Seeing Zander is disconcerting, but on the whole, the showing of friends elates
her. More than most, they understand the risks associated
with seeing a friend's first play, and they have come out in
spite of that. They have even hired baby-sitters!

Meanwhile, outside the theater, Phil and Charles—who
have not seen each other since Phil was a graduate student—
arrive at the same time. In fact, Phil enters the revolving door
one segment behind Charles and one ahead of Ellen. When
Charles steps out and turns to offer a shaky elbow to his wife,
Phil recognizes the older man from photos and, vaguely,
from the lab at OSU all those years ago. Unfortunately, he
does so one click past his own optimum exit point from the
whirling door. Charles hasn't been in the same room with
Phil since 1974, so he just sees a tall man staring rudely, then
mouthing his name, then revolving himself back out of the
building. Ellen exits the door and watches in a state of hilar-
ious disbelief. When Phil is redeposited in the lobby, both
men start to speak at once. In the moment of hesitation before either speaks again, Ellen says, "You must be Phil."

Unfortunately, Denny never sees this little comedy, and
none of those involved will ever bother to narrate it for her.

As the audience settles, Denny scoots herself up the left-
most aisle to the front of the house, avoiding the eyes of anyone she might need to greet. She wants to wait until it's all
over, so that if they have nothing nice to say about the play itself, they will at least have the inherent goodwill of greetings
to fall back on. She does glance in the direction of Lily and
Luke as she passes their row. They appear to be engaged in

conversation—about what, Denny cannot remotely imagine. For now, however, this allows her to temporarily cross two names off the list of people she may need to propitiate tonight, so she lets them be.

Charles, Ellen, and Phil enter the auditorium just as Denny is making her way backstage. They are too preoccupied by the process of finding their seats to see her, and she is too preoccupied with the imminent curtain to see them.

Behind the scenes, Denny thanks the cast members quickly and tells them she knows they'll be great. They take their positions. Sean reaches for her hand as the curtain goes up, as the audience goes silent, as the actors become the characters for one breath before the play begins.

Luke, who has been sitting in rehearsals for three days, realizes he has no idea what he is about to see. He has never sat through the scenes in sequence and he has never bothered to imagine what was really going on in the play. He has a vague impression that it will be something like a hospital show on TV, only with more talking. He doesn't expect to be interested, let alone entertained, but the first scene makes him laugh several times. In it, Beatrice teaches an undergraduate seminar on the idea of comedy. Her students are presenting their research. One speaks quite seriously about the way cartoon creatures die (run over by steamrollers, exploded by TNT, falling from impossible heights) and return in perfect health in the next frame. Another analyzes the nonsense poems of trumpet player Ish Kabibble. Luke finds his eyes tearing as he laughs—to learn that Ish was a real man, with what the student calls his own "shtick" (yet no stick: not, after all, a lollipop), is like an elbow in the ribs from his mom. Maureen had resurrected the wisecracking all-day sucker for her son when he was three.

As the scene continues, Sam comes forward to talk to Beatrice—he's been sitting in the back of her classroom and is full of delighted riffs on the students' ideas. This is the first time Luke has seen Sam's "before" character—he's a totally different guy! Beatrice and Sam get a kick out of each other. You can tell they were once in love. Later, when Arthur explains to Sam that he is, in effect, going to kill him in order to save him, Sam makes jokes, tries to tease Arthur, and generally so diminishes the idea of death that the experienced theatergoer can only assume nothing good will happen to him. But Luke is so happy to see the happy version of Sam, he almost forgets about the gloomy wretch he met first.

What follows is a scene in the operating theater. While Sam's body is cooled to the point of near-death, Luke strains to hear the sounds of the monitors and the murmuring of the surgical team. At first, the remarks made by the doctors and nurses are only factual reports. The silence is only really broken when one masked resident notices that there is no music playing in the O.R. "Hey, where's Mozart?" he asks, but no one answers. A few moments later, he tries again. "I thought you always played Mozart during bypass, Dr. Fisk." The nurse standing beside the young resident kicks him and the audience sees this. Then, a light comes up on Beatrice, who stands off to one side. She appears to narrate, though it's understood that she is narrating inside Arthur's head.

"He's clinically dead," she says. "You could be listening to the Rolling Stones, for all he knows, isn't that right?"

"That's ten minutes," announces the anesthesiologist.

"We'll start bringing him back in any time now," Arthur says.

"But usually it helps to have a little Mozart? A little distraction from the mighty task of resurrection?"

"Usually I'm not working on someone you used to love, Bea."

Another silence follows, broken only by the gradually increasing staccato of one of the monitors.

"You can't have it both ways," Beatrice says, largely to herself.

Luke, like everyone else, is relieved to learn that Sam's surgery is successful, but the reappearance of the depressed character he knew in rehearsals is a blow. It's almost too much when—right before intermission—he learns that Sam has killed himself. Luke finds that he is weeping and quickly wipes his eyes, but that tight feeling in the pit of his stomach won't let go. It occurs to him that he should really have forgiven Denny for embarrassing him at the library. She was only trying to protect him. You never know when you're going to lose someone and not have the chance to say anything else to them ever again.

Denny watches the audience as the lights come up: They seem drained. They're not interested in standing in the lobby to debate the play's issues until they find out what happens and where things really stand. As an audience member, Denny always disliked intermission, with its panic at the ladies' room and its lukewarm glasses of jug wine at five dollars apiece. As the playwright, she sees its value. It's good to let everything stew a little.

A stagehand brings her a waxed paper cup with a straw in it, telling her it's "from Phil." Sipping it, she discovers it's an orange float. It takes her a minute to realize why this particular beverage. It still tastes dubious, but is nonetheless soothing—touching, even. That night, outside her old house in Bexley, she felt seen and understood in a way that was rare for her. She felt like she had an ally. She peeks out to see if she should thank him, and there he is, on the aisle, flanked by Lily, then Luke. Luke is talking to the tall gray-haired man on his other side. The man is wearing a pumpkin-colored sweater knotted around the shoulders of his white shirt. This is odd because it's hot in the theater and because it's not a look you see on men in New York very much. He looks like her father and the woman next to him looks like—no, *is* Ellen. Denny sucks hard on the float. Dropping her plan to visit their row, she sits down on a folding chair. The professional hubbub on the "wrong" side of the curtain is a both a barrier and a relief.

Charles has had the wind knocked out of him by the revelation of Sam's suicide, with its implied reference to Ellen and her postsurgical depression. He is afraid to look at his wife, but she anticipates this, taking his hand.

"Smart kid you've got," she says.

Relieved, Charles smiles and turns to his left, to Luke. The boy's face reminds him, suddenly, of Maureen—of her death out of the blue not that long ago, which he learned about from Denny. This is what prompts him to open a conversation with Luke as follows:

"I'm sorry about your mother, Luke. I'm sorry I didn't make it to her funeral."

Luke barely remembers his mother's funeral, much less

who was and wasn't there. He was far from keeping score at the time. Anyway, he thinks this shaky, tan guy is Denny's father, who lives in California. But he seems sincere.

"How did you know my mother?"

"She used to work for me. A long time ago, before you were born."

Luke can't think of any reason for this man to lie, but his white-haired "long time ago" seems like it must have been before his mother was born, as well.

"She used to remember my wife's birthday for me, and tell me what to buy her." Charles shakes his head ruefully, remembering what a jerk he used to be.

"She remembered everything," says Luke, becoming fidgety. "Uh, can you excuse me?" he asks Charles. "I want to take a walk around before they turn off the lights again."

Charles makes way, realizing too late that maybe he could have started with small talk.

Luke gets as far as the lobby and wonders where the hell he is going. To the men's room? Back to Phoenix? Instead, he makes his way outside and dribbles an imaginary soccer ball among the cigarette smokers.

Lily turns to Phil and smiles at him. He is surprised at her ease—doesn't she see herself in this character of Beatrice? Doesn't she feel the immense rage building to a head between Arthur and Beatrice as Denny's commentary on their own marriage? But Lily is fine. She thinks the play is smart and insightful. She fails to recognize the versions of her own marriages it portrays. She *does* see Charles in Arthur, but that's irrelevant. She couldn't possibly see Phil in Sam—he is too well hidden.

Luke can't figure out what it is about the play in its full performance form that's so much more intense than anything he saw in rehearsals. It's simultaneously reassuring and wrenching. All he's been able to conjure is that it makes him happy and sad at the same time, like the knickknack store on 14th Street that Denny pointed out to him the other day, "Funny Cry Happy."

After the show, Denny is mobbed by her friends and by friends of the actors, of Sean, of everyone. She barely gets to see her father, but he gives her a terribly goony hug and kiss, and she can tell that he is besotted with pride. Ellen seems positively chipper, which is extremely good news. There was a possibility that she would have been angry about the use to which Denny has put her misfortune. Not so.

"Thank you!" she tells Denny. "You got it so right!"

Denny's glad they're flying out at six in the morning (Charles is dedicating a building at UCSD), because she has no idea what to say to them after "Thanks for coming." Luke falls asleep on a folding chair backstage, and Lily and Phil take him home with them so he can have a real bed and Denny can stay out as late as she wants. She didn't ask them for this favor, but when Lily offers it, she is unable to think of a reason why not. As Luke follows them out, sleepy-headed, she asks him quite genuinely, "What'd you think?"

Luke's opinion matters to her more than anyone else's right now—even if he hated it, she genuinely wants to know.

"I didn't understand all of it," he starts out.

"No, I know, there's a lot of yakking."

"But I liked it," he adds.

"Really?"

"Yeah, it made me remember my mom." His voice cracks as he says this and he has to look away. Denny is touched. She had not consciously written a play about Maureen's death, after all, or even about Maureen's sensibility—except maybe that thing about Ish Kabibble, which just fell in incidentally when she was doing research. But she has the sense that Luke is right—Maureen is in there somewhere, and to hear him say so is an enormous relief. Maureen is the one who shows up, whether or not Denny's parents do, and Maureen is the one who taught her not to listen to the idiotic voices in her head, just the smart ones. There are smart ones, she is starting to believe.

Denny, Sean, and some of the actors first go to the bar of a designer hotel uptown. As they make their way there, Denny realizes that Sean still does things like hold doors for her. Of course he is from some old-money family and probably learned it all at dancing school or riding academy or whatever happens to young boys in Connecticut. When Mace gets up to buy a round and leaves Denny and Sean sitting together beside an incongruous-seeming fireplace, Sean turns to her and says, "So, is he going to stay with you?"

"Sean, I don't know how to be a parent."

"No one does. I certainly don't."

"What happened to your . . . your son's mother?" It feels all wrong to ask, but it's information she knows she needs.

"Nothing. She lives in Los Angeles."

"Oh."

"Oh?"

"I thought she was dead."

Sean looks at her with a combination of suspicion and amusement. "Not everyone who's absent is dead."

"Not everyone who's absent is dead." She repeats it to herself. There's something about this remark that snags in her brain.

"Okay, that's true. So, even if she's in L.A., she exists, she's part of your equation. That's got to make it easier."

"You exist. And from what I can tell, you have friends and relatives who exist, too."

"No one who's going to coach me through it on a daily basis . . ."

"How do you know?"

"How do you know what kinds of friends and family I have?"

"Well, it's true you don't spill much, but I've seen this play you wrote. You clearly come from the world of people."

"As opposed to?"

"Oh, cut me some slack. I may look like a narcissistic ego-maniac, but I manage to pick up the occasional nuance if I run into it often enough."

Denny looks at him, hard, and starts to feel something. "Well, that explains the bruises," she says.

"Exactly."

Much later, in an Irish bar on 8th Avenue, Denny finds herself kissing Sean. They are both drunk, but the kiss makes sense to her in a way she hadn't anticipated. They seem to fit. There is a moment of eye contact afterward, but it offers information that she decides to store for later inspection, when she is sober. She tries to remember what it felt like to look at him when all she could see was "handsome." She can't.

Outside the bar, Sean makes sure Denny gets the first taxi. Before she gets the door shut, Mace and the actors who play Arthur and Beatrice's students trot up to the cab and thank her, each in turn, for writing a brilliant play. Riding down West Street, she leans her head back and looks out the rear window at the purplish late-night sky. She remembers yelling at the man at the library yesterday, and Luke's horrified face, but she is not ashamed. That moment of fear and aggression came from deep inside her, from a place she rarely has access to but which, tonight, she sees that she must trust: It is the part of her that loves.

CHAPTER

22

Denny wakes up having dreamed about Maureen. She can't remember what happened in the dream exactly, but she lies in bed enjoying the bizarre sensation of waking up happy. She remembers kissing Sean and she also remembers her dad, shaky as hell but beaming. She doesn't re-experience the dread of the phone call from Naomi, which has haunted her for so long. Not everyone who's absent is dead and, more important, not everyone who's dead is absent. The siege of sad mornings is lifting.

Now seems like a safe time to face the reviews, if there ever will be such a thing. Of course, she has a fantasy that they will be fabulous and mostly positive, but she's old enough to know it's far more likely they will hurt her in ways she can't even anticipate. It's the paradox of putting your work "out there." You want the approval so badly you think you can bear the pain, and you *can* bear it, of course—it's rarely something you haven't at one point said to yourself, but you work so hard not to listen to that voice, it really shouldn't get the last word. She pulls on some clothes and heads for the newsstand.

Luke wakes up in Phil and Lily's study, which has a very comfortable couch in it. He still doesn't really want to, but he has decided his best bet is probably to go home. Not to Phoenix, but to Columbus, where he has friends at school and he knows his way around and his reappearance will not require any elaborate explanation. After the play last night, he felt awkward telling people he was "a family friend," but he couldn't think of a better thing to say. For the first time, he saw how many people Denny knows and calls friends, and it made him realize how weird it is for him to suddenly start pretending to be her kid—or not even pretending, just plopping himself down in the middle of her life. And, if the scene in the library the other day is any indication, his presence is definitely bugging her out. In Columbus, he can stay with his friend Patrick, in Bexley. Pat's older sister is away at college and has left an empty bedroom. Pat's mom invited him to stay the last time he called—she's used to having five kids around, so it would be no trouble, she said. Columbus isn't even *that* far from Baton Rouge, where his father lives. Well, it's closer than Phoenix or New York. He could maybe go down there for a weekend sometime. He and Maureen once went to Oumar's for Sunday dinner and Luke got scared by the unfamiliar food, rules, prayers, and siblings. But he was just a little kid then, only six. He is thirteen, now—today. Lily and Phil are going to take him with them to Morocco over Christmas, so after that he may finally have something to talk to his father about. Maybe. He would like it a lot better if Denny was coming, too, but Phil is cool. Lily scares him a little.

Denny shows up at Phil and Lily's at noon to pick up Luke, but when she gets there, Lily is the only one at home. Luke and Phil are in the park, looking for a soccer game to crash—it's one of those fiercely clear fall days.

"How did it go?" asks Denny.

"He's suspiciously well-behaved."

"What's that supposed to mean?"

"Sooner or later he's got to get angry, don't you think?"

"Not if we don't piss him off."

"Don't you think losing your only parent at that age is enough to make anyone mad?" asks Lily.

Denny finds it alarming that she's almost forty and a so-called writer and has somehow missed an idea as elemental as this notion that death could make you angry and not just sad. It's *so* obvious.

On the kitchen table are today's newspapers, all of them. Lily has been reading Denny's reviews, too. Lily sees her daughter's glance stray over to the pile of newsprint.

"The reviews were awfully good, weren't they?"

Denny shrugs. "The *Daily News* critic said I tried to sugarcoat things with humor and just wound up making them brittle."

"What's so awful about that?"

"And the guy from *Variety* hated it."

"Who reads *Variety*?"

"Movie people. My friends in L.A."

"The *New York Times* guy said you handled potentially leaden issues with 'unique delicacy and wit.' "

Denny smiles. It did say that. She can hang on to that.

"Let's go to the park. It's so gorgeous outside," Lily says.

"Can we bring some food?" asks Denny.

Heading for the refrigerator, she has a déjà vu of being a teenager in Bexley. She was always doing this kind of thing: packing the lunch her mother hadn't thought of so they wouldn't have to stop on the way to buy something dreadful at a quick-mart. In Phil and Lily's New York fridge, there are cold cuts, pickles, even a tub of potato salad. Phil's influence. Laying out the sandwich makings, Denny glances through the kitchen window and across the park. Her eyes land on a building she has looked over at many, many times before. She picks up the phone and dials Sean.

"Hello?" he answers.

"It's Denny. I think I may be looking at your building."

"Where are you?"

"At my mother's. Eighty-third and Central Park. I'm looking straight across the park. Is that you?"

"What do you see?"

"Buildings. One is yellower than the others and has cornices."

"The next one's ours."

Ours? Denny gets stuck on the word.

"Me and Matthew," Sean explains, hearing her hesitate.

"Right. Anyway. I just wanted to thank you for the play. For your work."

"My pleasure. Thank you for yours."

She spreads first mayonnaise, then mustard, on half of the slices of bread. She has no idea whether Luke likes it this way, but it's the way she always makes sandwiches.

"I don't know why I called. I was just looking at that building . . ."

"I guess I should invite you over sometime, huh?"

"Okay." She is feeling panicky now. Is this why she called? Did she manipulate him into inviting her over? That wasn't what she meant to do, was it?

"I'm a lousy cook, though."

"What'd you think of the reviews?" she asks, opening drawers in a quest for sandwich bags.

"I thought they were very good. What about you?"

"Did you see Isherwood?"

"Yeah, well, that was a little harsh, but he blamed the worst of it on Lindstrom—or I guess I should really take credit for the shrillness factor, shouldn't I?"

"Isn't he usually nicer to first plays?"

"Forget about it. Bruce Weber liked it."

"I know. I just keep thinking about everybody in L.A. reading *Variety,* and I get upset."

"Stop thinking about that."

The sandwiches are done. There are five of them. She appears to have made one for Sean, too.

As they walk toward the park, Denny asks her mother the question she was avoiding asking earlier.

"Tell me what *you* thought of the play, Mom."

Though she knows it has little bearing on the quality of

the play as a whole, Lily was deeply hurt by the portrait of
Beatrice once it sank in. Ironically, in Denny's mind, Arthur
was the character to whom she had given her mother's more
odious qualities: intransigence, hyperrationality, disdain for
the everyday jobs of life.

"Obviously, I recognized certain traits," Lily states, before
heading across Central Park West against the light.

"He's not you, Mom," says Denny, defending Arthur
while trying to visualize a route through the oncoming cars
her mother seems not to have noticed.

When Denny catches up, Lily continues. "No, of course
not. But she does have some of my less wonderful qualities,"

Hearing her mother's choice of pronoun, Denny registers
that Lily has not made the connection to Arthur. She is not
well prepared to argue the question of whether Beatrice's
character is too much like her mother, but she comes out
swinging. "And some of mine. And some of Sandy Lindstrom's . . . and she has some of your more wonderful qualities, too."

"Such as?"

"Such as? She's brilliant and beautiful, and she tries to
make her choices based on what she believes is right."

"And narcissistic and addled-seeming and a lousy mother."

"Beatrice doesn't have any kids, Mom."

"She tries to be a parent to Sam, though."

Well, yeah. She sort of does. Who knew? They are inside
the park now, and a cool autumn breeze rustles past. The
brilliant sunshine feels good.

"You have to accept my promise that it's really not a play
about you, Mom."

"What *is* it about, to you?"

This sounds more like a peace offering than a challenge but, of course, it's both.

"Well, it's about marriage, and the deals people make with each other in order to live under the same roof."

"Right. And your experience of marriage comes from . . . ?"

"From living in the world for thirty-eight years. I mean, fuck marriage, it's about how hard it is to live with other people—and how easy it is to screw things up with the people you love."

To Denny's surprise, this interpretation succeeds in rerouting Lily. She watches her mother's eyes focus on nothing, then slide over to look at her daughter's face—which is not her own face, after all. Lily looks at Denny in the eye and says, almost sheepishly, "I can see that."

They find Phil and Luke near the baseball fields, playing Frisbee with some hippie-throwback types, including a white boy with dreadlocks. Phil is running and looking surprisingly athletic. Lily isn't seeing this, but Denny is. She whistles to get their attention, then yells, "Over here!" and waves.

Luke turns to the sound of Denny's voice and tosses the Frisbee back to the dreadlocked kid. He feels much better about New York than he did when he woke up this morning. Running around definitely helps. As he walks toward Denny and Lily, he sees that Denny is spreading her arms wide in a "hug me" gesture that surprises him. They're in public, after all.

Phil falls in beside Luke and, seeing the bag in Denny's hand, smiles.

"I think they brought sandwiches!" he says.

Luke ducks Denny's hug, so she swats him across the arm to get his attention.

"Hey, happy birthday!" she says.

"How did you know it was my birthday?"

"Uh, because I send you a card every year?"

"Yeah, I guess you do. Thanks."

"Here, a small token of my esteem," Denny says, producing a gift from the bag of sandwiches. It's a book, wrapped in yellow legal paper with a red bow.

Phil and Lily spread a blanket in a sunny spot as Luke unwraps his present—they're a little miffed that they were not let in on the birthday. As Luke tears off the wrapping he reveals *My Subway Right or Wrong: An Underground Guide*.

"Hey," says Luke. "This is great!"

Phil raises his eyebrows at Denny in recognition of the apparent success of her gift.

"Thanks. I thought it was pretty funny when I looked at it in the store. Check out what he says about the C train."

Luke seats himself on the blanket and starts looking.

"That's the train we took to their house," Denny adds.

"I know that," says Luke.

Denny points at the bag of food. "Picnic?" she asks.

"Of course," says Lily, tearing herself away from the sight of the obviously engrossed Luke to find Phil rooting around in the bag, identifying Denny's sandwiches and in some sense claiming them—usually he's the one to make the sandwiches.

"Turkey and cheese or salami and cheese?" he asks.

"Hey, here," Luke says, reading, " 'The C train, once known as the stuttering AA, runs a pokey backwater of a line.' "

"It gets better," says Denny. "Anyone want a soda?"

"I'll take a Coke," says Phil.

Luke nods. "Me, too," he says, then he continues reading: " 'On a weekday afternoon, your fellow passengers are a mittel-Urban fruit salad of schoolkids, food-service personnel, and workers in the construction trades—you're lucky if you step off the train without some lingering trace of Sheetrock or Cheetos dust on your pant leg.' That's harsh!"

Denny, pleased with herself, heads off toward a nearby hot dog vendor. She buys three sodas and can barely carry them, they're so cold. As she half trots back to the picnickers, she observes the little quasi-family in all their awkward intimacy—her mother somewhat obsessively arranging napkins and sandwiches as though setting a table, Phil staring at Luke, Luke—now lying down—reading his book. Luke glances up, sees Denny coming, and smiles at her. A feeling comes over her that takes her completely by surprise: pride? gratitude? She doesn't even know the name of it. It thickens the back of her throat and makes her want to skip—but she doesn't want to shake up the sodas.

She sits down beside Luke and hands him the first Coke, then offers Phil his. He "trades" her for a turkey sandwich with tomato no lettuce—the one she likes.

"Thanks," she says and nudges Luke, meaning to offer him a choice of sandwiches. He gets back into a seated position, his finger holding his place in the book. Denny's face looks serious to him—he was willing to accept turkey or salami with equal enthusiasm but, seeing her eyes, felt he should sit up.

Denny speaks like it's just between them, but he can feel Phil and Lily listening as they unwrap their sandwiches. "Luke, I really want you to stay in New York," she says. "At my place. With me."

Luke knows he is surrounded by three curious faces. He thinks of the five boroughs on the subway map. No one seems to know why the Bronx is called "the" Bronx.

"That'd be good," says Luke, "but . . ."

"But what?"

He's not sure what. She looks like she means it.

"But I'm going to need some more of my stuff with me."

Denny's not sure if she's been accepted or rebuffed.

"And I have to have my own bed," adds Luke, which makes Phil and Lily laugh. Denny, taking their laughter as cover, wraps Luke in a hug. He hugs back, just for a second. He is too old to cry, but his eyes hurt anyway. He has not been hugged by someone he loves in a long time.

ACKNOWLEDGMENTS

Nina Collins, Nina Collins, Nina Collins! She is the primary reason this book is not in a box under my bed and I love her. While substantially altering the course of my life, Nina was supported and aided by Leslie Falk, Matthew Elblonk, and Britt Carlson, and I am grateful for their every comment, e-mail, and encounter with the photocopier.

Second only to Nina: Dan Menaker, the long-lost friend I never met the first time. In addition to making me laugh (and cry, but only with his own writing), Dan's deft and gentle hand with this manuscript left me very nearly convinced that all his good ideas were really my own. Where Dan left off, the responsive and thoughtful Stephanie Higgs began. Deirdre Faughey also helped immensely. Early—and pithy—editorial insight came from Andrea Chapin, and I was insufficiently grateful at the time. Sorry/Thanks.

I have pressed many friends into service on this project—as readers, researchers, skilled practitioners, and road-trip copilots. I am indebted to the following for their particular contributions: Julie Applebaum, Rachel Cavell, Henry Cline, Tamar Cohen, Michael Duffy, Daniel Kaizer, Judy Katz, Kara Lindstrom, Kate Manning, Adam Moss, Susan Prekel (for the muffin story), Naomi Rand, Kate Rousmaniere, Oren Rudavsky, Julia Schacter, April Starr (for her response to the muffin story), and Patti Wolff. In the role of "hand of fate," I must thank Beth Bosworth, gifted editor of *The Saint Ann's Review* and no mean sentence crafter herself.

My family, including Katherine Cline and various Wolffs, have been a great source of love and support. In the category of extended family, my thanks to Betsy Causey, Weisbergs-at-large, and Sheila Ladden Colon, who saw the light at the end of the tunnel long before I had even admitted I was going underground.

Finally, I am grateful to the Corporation of Yaddo for my time there. It was kind of like going to heaven without the bother of having to die first.

WHAT TO KEEP

A Reader's Guide

Rachel Cline

A Conversation with Rachel Cline

Diane Goshkerian of *Books & Authors*

Diane Goshkerian: What would you say is the theme of this book?

Rachel Cline: Well, there are a few. One of them is "Life is what happens when you're making other plans." In other words, what turn out to have been the important decisions in life are rarely the things we are obsessing about at any given moment. A related theme is "brains that misbehave." Denny is always saying and doing things she didn't expect to—and it's those actions that really give her life its shape. Another example is Lily's car accident. She's this highly trained scientist who can't be bothered with her appearance, but when her brain isn't quite working, she spends her whole day getting beauty treatments. And then Maureen, who is incredibly competent and organized and has a preternatural capacity for understanding other people's lives, can't even leave her own apartment.

The other big theme is the question of what makes a family, or, What does family mean? There's the family we're

born with and the family we choose as adults, and the family
we almost accidentally cultivate out of the people we run into
along the way. For example, Maureen starts out as Denny's
parents' secretary, but she winds up being one of the most
important people in her life. A Peace Corps volunteer invited
Oumar to visit him in Columbus—probably without really
meaning it—and so that's where Oumar settles and meets
Maureen. Lily and Phil connect because they happen to be
on the same airplane. But your birth family is what you wind
up with, whether you like it or not, and in the end those relationships really are important, even if they're problematic.
And they're always problematic.

DG: So, what does the title mean to you?

RC: It's related to that "life is what happens" theme. When
you think about what to keep, you can worry it to death, but
life really makes the decisions for you. Denny goes home to
help Lily pack and spends the entire time worrying about
what to wear to her audition. She sets off on this mission to
the mall, where she works herself into a frenzy. She burns
through the whole weekend without even really talking to
her mother, whom she rarely sees at that point in her life.
And, ultimately, that audition turns out not to matter in the
least.

I used to have a recurring nightmare about having to
pack up all my belongings. And the suitcases aren't big
enough and the airplane is leaving in five minutes and I have
to let go of all these things from my past that seem so incredibly important. I would always wake up then—in that state of

crisis. Then, one day, I dreamed that I let all the keepsakes and treasures go, and it turned out that they didn't really matter. So the title came from that dream, actually.

DG: If you asked Lily where her main passion lay, would that be with her daughter or with her work?

RC: The words "Lily" and "passion" in the same sentence are almost an oxymoron. She is a totally cerebral person—she's comfortable only in the realm of research and science. That's where her real strengths lie and that's where she's masterful and forgets herself. She's essentially unsentimental. I guess she's just missing that gene, and I'm not sure she even knows that about herself. On the other hand, her connection to Denny *is* passionate. She's torn, as all working mothers are. There's no right way to do that balance. And in Lily's field, neurosurgery, there are so few women and the competition is so cutthroat that she really can't even pretend to do both things well.

DG: Was your mother a neurosurgeon?

RC: No, but she wrote a layperson's history of the birth of quantum mechanics, which was a pretty brainiac thing to do in 1963, especially for a woman. But she wasn't trained as a scientist. I was very close to my mother growing up. She was my best friend. She was also a woman in her forties when I was a kid of ten, and that's not really a natural alliance. So I spent a lot of my childhood trying to understand ideas and situations that were really beyond my ken. And then I spent my young adulthood trying to differentiate myself from her as much as I could, which was a waste of time, because, of course, we're totally different people. But I think a lot of girls go through something like that struggle.

DG: Maureen is a very prominent influence in Denny's life. What does she provide for Denny that Lily can't?

RC: First and foremost, spontaneity. If Lily is wholly cerebral, Maureen is truly emotional. She lives in her heart and her body—to the point where her body traps her in her apartment for a year. I think Denny's a bit that way also; she acts before she thinks. That's really their common ground. Denny feels unfairly judged by Lily, whether or not she really is. If you're somebody who is always thinking, other people often assume you're thinking mean thoughts about them, even if you're just making a grocery list—I know this from personal experience.

DG: Which character in the book is most like you?

RC: All the characters in the book are me. Really. When I'm in their heads, they're me and I'm them. It's interesting how it evolved, though, because before it was a novel, it was a screenplay. And it was about a day in the life of this forty-one-year-old woman. Then, when I turned it into prose, Denny kind of took over. And then I had this mother who wasn't really a mother and I had this daughter who was very important, so who was actually doing the mothering here? Enter Maureen. In the screenplay, I could have Lily running around with a concussion and Denny at home, and cut back and forth and I never had to explain how Denny got to school that morning. You didn't need to know. I guess that's my version of "life is what happens when," because without Maureen, there wouldn't really have been much of a story, but she wasn't part of my original plan.

DG: What about Luke, Maureen's son? Doesn't he wind up being family to Denny, too?

RC: Luke takes bus across the country for three days to show up on Denny's doorstep. When he gets there, he discovers that New York City isn't necessarily the greatest place to just show up when you're thirteen years old and you don't know anyone there. He's also on one of those missions that don't turn out the way we planned. But he finds something he needs with Denny, and at the same time he presents her with exactly the problem she needs to solve about herself at that point in her life. I wish Luke would show up on my doorstep sometimes!

DG: What do you think happens with Denny and Sean? Do they get together?

RC: I think so. I don't know if they live happily ever after, but I think there's a real alliance there and I think Denny's ready for it. Of course, it's also nice that he has all that money! I guess I wanted her to be able to go on writing, whether or not her play is really a success. In one version, I had Sean and his son both there at the end, in Central Park, but it was just too neat and tidy. And it wasn't really what the book was about, so I left it open-ended. That felt truer to me.

DG: Were you trained as a creative writer?

RC: Gee, was I trained? [*Laughs.*] I majored in English. I was always a reader and from a young age wanted to be a writer. But growing up in a writer's household in New York City, the economic realities are hard to miss. So I put that out of my mind and did a lot of other things. I was a proofreader and a copyeditor, and I was a publicity secretary and a word-processing temp and things like that. And I hated most of those jobs. Finally, I decided to apply to film school to learn screenwriting, because I thought then I could be a writer *and* make a living, which was tremendously naïve. It turns out that to be a screenwriter you have to wait tables for ten years, just like in any other creative pursuit.

DG: Did you have any success in screenwriting?

RC: Well, yes and no. I sold a couple of scripts to independent producers, but none of them even came close to being made into movies. The most success I had was when I worked in television for a couple of years. I wrote for *Knots Landing* for one season—that was the pinnacle of my show-biz experience.

DG: What would you say is the difference for you between screenwriting and writing a novel?

RC: I don't know that I really have an answer to that. There's one alarming similarity, which is "Show, don't tell." It's the cardinal rule of screenwriting—I taught for years and I must have said it a hundred thousand times to my students. Then I sat down to write a novel and the first comment I got was "Show, don't tell." It was humiliating. And I hear it in my head all the time now, as I'm working on my second novel. It's the hardest thing, I think.

Reading Group Questions and Topics for Discussion

1. Lily set out to be a pediatric neurosurgeon but shifted her focus to research when Denny was young, in part because the schedule was more flexible. Later, Lily has an impressive career in scientific research. Is Lily a good scientist? Does it matter that research wasn't her first choice of career? Did her career change make her a better mother? Might her life have been more satisfying if she'd stayed with surgery?

2. Denny's parents, Lily and Charles, are professionals in the same field. Was this a strength or weakness of their marriage? Why didn't they stay married?

3. When we first meet Maureen, she is suffering from severe agoraphobia—she's afraid to go outside. She isn't married or apparently close to her own family, nor does she have children of her own. Why does Denny get along so much better with Maureen than she does with Lily?

4. Denny chooses a different—some might say opposite—career path from her parents. What makes her unlike her

parents? How do her parents' choices and personalities influence her own?

5. Is Maureen crazy at first, or just depressed? What's the difference? Did her sexual encounter with Jamie (the guy from the record store) cause her agoraphobia, or did her emotional problems make her particularly susceptible to the type of experience she had with Jamie?

6. Lily has a car accident that leaves her with a mild concussion and temporary amnesia. What, if anything, does Lily learn from her accident and its aftermath?

7. In the long run, does it matter that Lily misses Denny's performance in *Damn Yankees*?

8. In Book Two, Lily calls Denny home to help her pack up their house in Bexley, the house where Denny grew up and where she lived with her mother and father before their divorce. Lily expects Denny to stay for a week and to make an effort to get to know her new stepfather, Phil. Why is Denny so impatient with her mother in this section of the book? Does Lily deserve it? How could Denny be doing a better job of being a daughter?

9. At the end of Book Two, after Lily and Phil have been fighting and Denny has been reunited with Maureen, Denny and Phil go out for ice cream and wind up kissing each other briefly. Phil is actually closer to Denny in age than he is to Lily. How do you feel about Phil and Denny's kiss? Is it

wrong? Should one of them have stopped it? What do you think was really going on there?

10. In Book Three, Lily and Phil are living together in New York City and trying to imagine what it will be like to retire. Why does Lily and Phil's relationship last? What's in it for each of them?

11. The director of Denny's play is an extremely handsome former film actor named Sean. He's a divorced father and comes from what sounds like a privileged background. Initially, Denny mistrusts him and it seems as if her reason for this is simply because he's so good-looking. Are her instincts right or wrong? Where do you think those instincts come from?

12. Denny leaves California and the movie business to come to New York and direct her play. What's different about New York? Why might it suit Denny better? Is it merely a coincidence that Denny and Lily settle in the same place?

13. At the end of the book, thirteen-year-old Luke has come to stay with Denny in New York. Will Denny be a good parent for Luke? Does it make sense for Luke to stay in New York? What will Denny have to change about her life that she hasn't foreseen?

14. This book is full of families of various kinds, some makeshift, some formal; some functional, some less so. Who are the best parents in this story and why? Discuss some of the

minor characters who sometimes act like parents—people like Denny's drama teacher and her school principal in the early part of the story, and later, her agent, Luke's grandmother, Sean, and even Simon (the guy at the library). What are some of the qualities that do and don't make a good parent in this story?

15. This story is structured in three parts, each a different time in Denny's life, with many years skipped in between. Why do you think Rachel Cline told the story this way?

16. One reviewer called *What to Keep* "chick lit for smarties." Do you agree? How does *What to Keep* fit the category, and how is it unique?

ABOUT THE AUTHOR

RACHEL CLINE spent almost a decade in Los Angeles writing screen- and teleplays and teaching screenwriting at USC. She returned to New York in 1999 and settled in Brooklyn. She plans to stay.

http://rachelcline.com